Praise for

BETH KENDRICK'S NOVELS

The Pre-Nup

"In the exceptionally entertaining and wonderfully original
THE PRE-NUP, Kendrick writes with a wicked sense
of humor and great wisdom about the power of friendship,
the importance of true love, and the very real satisfaction of
romantic revenge done right." —*Chicago Tribune*

"The three female leads all captivate." —*Romantic Times*

"Beth Kendrick creates a careful examination of a contentious contract
in this highly entertaining story." —Freshfiction.com

"[Kendrick's] heroines are easy to like." —*Booklist*

"Clever, wise, and wonderful, THE PRE-NUP is Beth Kendrick at her
best." —Jane Porter, author of *Easy on the Eyes*

"Witty, juicy, and lots of fun! Say 'I do' to THE PRE-NUP."
—Susan Mallery, *New York Times* bestselling author of *Lip Service*

"A smart, funny spin on happily-ever-after!"
—Beth Harbison, author of *Hope in a Jar* and *New York Times*
bestseller *Secrets of a Shoe Addict*

Nearlyweds

"A fun and funny look at marriage, commitment, and figuring out what your next best step is...whether it be down the aisle, or not." —Alison Pace, author of *City Dog*

"Very funny." —Carole Matthews, author of *The Chocolate Lovers' Club*

Fashionably Late

"Wickedly clever." —*Booklist*

"Kendrick gives chick lit clichés an adroit turn." —*Publishers Weekly*

"Kendrick's keen sense of humor and pitch-perfect gift for dialogue are excellent accessories to this fun and frothy tale." —*Chicago Tribune*

Exes and Ohs

"Breaking up is hard to do, but *Exes and Ohs* is hilarious! You won't be able to put this book down."
—Cara Lockwood, author of *Every Demon Has His Day*

My Favorite Mistake

"Absolutely fabulous! Beth Kendrick is a major new talent."
—Melissa Senate, author of *The Secret of Joy*

"A laugh-out-loud treat as frothy and appealing as a raspberry sorbet." —*BookPage*

Also by Beth Kendrick

The Pre-Nup

Nearlyweds

Fashionably Late

Exes and Ohs

My Favorite Mistake

Second Time Around

A Novel

Beth Kendrick

Bantam Books Trade Paperbacks
New York

A Bantam Books Trade Paperback Original

Copyright © 2010 by Beth Macias

Published in the United States by Bantam Books, an imprint of The Random House Publishing Group, a division of Random House, Inc., New York.

BANTAM BOOKS and the rooster colophon are registered trademarks of Random House, Inc.

Library of Congress Cataloging-in-Publication Data

Kendrick, Beth.
Second time around / Beth Kendrick.
p. cm.
ISBN 978-0-385-34224-7 (alk. paper)
eBook ISBN 978-0-553-90712-4
1. Female friendship—Fiction. 2. Chick lit. I. Title.
PS3611.E535S43 2010
813'.6—dc22
2009047665

Printed in the United States of America

www.bantamdell.com

6 8 9 7 5

Book design by Carol Malcolm Russo

For Catherine,
best roommate ever and creator
of the original Richard III *flowchart.*

Acknowledgments

I did lots of research on the history of baking while writing this novel, but by far the most in-depth and entertaining resource was Linda Stradley's website: www.WhatsCooking America.net. If you would like to duplicate some of Anna's retro desserts in your own kitchen, this site is a great place to start.

Pastry chef Michael Dory set me straight about what it takes to make it as a professional baker and how, exactly, one constructs a tiered wedding cake.

My dad taught me everything I know about knob-and-tube wiring, thermodynamics, drill bits, and the horrors of cast-iron toilet flanges. Thank God for engineers!

There is not enough gourmet chocolate in all of Manhattan to amply reward Christina Hogrebe, Meg Ruley, Danielle Perez, and Marisa Vigilante for their guidance and support. Ladies, you give English majors everywhere a good name.

Finally, I owe undying gratitude (along with a lifetime supply of "vodka juice and cranberries") to the fabulous Kresley Cole, who gave me a crash course in penning historical romance. If you like kick-ass heroines and white-hot love scenes, I highly recommend her books.

Second Time Around

Chapter
1

"The only way not to think about money is to have a great deal of it."
—Edith Wharton, *The House of Mirth*

We all should have gone to law school." Jamie Burton plopped down on a white rattan rocking chair, kicked off her flip-flops, and gazed out at the lake. "I'm telling you. Everyone who warned me about majoring in English was right. If I'd gone to law school, I wouldn't be flashing my décolletage for tips. If I'd gone to law school, all my student loans would be paid off, and I'd be swanning around in the trinity of Christians: Dior, Lacroix, and Louboutin. If I'd gone to law school, I'd be—"

"Careening down the slippery slope of insanity," said Arden Henley, who had a framed J.D. diploma from

Georgetown and a plushly appointed office in a prestigious Manhattan law firm. She'd hosted a girls' weekend reunion here at her family's cottage in the Adirondacks every Fourth of July weekend since they'd all graduated from college ten years ago. "You'd hate being an attorney. Trust me."

"You're probably right." Jamie stretched out her long, tanned legs and swatted away a mosquito. With her bleached blond hair, freckles, and disproportionately ample bustline, she wasn't classically beautiful, but she was so cocky and outspoken that beauty was beside the point. Jamie made it clear that she didn't care what anyone thought of her and so, paradoxically, most people fell all over themselves trying to earn her good opinion. "I'll admit that my brief foray into corporate America wasn't exactly a rousing success. Just the thought of being stuck in a cubicle makes me break out in hives. But I'm sick of bartending and getting home from work at three A.M. and being ogled like some airhead model." She paused. "Okay, maybe that part's bearable. But the rest..."

Brooke Asplind stopped painting her toenails long enough to strike a match and light the citronella candle next to the chaise longue on the porch. The sharp citrusy fragrance mingled with the scent of the pine trees surrounding the cottage. "You're burned out, that's all. This little vacation is perfect timing. Stop talking about how the glass is half empty and grab a cold drink."

"Twist my arm." Jamie grinned. "What're we drinking? Microbrews? Wine?"

"Wine *coolers*." Arden rummaged through a large metal washtub filled with ice and extracted a bottle of peach-flavored booze with a pastel label.

Jamie wrinkled her nose. "Are you serious? I haven't had

a wine cooler since...last summer, when you lowbrow degenerates peer-pressured me. We're not twenty-one anymore, ladies."

"No, we are not," Arden said. "We're more mature..."

"...more worldly and alluring..." Brooke added.

"...and still paying off those student loans," said Caitlin Johnson, who had leveraged her B.A. in literature all the way to a Ph.D. and an assistant professorship at tiny Shayland College in Connecticut. "But all that debt was worth it, don't you think? We had some good times in college."

"We're still having good times." Arden took a long swig from her wine cooler.

Brooke's forehead creased in concern. "Should you really be drinking that? Since you just took your pills an hour ago?"

Arden tucked her feet up under her and settled back in her cushioned wicker chair. Her baggy beige cargo shorts and threadbare Thurwell College T-shirt only served to emphasize the gauntness of her frame. She had always been pale and petite, but now her complexion looked ashen and her cheeks had hollowed out underneath those huge hazel eyes and glossy black hair. "Don't you worry your pretty little head about me. If I gotta die young, at least I'm gonna die with a good buzz on."

The four women lapsed into silence for a moment, watching the sun sink down toward the jagged silhouette of pine trees lining the lake. Then Jamie shook out all her long, yellow hair and said, "Give me a break, girl. You're not going to *die*."

"Certainly not." Brooke waved her pedicure brush for emphasis, splattering tiny pink drops across her bare foot.

Caitlin, who had gotten a late-night phone call after Arden's latest round of doctors' appointments, said nothing.

"You caught me; I confess." Arden fanned her face with her hands. "I just made up the whole lupus thing to get attention and an extension on Professor Clayburn's final paper senior year."

The undertone of anxiety ebbed away as they started reminiscing about the professor they used to refer to as the Mr. Darcy of Thurwell's English department.

"I just saw him last week," said Brooke, who still lived in the tiny town where they'd attended college and who worked as a coordinator for the school's alumni affairs department. "In the produce aisle at the grocery store."

"Is he still all swarthy and rough around the edges?" asked Cait. "Don't tell me he's turned into one of those pompous, sherry-swilling blowhards."

Arden arched an eyebrow. "Sounds like someone's gone sour in the Ivory Tower."

Jamie snorted. "Wouldn't you, if your dating pool were reduced to guys like Cheerio Charles?"

Brooke and Arden dissolved into laughter along with Jamie. Cait clapped her palm over her eyes. "I so regret ever telling you guys that."

"You have to admit it's the last word in pretension," Brooke said. "Breaking up via email is bad enough, but signing the breakup email with 'Cheerio, Charles' is—"

"Acceptable only if you're a British aristocrat wearing an ascot," Jamie finished. "And your peers address you as 'old chap.'"

"Judgy McJudgersons." Cait slathered on a fresh coat of bug repellent. "How quickly you forget what intellectual snobs we all used to be."

"Yeah, but we grew out of it," Arden said.

"I was never snobby to begin with," Brooke protested. "I'm the one who couldn't make it through Shakespeare's histories without CliffsNotes, remember?"

"And I'm the one who currently spends every night pouring tequila infusions for people who think *Middlemarch* is a war epic starring Gerard Butler and who could buy and sell me ten times over with their black AmExes." Jamie shrugged one shoulder. "We're not being snobby; we're stating the facts. And the fact is, you were way too good for that old chap."

"Yeah. He was just distracting you from writing your novel," Brooke said. "Which you can now finish, publish, and rub in his face when you win the National Book Award."

"Well, National Book Award might be a stretch," Cait hedged, but Arden waved this away.

"All I know is, Professor Clayburn would never break off a relationship through such cold, impersonal means. He'd probably write a long, poetic letter suitable for framing and handing down to your grandchildren."

"That he would." Brooke sighed. "Swoon. He's getting even better with age."

"That man was hott with two *t*'s," Jamie declared. "Plus, he had ridiculous amounts of self-control. No matter how short my skirt was or how tight my top, he never even looked my way. Damn him."

"You're insatiable," Brooke said. "Every guy on that entire campus looked at you constantly. Even President Tait. And he was *married*."

Jamie choked on her wine cooler and flushed bright red. "President Tait did not look at me! You're getting a contact high from nail polish fumes."

Arden intervened. "Wait, wait, I'm not done with my interrogation of Professor Johnson. Spill it, Cait. Any promising new prospects on the horizon?"

"None whatsoever," Cait said. "Every eligible male I know on campus is either under twenty-one or over fifty. I'm so desperate, I'm considering reactivating my Internet dating account."

"Don't do it," Jamie advised. "That's how I met my second fiancé, and we all know how that turned out."

"I thought that was a blind date?" Brooke said.

"'Blind date' is code for 'We met online and don't want to talk about it.'"

Caitlin tuned them out and focused on Arden, who had dropped out of the conversation and was trying to hide a wince of discomfort. Arden rubbed at her eyes with shaking hands, then gripped the wooden slats of her chair.

Cait leaned in and whispered, "You okay?"

Arden immediately unclenched her hands and jerked her face away. "Fine. My eyes are a little dry."

"Do you want me to——"

"I'm *fine*. Can we please just have a good time?"

The crunch of tires on a gravel road drowned out their whispering, and Arden glanced toward the driveway with evident relief. "Look who finally decided to grace us with her presence."

Jamie let out a whoop. "Reunion weekend can officially begin—it's the late, great Anna McCauley!"

They heard a car door slam and a quick succession of footfalls on the path.

"We're out on the deck!" Jamie hollered. "Hurry up; fireworks are starting as soon as the sun goes down."

Anna rushed into view, bustling and breathless as usual.

Short and plump with wild curly hair and an adorable snub nose, Anna combined an innate tendency to nurture with never-say-die tenacity. She started doling out hugs and compliments as soon as her foot hit the porch.

"Sorry, sorry, I meant to be here hours ago," she said. "We saw a new endocrinologist today and she could only squeeze us in at four forty-five and traffic on the Northway was a nightmare."

Brooke's eyes widened. "Endocrinologist?"

"Reproductive endocrinologist."

"Ah." Brooke paused. "May I ask how everything's going with that?"

"Here, I brought cupcakes," Anna said brightly. "Red, white, and blue for the Fourth. Ooh! Wine coolers!" She deposited a platter of baked goods on the rickety table next to the chaise, then helped herself to a bottle from the ice bucket. "Ahh. Tastes like youth and reckless abandon."

Jamie grimaced. "It tastes like a wicked hangover in the making. That's it; I'm making mojitos. Who's in?"

"I'll have one," Arden said.

Cait's vow to leave her friend in peace lasted less than two minutes. "Arden, seriously, don't you think—"

Arden narrowed her eyes at Cait, then told Anna, "Throw your bag in the house, pull up a chair, and make yourself at home. We were just telling tales of the glory days. Namely, Professor Clayburn."

"So dreamy." Anna clapped her hands over her heart. "But Cait was always his favorite."

Cait blinked. "I was not!"

"You totally were," Jamie said. "Life is so unfair."

"Mostly in your favor, blondie," Anna pointed out. "So what else is going on in our old stomping ground?"

"Not much, really," Brooke said. "The usual town-versus-gown drama. The grocery store finally started stocking organic produce and gourmet coffee...."

Arden cleared her throat. "The college is selling Henley House. To raise money for a new state-of-the-art fitness facility."

Cries of outrage rang out through the twilight.

"What? Shut yo' mouth!"

"Blasphemy! How dare they?"

"Not *our* Henley House!"

"Yep. One of the deans called my dad last week," Arden said. "To break the news tactfully and to let us know that it was nothing personal and they appreciate our continued endowment."

"But Henley House was *our* house," Brooke repeated. "Site of Primal Scream Thursdays! Site of Pack-a-flask Fridays!"

"Site of your deflowering," Arden added.

Brooke flushed. "That, too. I'm an employee of the college, for goodness' sake. How have I not heard about this?"

"What a shame," said Cait. "What's going to become of the building?"

"I have no idea," said Arden. "But now that they've finished construction on some new dorms, Residential Life decided it's not cost-efficient to maintain the off-campus houses."

Brooke shook her head. "If I had any money, I'd buy it."

"And do what with it?" Jamie scoffed. "It was built to house like fifteen students."

"I'd renovate it and open a bed-and-breakfast. I've always wanted to run a B and B. I'd decorate every room differently and serve tea every afternoon and homemade biscuits every morning." Brooke, a rosy-cheeked natural blonde who'd been raised in Alabama, had always been a firm believer in the restorative powers of hospitality and baking-powder biscuits. Fifteen years of living amongst the Yankees had eradicated all but a trace of her lilting Southern accent, but when the booze kicked in, so did her drawl.

"Why a bed-and-breakfast?" Cait asked.

"Because I like making people feel at home."

"*Why?*"

"Don't be a dream crusher," Arden admonished. "I think it's a lovely idea."

"Yeah, don't let the misanthropes gang up on you, Brooke. I like people, too," Jamie chimed in. "Sometimes, I like 'em a little *too* much, actually. But, look, with age comes wisdom. Please note which finger is naked." She waggled her ringless left hand at them.

Anna nodded her approval. "Hearts must be broken all over Los Angeles."

"Only those belonging to overpriced wedding planners, florists, and caterers," Jamie said. "In fact, if *I* had any money, that's what I'd do: start my own event-planning business. I can see my business cards now: *Let Jamie Burton's three failed engagements add up to your one perfect day.* Anna, you could be my cake supplier."

"Oh, I'm not doing the birthday cakes anymore," Anna said.

"Why not? Those were works of freaking art!"

"It just got to be a little too..." Anna's good cheer finally faltered. "Last month, one of the members of my book club asked me to do an Eiffel Tower cake with a pink poodle for her daughter's fourth birthday, and while I was finishing up the detail work on the icing, I realized that I'd made a cake for this little girl every year since she turned one. Three years, three rounds with in vitro, enough fertility drugs to stock a pharmacy, a maxed-out home equity loan, and still nothing."

Brooke didn't hesitate for even a nanosecond. She looked Anna square in the eye and said, "It'll happen for you and Jonas."

Arden touched her elbow. "Absolutely."

But Anna shook them off. "Maybe it won't. I'm so tired of people telling me to 'just relax' and 'it'll happen when you least expect it.' I'll probably never be able to have a baby, and eventually I'm going to have to face that fact. But right now, it kills me to spend my weekends making cakes for other families. Selfish, I know, but there it is."

Cait nudged Anna's bare foot with her own. "It's not selfish at all."

"It actually works out perfectly for my new fantasy career," Jamie said. "I need you to whip up the dessert trays for all my five-star shindigs."

"And I need you to make crumpets and watercress sandwiches for my B and B," Brooke said.

"And what am I supposed to do while you're all colluding with crumpets?" Cait demanded. "Don't leave me stranded up in the Ivory Tower with Cheerio Charles and an angry mob of freshmen who're pissed because they've never gotten less than a B+ on a paper before in their lives."

"We would never," Brooke said. "You'll be up in the B and B garret, plugging away at the Great American Novel. We'll keep you fully supplied with pastries and tea."

Cait closed her eyes and indulged the fantasy for a moment. "Sounds heavenly. When do we start?"

"Never, because we have no money and no business acumen because we all majored in English."

"Silence, dream crusher!"

Jamie started belting out Cher's "If I Could Turn Back Time."

Their laughter rang out over the black, still lake as the first firework of the night exploded into the dusk.

Arden held up her wine cooler. "Here's to ten years of friendship and fine literature."

"And many more!"

"Cheers!"

"Cheers!"

"Cheerio!"

*L*ater, after the other girls drifted off to bed one by one, Arden and Cait remained on the porch, hugging their knees against their chests to ward off the damp midnight chill and watching the rippling reflection of the huge white moon on the lake.

They sat in silence, listening to the steady lapping of the waves, until Arden yawned loudly. "Last Fourth of July. Couldn't have asked for a better night. Jamie was right about those wine coolers, though; I can already feel an epic hangover coming on."

Cait stared straight ahead and addressed the fearless, frail girl who had started out as her freshman year roommate and ended up as her best friend and bonus sister. "You're not going to die, you know."

Arden's laugh was wry but gentle. "Of course not. I'm only taking an extended leave of absence from the firm because I'm bone idle."

"That's not what I meant; I just—"

"I know exactly what you meant, Cait. I know what you

mean and you know what I mean." Arden exhaled slowly, her breath barely audible above the breeze. "Let's change the subject. How's the book coming?"

Cait frowned. "What book?"

"That novel you keep saying you're going to write."

"Oh. That. Well, between teaching and going ten rounds with the B+ brigade and trying to publish all those esoteric articles in all those esoteric journals, I don't really have time to write fiction right now."

Arden shifted in her seat and quoted Marvell. "*'Had we but world enough, and time...'*"

"Exactly. I'll get to it someday."

"Well, you better buckle down, sugarplum, because all the best writers kick off young: Keats, Shelley, Plath..."

"Those are poets," Cait pointed out. "Totally different. Poets do their best work before thirty; novelists don't even get warmed up until then."

"Says who?"

"Professor Hott-with-two-*t*'s Clayburn."

"I see." Arden changed position again, but Cait couldn't tell if the cause of this restlessness was physical or psychological distress. "Well, correct me if I'm wrong, but you just had a birthday, didn't you? Thirty-two?"

"I prefer to think of it as twenty-twelve."

"Always with the excuses." Arden's voice dropped to a thick, slow murmur. "Here's the thing: Time is a luxury. Time is precious. And this is coming from the queen of procrastination. No more extensions. No makeup tests."

Cait bowed her head to hide her tears. "Can we please talk about this?"

"Absolutely not." Arden snapped back into her customary flippancy. "And if you start singing 'Wind Beneath My

Wings,' I'm kicking you out of the cabin. You'll have to sleep on the beach."

"Can I just hum a few bars?"

"You'll be a tasty bear canapé in your sleeping bag." Arden shivered. "Let's stay up late and look at the moon. Pull an all-nighter, just like back in college."

"You're on." Cait ducked into the house long enough to grab two thick woolen blankets, which she wrapped around Arden and herself. They huddled together on the chaise in silence, sharing a cocoon of warmth and gazing up toward heaven. Cait vowed to stay awake, to safeguard Arden with her own vitality, but sometime before dawn, her vigilance lapsed and she slipped into slumber.

Two months later, Arden slipped away, too. She did so in classic Arden Henley fashion, quietly and on her own terms, and not before springing one last, life-changing surprise on her friends.

Chapter
2

A million dollars?" Jamie slid down against the bar's break room wall until she was sitting on the booze-sodden floor mats. "You're yanking my chain."

"Well, a million dollars split four ways," Anna explained on the other end of the phone line. "So two hundred and fifty thousand."

"But that's too much! She can't do that!"

"She already did. According to her estate attorney, she wants us to pay off our student loans and our credit cards— or, in my case, home equity loans taken out to pay for in vitro—and use the rest to start over. Follow our bliss. Fight the power."

Jamie pushed off the wall, grabbed her handbag from her employee locker, and dug out a cellophane-wrapped pack of cigarettes.

Anna paused when the lighter sparked. "Are you smoking?"

"No." Jamie closed her eyes and inhaled. The initial hit of nicotine rendered her light-headed for a moment, reminding her of how hard it had been to quit two years ago and why she shouldn't have surrendered to the temptation to buy this "emergency reserve" pack on Monday when Cait had called to break the news about Arden.

"Liar. Don't make me send you another ashtray shaped like a blackened lung."

"Ugh. That thing was grotesque." Jamie shuddered at the memory and stubbed out the smoke. "Listen, I can't talk now because I've gotta start my shift, but you tell the powers that be that I don't want any of Arden's money. I already owe her more than I can ever repay. You, Brooke, and Cait can split it three ways."

"But her will says—"

"I don't care." Jamie's tone was sharper than she'd intended. "I'm not taking any of that money."

"But—"

"No. *Non. Nyet.* End of discussion."

Anna paused, then asked, "Did something happen? Between you and Arden?"

Fuck it. Jamie extracted a fresh cigarette and lit up again. "No. Of course not. What are you talking about?"

"I don't know. But why are you so adamant about this?"

"I love that girl like a sister and she's only thirty-two and I will not profit from her death. There is no upside to this. Not for me."

"We all loved Arden," Anna said softly. "But refusing this inheritance isn't going to bring her back. This was her wish, Jame. She wanted to give us a gift."

"Well, I don't want any part of it." Jamie dragged on her cigarette and watched the ash crumble down onto her tight black halter top.

Anna resumed her usual authoritative attitude. "Don't make any final decisions right now. You'll have time to think it over later when you're not so shell-shocked."

Jamie finished her cigarette and tossed the rest of the pack into the trash with a physical pang of longing. "That's a good word for it. The whole thing is still so surreal. My brain can't process anything beyond the most superficial details. Like, you know what I was thinking while I was driving to work tonight: *What am I going to wear?* Honest to God. I can't believe I'm going to go home tonight and open my closet and try to find something appropriate for Arden Henley's funeral."

"Knowing Arden, she'd probably want you to show up in that micro-mini leopard print number and four-inch red heels. With a six-pack of wine coolers." Anna's laugh ended in a sigh.

"Yeah, I'm sure her parents would really appreciate that. Not to mention the minister. I think I'll stick to basic black and a purse full of tissues. Are we still on for the airport pickup tomorrow?"

"Text me when you land. I'll pick you up at the curb."

"Is Jonas coming with you?"

Anna hesitated. "Um, I don't think so."

"Oh?" Jamie waited a few seconds for Anna to elaborate, then prompted, "Everything okay with you guys?"

"Mm-hmm."

"I know you're holding out on me."

"And I know you're smoking again."

"Well, aren't we all just jam-packed with knowledge?"

"Love you, Jame. Have a safe flight."

When Jamie emerged from the break room, the bar manager was waiting with the latest copy of the employee schedule in his hand and an irritated expression on his Botoxed, exfoliated face.

"Why are your shifts X-ed out for the next three days?" he demanded. "We've been over this. I let you take Fourth of July weekend off because I'm a nice guy, but you have to work Labor Day. Those are the busiest weekends of the summer, and we need all hands on deck."

Jamie glanced down and let her hair shield her face. "I get it, but it's not like I'm traipsing down to Cabo for vacation. It's a *funeral*."

"Family member?"

She started to nod and had to correct herself. "Well, not technically. One of my oldest and dearest friends from college."

"If it's not a family member, then I'm sorry, but I can't give you the time off."

Her head snapped back up. "Okay, fine, it's my grandma."

The bar manager crossed his arms. "You just told me it wasn't."

"Pretend I didn't."

"Jamie." He closed his eyes and massaged his temples.

"You're my best bartender, and the customers love you, but I can't deal with your drama all the time. If you don't show up to work this weekend, you're making a choice."

Her fingers twitched, itching for a cigarette. "I'm sorry, but I have to go to New York tomorrow. It's not optional."

"Then you'll have to find a new job when you get back."

"Probably for the best." She lifted her chin and tossed out a little T. S. Eliot. "I've been measuring out my life with coffee spoons for too long."

He narrowed his eyes. "What's that supposed to mean?"

"It means you can't fire me, because I quit." She threw back her shoulders and marched toward the break room to collect her belongings. "Dare to eat a peach!"

*O*n the flight from LAX to JFK, Jamie sweet-talked her way into first class and gratefully accepted the flight attendant's offer of red wine, even though it was only ten A.M. She hadn't been able to sleep at all the night before, and hadn't bothered with a shower or makeup, so she looked like crap, the upside of which was that she'd be left alone to read in peace.

Or so she thought.

Five minutes after takeoff, the businessman seated next to her leaned in so closely that she could smell the starch in his crisp white shirt. "Good book?"

"Mmm." She didn't raise her gaze from the text.

He squinted to read the title on the back cover. "*Wings of the Dove?* Never heard of it. What's it about?"

"A beautiful heiress who dies young and leaves a ton of money to her ratbag friends who don't deserve it."

"Pretty heavy stuff for a plane ride." He took in the

bright blond hair and the boobs and asked, "Are you an actress?"

"Nope. Unemployed bartender."

"Well, do you have any interest in acting? Because I'm starting a production company and I could really—"

"Look, no offense, but I'm having a bad week and I just need a little downtime."

"Sure. I'll leave you alone. Sorry."

"No need to apologize." She turned the page and sipped her wine.

He managed to contain himself for a few more minutes, then leaned in again. "You headed to New York for business or pleasure?"

Jamie put down the book and looked him straight in the eye. "Funeral."

She spent the next five hours reading in undisturbed silence.

Arden's memorial service was even more wrenching than Jamie had anticipated. After the last "amen" echoed off the arched stone ceiling of the Upper East Side cathedral, she straggled back out into the sunlight with Brooke, Anna, and Caitlin by her side.

Anna wiped her nose and drew a shuddery breath. "Well, that was..."

"Devastating," Cait said.

"Draining," Jamie said.

"Beautiful," Brooke insisted bravely. "A beautiful tribute to a beautiful spirit." Then her lower lip started to quiver. "God, that was horrible. Her mother's face..."

"Enough," Anna took one more swipe at her eyes, then

crumpled up the tissue and addressed the other three sternly. "No more crying. We're supposed to be celebrating her life, not dwelling on her death."

"I have never felt less celebratory," Jamie said.

Brooke motioned them in, glanced at the mourners still streaming down the cathedral steps, and murmured, "Did you see who was sitting in the very last row?"

They all crowded closer together. "Who?"

"Jeff Thuesen. He ducked in after the service started, hoping no one would notice him. But I noticed, all right."

Jamie's stomach lurched.

"Jeff Thuesen?" Anna's eyebrows snapped together. "Are you sure?"

Brooke held up her right palm. "I swear on a stack of Bibles."

"I didn't see him," Jamie said softly.

"Oh, it was definitely him," Brooke said. "He slipped out while the minister was winding down. Afraid to face our wrath, no doubt."

Anna crossed her arms. "As well he should be."

"Jeff Thuesen." Cait scowled. "What a piece of work."

Jamie stared down at the concrete and concentrated on the cacophony of idling diesel engines and car horns in the street behind them.

"Seriously," Anna said. "He breaks Arden's heart, ignores her for ten years, and then has the chutzpah to show his face at her *funeral*?"

"I don't know who he thinks he's fooling." Brooke clicked her tongue. "It's a little late to be playing the contrite exboyfriend now. He ruined her life."

"Let's not get carried away here." Cait tilted her head.

"I wouldn't say he *ruined* her *life*. I mean, don't get me wrong, I'm not defending him, but Arden had a lot going for her: a great job, a great family, great friends."

"Okay, then, he ruined her love life." Brooke's eyes flashed. "Who did she date after they broke up?"

Cait sighed. "Well…"

"Exactly. No one. She spent the rest of her life alone. Completely and utterly alone."

Jamie covered her face with her hands and started to shake.

"Jamie? You all right?"

"It's okay." Cait pulled her in for a hug. "I feel the same way. I just want to go back to the hotel, close the curtains, and spend the rest of the day in bed."

The four friends huddled in silence for a minute, keenly aware of the absence of the fifth.

Then Anna straightened up and said, "No one's going to bed. We're all spending the rest of the day together, because that's what Arden would have wanted. No roommate left behind."

Cait rolled her eyes. "What a tyrant. You can't force camaraderie at a time like this."

"True. But I can force you all to eat dinner. We need to keep up our strength. Come on, we'll find someplace dark and quiet."

"You're so practical," Brooke marveled.

"Well, one of us has to be, and since you're too sweet to be bossy, and Jamie has impulse control problems, and writers like Cait are impractical by definition, I'm it by default." Anna strode toward the corner and shepherded them along.

"I'm not a writer," Cait protested.

"And I'm not that sweet," Brooke said. "Just well-mannered. There's a difference between being polite and being a pushover."

They turned to Jamie expectantly.

"What? We all know I have impulse control problems." She shrugged. "I don't think anyone can dispute that."

A tinkly ringtone emanated from Brooke's black patent leather clutch. "That's my cell phone." She opened her bag and checked caller ID. "Excuse me for one second. This is important."

While Brooke stepped away, the conversation turned to the million-dollar bombshell Arden had detonated via her will.

"I still can't wrap my head around it," Anna said. "When her lawyer called, I was just...poleaxed."

"'Poleaxed'?" Cait grinned. "Do you get a triple word score for that?"

"I already told you, I'm not taking that money," Jamie said. "You can have my share."

"Mine, too," Cait agreed.

"No, I can't!" Anna cried. "Don't you see? She wasn't just giving us money, she was trying to give us an opportunity. Cait, you could take a sabbatical and finally pound out that novel. Think of it as the Arden Henley Literary Fellowship."

"I can't." Cait fidgeted with the pearl pendant at the hollow of her throat. "I have a job. I have responsibilities."

"I don't have either, as of yesterday." Jamie recounted the details of her termination.

Cait looked incredulous. "And you still refuse to accept an inheritance?"

"Do you have any idea how many overpriced bars there are in Los Angeles?" Jamie said. "I'll be serving up shots to the black-AmEx crowd again by the end of the week. Or, you know, my apartment lease is up at the end of the month. I may just pack it in and move on. I'm sick of the Hollywood scene. I've been thinking about Santa Barbara or maybe Vegas."

"Well." Brooke had finished her phone call and was waiting patiently at the periphery of the discussion. "You could always come live with me."

Jamie waved this away. "Thanks for the offer, hon, but I've seen your apartment. I'd have to sleep in the closet, and I wouldn't want to displace all your shoes."

"Don't worry about space. I've got lots of problems, but space isn't one of them anymore." Brooke's smile flickered, and Jamie couldn't tell if she was excited or dismayed. "In two weeks, I'm going to have a spare room. Six spare rooms, actually."

"You're moving?"

Brooke nodded, her blue eyes huge. "That was my real estate agent on the phone. I just agreed to buy Henley House."

Chapter 3

"'Home' is any four walls that enclose the right person."
—Helen Rowland, *Reflections of a Bachelor Girl*

*B*rooke Asplind had spent most of her life searching for home. Raised in a big white house by a creek in rural Alabama as the youngest of five sisters, she had been the bashful bookworm in a family of athletes and extroverts. As her mother frequently remarked, "Our little Brookie's no Southern belle. She's too busy daydreaming to date."

Brooke had shocked everyone—herself most of all—when she turned down admission to Tulane and Ole Miss to attend Thurwell College, a tiny liberal arts school in upstate New York. Thurwell's reputation for academic excellence held no sway with her family and friends. "Why on earth would you want to go so far away?" they asked. "You'll drop out and come home crying before Thanksgiving." At Thurwell, her accent relegated her to the role of a dainty hothouse flower who didn't stand a chance amid the crush of cutthroat competitors from the finest prep schools in the Northeast.

The sweet, soft-spoken 'Bama blossom didn't argue when other people tried to define her. She just smiled and daydreamed and graduated summa cum laude with a B.A. in English. Then she shocked everyone again when she chose to remain at Thurwell, working as a coordinator in the alumni affairs office.

All the people who had originally tried to talk her out of going to Thurwell were quick to let her know that she was wasting her potential by staying there. "You could be making beaucoup bucks in PR or advertising. What are you waiting for?"

"I'm not entirely sure," she replied. "But I'll know it when I see it."

Home. That was what Henley House had been to Brooke, with the spindly white porch railing and the stained-glass panel over the stair landing and the newel post topped by a hideous bronze finial shaped like the Greek god Hermes, whom they'd dubbed "Mr. Wonderful." She had shared a triple with Cait and Anna during senior year; Jamie and Arden had roomed just down the hall. Jamie had smuggled in a contraband air conditioner to get them through the stifling humidity at the beginning and the end of the school year. Anna sustained them through midterms and finals with her signature "caffeinated cupcakes." Arden offered up her array of designer clothing and accessories as date night artillery. And Cait, with her gift for teaching and her love of poetry, had hunkered down with Brooke night after night and patiently talked her through the political machinations of *Henry V.* (When Brooke had twelve hours until deadline and a nervous breakdown over her inability to plow through *Richard III,* Jamie had stepped in with a stack of CliffsNotes and a six-pack of Red Bull, and together, they toiled through the night on the only English paper Brooke ever received less than an A on.)

At Henley House, Brooke became part of a group of girls who complemented one another without having to conform. And after graduation, when the five of them all went their separate ways, Brooke lingered in Thurwell, hoping to hang on to that sense of belonging.

It hadn't worked. She became, once again, an outsider in the community in which she felt most familiar.

But now Henley House was going to be home again. Literally.

She tried to explain this to Anna, Cait, and Jamie as they slid into a booth at a cozy Irish pub near the church they'd just left. "I know this seems sudden."

" 'Sudden' is an understatement," Cait said.

Jamie shook her head. "And you say *I* have impulse control problems."

"We need a round of pints," Anna called to the waiter. "Immediately, please."

"When Arden mentioned the college was selling it, I couldn't bear the thought of some developer bulldozing it. I kept daydreaming about how the house would make the perfect, quaint little inn. Patchwork quilts, hand-stitched throw pillows, baking-powder biscuits...So I used my contacts in administration to find out how much they were asking, but when I heard the listing price, I knew I'd never be able to swing it. Then Arden's lawyer called me, and I called a realtor, and next thing you know, I was making what I was assured was a ridiculously lowball offer, and…" She gnawed her lip. "Oh dear Lord. What have I done?"

Anna put an arm around her and squeezed. "Exactly what Arden wanted. She loved the idea of turning Henley House into a B and B. I can't think of a better way to honor her memory."

"This is why we call you the Stealth Magnolia," Cait said. "No talk and all action."

Brooke let her head loll back against the back of the worn wooden booth. "I should call the realtor back. Maybe she can still rip up the sales contract. I didn't think this through."

"And that is exactly how you know you're doing the right thing." Anna wrestled Brooke's cell phone away. "You're following your heart. Turning your dreams into reality."

"Yeah, but the reality is, I don't know the first thing about running a bed-and-breakfast. I'll need a bookkeeper and a contractor and, presumably, some sort of business license."

"Okay, let's just calm down and take this one step at a time," Jamie said. "You'll get all those details squared away. You're organized. You're diligent. You're whip-smart."

"I'm only selectively smart! I had to drop out of Intro to Physics sophomore year so I wouldn't destroy my GPA. I had to fulfill my science and math requirements with Technology in American Culture and Statistics and the Media."

"Who cares?" Jamie flipped back her hair. "You don't need to be a physicist to open a bed-and-breakfast."

The waiter approached their booth with a tray of frothy dark pints, and while he distributed the drinks, Brooke closed her eyes and commenced hyperventilating.

She heard the server ask, "Is she okay?"

"She's fine," Cait assured him. "Just a touch of buyer's remorse."

"Brooke, look at me," Jamie commanded. "You can do this. You've got all the necessary skills, and now you have the funding. Your only problem is an inexplicable lack of confidence."

"Absolutely." Cait and Anna nodded their encouragement.

The dull roar in Brooke's ears finally started to subside. "You really think so? You're not just saying that?"

"I'm not known for my tact," Jamie said. "When have I ever 'just said' anything?"

"All right." Brooke pushed aside the silverware, reached across the table, and grabbed Jamie's hand. "But you have to help me."

"Me?" Jamie struggled to free herself but was no match for Brooke's immaculately manicured death grip.

"Yes! You just said you lost your job and your lease is up."

"Yeah, but—"

"Come back to Thurwell and help me." Brooke beseeched Jamie with her eyes. "You have enough confidence for both of us."

"Brooke." Jamie winced and extricated her fingers. "I'm a bartender."

"And I'm an alumni affairs coordinator who needs her bartending friend. Please. *Please!*"

Jamie opened her mouth, then closed it and shrugged one shoulder. "Fine, I'm in. What the hell."

"You're a lifesaver, Jame. The antithesis of a dream crusher. Here, take this as a signing bonus." Brooke wrinkled her nose and pushed away her pint. "I don't care for beer."

Jamie jerked her thumb at Cait and Anna. "What about these two? How come they're not getting roped into the B-and-B bonanza?"

Cait laughed. "You know I'd love to help, but classes start next week, and I'm teaching a senior seminar on the epistolary novel. Good old Samuel Richardson, a little Balzac, Laclos..."

Anna shuddered. "My condolences. *Pamela* and *Clarissa* were bad enough the first time around."

"Oh, I'm excited. It's my first self-designed upper-level course and I spent all summer compiling the syllabus."

Jamie shook her head. "Tell those poor, impressionable kids to save their sanity and stock up on Henry Fielding and Laurence Sterne." She turned to Anna. "What about you? Any reason why you can't pitch in here? I thought you said your workload's been pretty light lately."

"More like nonexistent." Anna, who had relocated three times during her six-year marriage due to her husband's job, had managed to establish a freelance career, writing and editing technical operating manuals and corporate handbooks. "Now that we've finally bought a house and settled in for the long haul in Albany, all my business has dried up because of the economy. Which is unfortunate because it leaves me with way too much time to obsess over Operation: Ovulation." Anna ticked off her to-do list on the fingers of her left hand. "Obsessively chart my basal body temperature, monitor my ovulation predictor tests, force my husband to perform on command—speaking of which, do you think there's any place around here where I could score fresh pineapple?"

Jamie glanced up at the chalkboard hung over the bar. "I don't see that on the specials menu. Should I be afraid to ask what pineapple has to do with procreation?"

"I read that pineapple is loaded with something called bromelain, which apparently helps to regulate the pH level of your cervical mucus."

Brooke blushed crimson and ducked behind her menu but listened attentively when Cait asked, "How much pineapple are you supposed to eat?"

"Well, some people say the whole thing, and some people say just the core. But everyone agrees that you have to eat it for at least five days a month for it to work."

"Who's 'everyone'?" Cait pressed.

"Oh, there's this online chat room for women having trouble conceiving. My ob-gyn says I should stay off the Internet, but at least I feel like I'm doing something proactive, you know?"

"What else do you have to eat?" Jamie wanted to know.

"Lots of oily fish, kiwi, honey, garlic—"

"Garlic?"

"Vitamin B," Anna explained. "I choke down a raw clove every morning with my tea." The spark in her brown eyes dimmed. "And still nothing."

Jamie pushed up her sleeve and offered up a salute. "Well, keep slugging back the garlic and pineapple, 'cause it's going to happen for you very soon. I can feel it. This is the year we stop dreaming and start living. This is the year the English majors make good."

Chapter
4

"What a strange thing is the propagation of life!"
—Lord Byron, *Detached Thoughts*

Anna fumbled with the clasp on her skimpy black lace bra, applied a fresh coat of lipstick, and dabbed perfume behind her ears and on her wrists. She sashayed down the hallway to the den and purred, "Are you ready for dessert, darling? I've got something delicious waiting for you in the bedroom."

Her husband was hunched over the desk in the corner, deeply absorbed in some online video game involving flamethrowers and aliens. Jonas spent his days working as a quality assurance engineer for a company that manufactured autopilots for commercial jet aircraft, and after a long day of implementing, documenting, and maintaining quality control systems at the office, he liked to unwind at home with a little virtual intergalactic warfare. "What's up?"

Anna leaned against the doorframe and struck a pose. "It's time."

Jonas flinched and returned his gaze to the computer screen. "Again?"

"What do you mean, 'again'? I only ovulate every thirty-three days! We've been waiting over a month for this!"

Jonas continued his alien annihilation without any sign of having heard her. Then finally, as she was preparing to repeat herself, he paused the game and stared up at the Edward Hopper print hanging above the desk. "Anna, I'm exhausted."

"I can think of a few ways to reenergize you." She smiled wider to hide her hurt feelings. "Come on, honey, we'll have fun. And this time it's gonna happen for us."

His shoulders slumped. "It never happens. If IVF didn't make it happen—three times—what makes you think that this one medically unassisted romp in the sack is gonna change anything?"

Anna closed her eyes and repeated what Jamie had said. "I can just feel it. This is our month."

"You say that every month," Jonas pointed out. "And I'm tired of spending all our time and money and energy on something that most people accomplish by accident."

So much for sensual seduction. Anna grabbed the green chenille throw blanket off the couch and wrapped it around her torso. "I know, honey. This is frustrating for me, too." She crossed the room and started kneading his shoulders. "And I really want to talk about it with you. But right now, can we please just go to the bedroom?"

His muscles tensed beneath her fingers. "Maybe later."

She exhaled slowly and made a conscious effort not to let his negativity feed her own. "Maybe now."

"I need to finish up here," he said tightly.

"No, you don't. The computer doesn't need you." She leaned over to whisper into his ear. "I do."

She knew he could smell her perfume and feel her breath tickling his neck, and for a moment, she felt his defenses weaken. But then he shut down and pulled away.

"Can't we do this tomorrow?"

"Jonas, *come on!*" The green blanket fell to the floor as she threw out her arms in exasperation. She didn't even bother trying to suck in her stomach. "I'm offering up sex on a silver platter here! Most guys would be ecstatic."

Finally, her husband snapped. "Most guys don't have to wait for a surge in their wife's luteinizing hormone to get lucky. Most guys don't even know what luteinizing hormone *is.* You don't want me. You only want my sperm!"

She gasped. "How can you—"

"Actually, you probably don't even want my sperm." His forehead gleamed with a sheen of perspiration. "You'd probably rather get it on with someone who has a chance in hell of getting you pregnant."

Anna sat down hard on the sofa. "Jonas!"

"What?" His dark eyes flashed, but she saw pain underneath his anger. "Are you denying it?"

"Of course I am! I only want you. I love you. I *married* you." Then she took a calming breath and added, "Besides, the doctors all said your sperm is totally fine. Why are you blaming yourself? It's probably me. It's because I'm overweight."

He furrowed his brow. "You're not overweight."

"Yes, I am. You heard the endocrinologist. My body mass index is on the high end."

"The high end of *normal.*"

"Then what is it? Why aren't I pregnant yet?"

He clenched the sides of his head with both hands. "What do I have to do to escape this conversation?"

"Get over here, rip off my panties, and have your way with me!" She knew she sounded more like a drill sergeant than a dominatrix, but she was too exasperated to care.

He paused, then muttered, "I can't."

"You can't or you won't?"

His face was still buried in his hands. "I can't. I won't. I just...I'm sorry." He abruptly turned back to his gaming and turned the volume way up.

She crossed her arms over her flimsy bra and listened to the juicy *splat* of alien flesh under fire. "You're not attracted to me anymore."

"Stop." His clipped, authoritative tone now matched hers. "We're tabling this for tonight."

"NO! I'm ovulating! If we 'table' it, that's one more month wasted. This is only going to get more difficult."

"I'd say it's difficult enough right now."

"Meaning?"

Jonas shoved his chair back from the desk, stood up, and gave her his full attention. "Meaning which would you rather have: a happy marriage with no kids or a crappy marriage and a baby at any cost?"

He stared at her. She stared back.

Finally, she said, "Don't ask me that unless you want an honest answer."

He nodded, his expression grim.

"We've been planning this for years. We specifically chose

this house because it's in the best school district in Albany. All the money we've spent, all the doctors and the hormone injections and the medications and the time. And you want to just quit."

"What I want is to start considering other options. We don't have to keep going through this, month after month."

"I can't believe I'm hearing this."

"Why are you so dead set against adoption?"

"I'm not *against* it. But I want to experience pregnancy and give birth. I want my body to do what it's supposed to do. I want to stop feeling like such a failure."

He stared at her, clearly mystified. "At the end of the day, we'll have a child. The biological details don't matter. Would it really be so bad to miss out on morning sickness and labor pains?"

Anna threw up her hands. "You're right. A child is a blessing, no matter what. That's irrefutable logic."

"I know. So why are you crying?"

"I'm not," she lied, turning her face away. "Are you really saying you've given up all hope we'll ever conceive?"

"Yes." He set his jaw. "It's time to get real and move on. Look at you, Anna. You're running on empty."

She nodded, swiping at her eyes.

He sat back down at the computer. "Both of us need a break. At least, I do."

Anna froze. "What kind of break?"

Jonas shrugged.

"Physical? Emotional? What kind of break?" Her voice broke.

He hung his head. "I don't know. But you have to make a choice, because I can't keep going like this."

She left him in the den, swapped her lingerie for

sweatpants and a T-shirt, and retreated to the kitchen. She flipped through her cookbooks for the most labor-intensive recipe she could find, some impossibly complex confection that would demand all her concentration.

The next few hours were spent mixing and whisking and doling out ingredients in precisely measured quantities. She was only dimly aware of Jonas's good night and the closing of the bedroom door. She soaked up the silence with sugar and spice, and before dawn broke, she left a perfectly executed mint parfait filled with chocolate mousse in the refrigerator along with a note on which she'd scribbled a Shakespearean ultimatum:

"Love is not love which alters when it alteration finds."
All or nothing at all.

Chapter
5

"Women are often under the impression that men are much more madly in love with them than they really are."
—W. Somerset Maugham, *The Painted Veil*

Cait found out about the other woman quite by accident. She was sequestered in her office on campus, where she'd intended to spend the afternoon compiling a list of journal articles to put on reserve at the college library, but she'd gotten slightly sidetracked. Her work papers had been pushed aside and her coffee had gone cold while she spent two hours making and breaking promises to indulge in "just one more chapter" of *The Captain of All Pleasures.*

Who needed Internet dating when you could have adventure on the high seas and sizzling Victorian sex at the flip of a page?

She startled when she heard the murmur of approaching

voices outside her door. She shoved the novel into her desk drawer and snatched up an article on literary criticism. No one knew about her secret vice of paperback romances, and no one ever would. Especially not her elitist ex.

Cait recognized the voices in the hall as belonging to professors Helen Nam (Renaissance studies) and Ritu Radhakrishnan (postmodern lit).

"How about that guest lecturer from Cal State?" Helen was saying.

"Well, I'm not sure about her academic credentials," Ritu replied, "but I can certainly see why the old guard flew her out and gave her the grand tour."

"Moll Flanders in a pantsuit," Helen scoffed. "I'm pretty sure her curriculum vitae isn't the only thing she's padding!"

They both laughed. "Exactly," Ritu said. "Since when does a heaving bosom and an affinity for creative corsetry make anyone an expert on the eighteenth-century novel?"

Cait flung open her door and poked out her head. "What guest lecturer? We hosted an eighteenth-century scholar, and I missed it?"

The snickers and smiles vanished and were replaced with blinks and stammers. Helen wouldn't even make eye contact.

"No, no," Ritu said hastily. "Nothing like that. Just a very informal, er, I think my office phone's ringing."

Both of them escaped down the hall. Cait listened to the clatter of high heels echoing off the empty corridor and tried to reason away a rising swell of panic. Surely her colleagues weren't deliberately trying to leave her out of the loop. To suspect otherwise would be to suggest department-wide subterfuge and that was just...paranoid.

But, as Jamie was so fond of remarking, just because you're paranoid doesn't mean they're not all out to get you.

Cait marched down the stairs toward the all-knowing or-acle of truth and wisdom: Penny Powell, the English depart-ment secretary.

Penny glanced up from her computer keyboard when she heard Cait approaching, but did not offer her customary wave or chirpy hello. Instead, she ducked her head and re-sumed typing. Alarm bells clanged in Cait's head, but she forced herself to remain casual.

"Hey, Penny. Um, I heard that the department had a vis-itor recently."

Penny's gaze slid away from Cait's and fixed on the jar of consolatory butterscotches she offered to students facing particularly dire circumstances: dismal exam scores, plagia-rism charges, revoked graduation eligibility. She tapped her pen against the desktop. "What sort of visitor?"

"Actually, I'm hoping *you* might be able to tell *me*. I just heard Professors Nam and Radhakrishnan discussing an eighteenth-century scholar flown in from California."

"I wouldn't know anything about that."

Cait's heartbeat kicked into an uneven gallop. "Is the de-partment planning to hire another early British lit professor?"

Still with the shifty eyes. "I wouldn't know anything about that, either."

"Penny, come on. Please!" Desperation won out over dig-nity, and Cait planted both palms on the secretary's desk. "You know everything that goes on around here. Why are we flying in scholars from the West Coast?"

Penny pushed her frizzy, honey-colored bangs out of her eyes and regarded Cait with poorly concealed pity. "You'll have to ask the department chair." Then she delivered the coup de grâce: She removed the lid from the glass candy jar. "Butterscotch?"

"Oh shit." Cait raced back up the stairs and rapped on the office door of the department chair.

"Charles. Open up. I know you're in there."

She heard the creak of a wooden chair, then the door swung inward to reveal the narrow, ruddy face of her Anglo-fetishist former boyfriend. He did not look happy to see her.

She barged past him and made herself comfy on the battered, corduroy-upholstered armchair next to the overflowing bookcases. "Who, may I ask, is the guest lecturer from Cal State?"

Charles ran his hands back through his thick, dark hair, which he insisted on keeping a few inches too long in the back. "The Arthurian mullet," Cait had heard Helen Nam call it.

"I suppose you're referring to Lorelei Alben?" he said.

"I suppose I am." Cait filed the name away for future cyber-investigation. "What's her deal and why wasn't I asked to meet her?"

Charles's lips thinned into an expression of almost paternal disapproval. From the moment he first met Cait at an academic conference in Chicago, he had adopted an air of authority, and she had gone along with it. He was so confident in his scholarly superiority that she never thought to second-guess him. He was older, he was tenured, and he had his Arthurian mullet and carefully groomed facial hair to bolster his image as a dashing man of letters. At first, it had been refreshing to date a guy who would rather talk about Foucault than football. She'd considered Charles to be her mentor; he had swept her off her feet and helped her land a job at his college.

In retrospect, Cait could see that the problems between them began the day she signed on as his coworker, but things really got shaky last year, when she initiated the review process for tenure. Suddenly, nothing she did was good enough. He dismissed her research interests as frivolous and lacking in scope. Her class lectures were pronounced "merely adequate." But she was no longer the impressionable subordinate straight out of grad school. And so, slowly, her view of him changed from worldly and erudite to affected and pedantic. But before she'd worked up the nerve to break things off with him, he'd made his preemptive strike via email.

Cheerio, my ass.

Charles waited until he had her full attention before he continued speaking. "I had the pleasure of meeting Ms. Alben at a symposium in Toronto, and her, ahem, *deal* is that she's a Ph.D. candidate about to defend her dissertation. She was on campus just before Labor Day weekend; if I recall correctly, you were taking a personal day."

"I was at a *funeral.*" Cait kicked up her feet and rested them on his bookshelf, watching him flinch as she grazed his treasured French edition of Roland Barthes's *Criticism and Truth* with the sole of her shoe. "So what exactly are you inviting her out here for?"

"Ms. Alben has authored some groundbreaking articles on feminist themes in Gothic and amatory fiction."

"It's interesting that her area of expertise happens to overlap with mine."

He unfurled his fingers as if tossing a set of imaginary dice. "Yes, well . . ."

"It's also interesting that just a few years ago, when I myself was a wide-eyed Ph.D. candidate, you introduced yourself at a similar conference in a similar fashion and suggested I apply for a teaching position here."

"Are you implying——"

Cait swung her feet back to the floor. "I'm not implying anything, I'm saying it outright: First you dumped me, now you're trying to replace me with some freshly degreed hottie. You know, I wondered why you ended things so abruptly last semester. I had myself convinced that everything was my fault, that I was too frivolous for someone of your intellectual stature." She snorted. "But now I see that my *brain* wasn't the source of your dissatisfaction."

"I categorically deny and resent that supposition." Charles pounded his desktop for emphasis. "Please understand, you've put the whole department in a difficult position, Professor Johnson."

"Don't 'professor' me." Cait rolled her eyes. "We've seen each other naked."

"Very well then, I'll speak frankly." He straightened his tie. "We've had some concerns about your performance of late."

"What are you talking about?" She'd received a glowing evaluation at her third-year teaching review in April. "And who's 'we'?"

"Well, for one thing, the students feel that you have unrealistic expectations. You do not enjoy a reputation as a generous grader."

"So what? They complain, but they learn. I'm happy to offer help to anyone who asks, and I'm always trying to innovate fresh new curricula."

Even the tips of Charles's ears began to redden. "Yes. About that. I'm afraid we're going to have to cancel your seminar on the epistolary novel."

Her jaw dropped. "On what grounds?"

"As of today, only three students have enrolled. But if

you'd like to pick up an extra section of freshman comp, I suppose we could offer you the eight A.M. class."

"Oh my God." Cait sat back, reeling. "Let's cut to the chase here. After everything you've put me through, you owe me that much."

He shuffled a few papers. "Very well. Your fourth-year review is coming up in October, and it's only fair to warn you that your contract may not be renewed for next year."

"*What?*"

"You're aware that you can be let go at any point in the review process."

Cait was stunned. The fourth-year review was usually treated as a mere formality, a friendly check-in after the grueling third-year review process. Her dreams of tenure evaporated.

"Additionally, the dean has received several letters of complaint regarding your"—Charles cleared his throat—"poor collegiality."

"Is that so?" She fixed him with a death glare. "Letters from whom?"

"That's confidential."

She opened her mouth to argue, but he cut her off. "Finally, I didn't want to bring this up until we had some concrete evidence, but there have been a few red flags lately. Financially."

She couldn't have been more shocked if he'd slapped her. "What on earth are you talking about?"

"Well, for example, your annual expense report was turned in a few days late."

"Along with half the department's! Where are you going with this?"

He picked up a gold pen and began fidgeting. "You're in charge of disbursing the colloquium speaker fund, are you not?"

"Yeah, because you assigned it to me last winter."

"As you're well aware, each speaker is entitled to a one-thousand-dollar honorarium, plus travel expenses." More throat clearing and pen tapping. "Questions have been raised as to whether those expenses have been properly documented and directed."

"Are you accusing me of *embezzling*? My God, Charles, I know we've had our differences, but you can't honestly believe I would—"

He held up his palms. "I'm not accusing you of anything."

"Then who is?"

"You know I can't divulge my sources."

"Oh, cut the bullshit. Are you or are you not interviewing Left Coast lightskirts for my replacement?"

He took a slow and deliberate sip from his coffee mug. "Nothing's set in stone."

Cait sat motionless for a minute, absorbing the impact and reviewing her options. This was completely wrong and unfair, and fighting it was going to require every iota of energy she had. She thought about the upcoming academic year, the endless battles she'd have to wage with Charles, and suddenly she remembered what Arden had said about time being a luxury.

She looked her ex-lover straight in the eye and asked, "What if I said I'd like to take some time off?"

Charles's whole body relaxed. "I'd say that's an excellent idea. Take as much as you need."

"Fine, I will. And before I go, I'll be sending the dean

documentation accounting for every single dollar I spent from that honorarium fund."

He inclined his head. "I applaud you."

"And don't expect me to come crawling back, begging for tenure. I have other offers."

He templed his long, smooth fingers beneath his chin. "Indeed. Like what, pray tell?"

She got to her feet and regarded him with all the icy hauteur she could muster. "I just found out I'm a recipient of the very prestigious Arden Henley Literary Fellowship. Keep your eye out for my name on the National Book Award short list."

Then she turned on her heel, stormed back to her office, and started piling textbooks and file folders into cardboard boxes. When she yanked open her desk drawer and glimpsed *The Captain of All Pleasures,* she smiled for the first time all day and slipped the novel into her handbag.

Twelve hours later, Cait pulled her battered old Honda hatchback up to the curb in front of Henley House, which now featured a small white clapboard sign hanging from the eaves of the front porch:

Paradise Found Bed-and-Breakfast

"Come in, come in!" Brooke greeted her at the front door with a mug of hot cocoa. "Do you like the sign?"

"Yeah, but you're not open for business yet, are you?" Cait glanced over Brooke's shoulder into the house, the interior of which was obscured in shadows. She had driven through the night, fueled by adrenaline and a six-pack of diet cola, to arrive almost exactly halfway between dusk and dawn. But the porch light provided enough illumination to see that the front room was empty and the walls bare.

"Not yet." Brooke covered her yawn with her hand. "But I got caught up in a whirlwind of enthusiasm when I thought of the name, and commissioned the sign from a local artist. Isn't it perfect?"

"It is." Cait stepped into the foyer and all her worries washed away in a wave of nostalgia. "Wow. Do you smell that? It smells like..." *textbooks and stale beer and a potpourri of snack foods ground into industrial carpeting* "...college."

"The painters are coming this weekend." Brooke turned up the collar of her fluffy pink robe. "Then on Monday, I've got the zoning board hearing and a meeting with an attorney about applying for a business license."

"Jeez. You're not wasting any time."

"There's a lot to do. A lot to know. A lot to pay for. And I'm trying to get it all done so I can open before prime leaf-peeping season." Brooke nibbled her lower lip. "I'll be happy when I get to the part where I can relax and pick out Laura Ashley duvets and brew afternoon tea for the guests."

"Well, don't worry about any of that right now. Go back to bed. I'm sorry to wake you up like this in the middle of the night."

"It's no trouble at all." Brooke flashed her dazzling charm school smile. "Here, let me take your bag. Once this place is up and running, I'll have to accommodate new arrivals at all hours. Oh, I'm so glad you came, Cait."

"Me, too. I need a change of scenery. Badly." Cait hadn't gone into the details of her abrupt departure from teaching when she called earlier, but Brooke didn't press her.

"Stay as long as you please. It'll be just like old times."

Brooke handed her the mug of cocoa. "Want me to rustle up a bite to eat?"

"No, I'm fine." Cait sipped the hot chocolate and announced, "I'm finally going to do it. I'm starting my novel tomorrow. No more excuses." This was the second time she'd voiced that goal in the last twenty-four hours. Saying it aloud made it real. Now she couldn't take it back.

Brooke clapped her hands together. "Excellent. We'll have a bona fide writer-in-residence at Paradise Found. How rarefied." She turned off the porch light, locked the front door, and led the way up the stairs. "I've ordered furniture for the bedrooms, but it hasn't been delivered yet, so we're roughing it with air mattresses and sleeping bags right now."

"Don't worry about me. I'm so tired I could sleep standing up." Cait trailed her hand along the banister. "Hey, it's Mr. Wonderful!"

The ornate bronze figure glinted in the moonlight streaming through the window above the landing.

Brooke smiled and patted Hermes's little winged cap. "Did you know he's the official god of travelers?" She tilted her head. "Well, actually, the book I consulted said he was the 'Olympian god of *boundaries* and of the travelers who cross them.'"

"Official god of boundary issues?" Cait laughed. "How fitting for this house."

Right on cue, Jamie's sleep-tousled head appeared at the top of the staircase. "Who goes there?"

Cait raised her mug in greeting. "A refugee from the Ivory Tower."

"*Cait?* But you..." Jamie rubbed her eyes and peered down at them. "What happened?"

"Long story." Cait reclaimed her overnight bag from Brooke and made a beeline for her old room at the end of the hallway. "With an unfortunate and unoriginal ending. Heed my words, ladies: Never, ever, ever date a college administrator."

Chapter 6

"...Without scheming to do wrong, or to make others unhappy, there may be error, and there may be misery. Thoughtlessness, want of attention to other people's feelings, and want of resolution, will do the business."
—Jane Austen, *Pride and Prejudice*

Never, ever, ever date a college administrator.

Cait's warning reverberated through Jamie's mind early the next morning as she shuffled into the kitchen to make coffee. Because Brooke had yet to select window coverings, the bright morning sunlight had awakened Jamie at an hour when she would typically be going to bed if she still lived in Los Angeles.

But she didn't live in L.A. anymore. She'd thrown away her job and her attempts to get her life together in California, just as she'd thrown away her jobs and relationships in Miami, Honolulu, and Atlanta.

Never, ever, ever date a college administrator. Jamie would add to that: Never, ever, ever date an investment banker, a chemical engineer, an auto mechanic, a sculptor, a zoologist, an actor, a computer programmer, or a social worker.

Hmm. Come to think of it, maybe the take-home message here was that no man in his right mind should ever, ever date *her*.

Though Jamie was always the first to make fun of her own romantic track record, she secretly harbored a growing sense of shame about her total inability to see anything through to its conclusion. When the tough got going, she quit, to the point that it was no longer an amusing postadolescent foible; it was a major character flaw. She hurt the people who cared about her. Not on purpose, not with malice, but the end result was the same, regardless of motive.

She thought about Arden and the thick cream-colored envelope that had arrived via certified mail last week, and her stomach churned.

Outside, she could hear birds chirping and a dog barking. The mornings were so quiet here. Careful not to slam the cabinet doors or clink the glasses, Jamie assembled a mismatched trio of coffee mugs. She leaned back against the chipped Formica countertop and gazed out the window at the clear cobalt sky and the copse of maple saplings in the backyard.

Thurwell, New York, billed itself as a pocket of tranquillity tucked in the foothills between the old-world gentility of Saratoga and the rustic charm of the Adirondacks. The streets were small and safe, the air clean and invigorating. The town's neighborhoods branched outward from the main thoroughfare of Pine Street, which boasted one major grocery store, two stoplights, a pair of boutiques featuring expensive outdoor gear, a few family-owned restaurants, a cozy little pub, and a single-show movie theater. Most local businesses catered to the college population and the tourists who came to enjoy foliage and apple picking in the fall, Nordic skiing in the winter, and antiquing in the summer. The Thurwell College admissions brochures featured photos of professors leading seminars outdoors on the grassy quad and groups of rosy-cheeked students frolicking through the fresh snowfall at the annual winter carnival. But, like most small towns, Thurwell constantly roiled with scandal just below the surface. You just had to know where to look.

"Morning." Brooke padded in wearing a pink chenille bathrobe and sheepskin slippers at least two sizes too big for her tiny feet.

Cait trailed in behind her, clad in a white ribbed tank top and a threadbare pair of blue plaid boxer shorts that looked vaguely familiar.

"Are those the same shorts you had in college?" Jamie shook her head. "Damn, don't you ever throw anything away?"

"After years of living on Ramen noodles and a grad student stipend? No. Besides, I look good in these. Right, Brooke?"

"They're very, uh, Robinson Crusoe chic." Brooke turned back to Jamie. "What's for breakfast?"

Jamie nodded toward the coffeemaker. "I'm a bartender, dearest, not a cook. If you need a killer mimosa or hibiscus, I'm your girl. You want eggs Benedict? I'm out."

"What's a hibiscus?" Cait wanted to know. "Sounds exotic."

"Champagne and cranberry juice."

Cait perked up. "Ooh, that sounds good. I might have to try that."

"No!" Brooke smoothed her disheveled blond hair and rummaged through the cabinet next to the refrigerator. "No drinking. Today is a workday. For all of us. I have to go into the office—"

"You didn't quit your job yet?" Cait asked. "I thought that was the whole point of this."

"Do you have any idea how much it cost to put a down payment on this place? Never mind legal fees, accounting fees, liability insurance, dishware, website design, mattresses, furniture..." Brooke's blue eyes got bigger and wilder with every word. "It's only been three weeks, and I'm practically in the hole already."

Cait nodded. "Point taken."

"I have to keep my day job at least until I open the doors to guests," Brooke said. "So I'm going into the office today, and Jamie's going to start researching how to start an event-planning business."

"I'll let in the inspector guy, too," Jamie volunteered. "And call the mattress place again and harass them about delivery."

"What about me?" Cait asked.

"Well, you'll be getting your muse on upstairs," Jamie said.

Cait looked at them blankly.

"Your novel," Brooke prompted. "You're starting today, remember?"

"Oh yeah." Cait poured herself a bowl of shredded wheat and shoveled in a huge mouthful.

Brooke put down her coffee cup for a moment and clasped her hands. Her face took on a radiant, peaceful glow. "I know start-up is a lot of work, but I shouldn't complain. We are all *so* lucky to have this opportunity. How many people ever get the chance to start from scratch and chase their dreams?"

"Mmph," Cait said.

"Exactly." Brooke nodded. "No more negativity. Come hell or high water, Paradise Found will flourish. As God is my witness"—she waved her fist like a fair-haired Scarlett O'Hara—"I am going to do Arden proud!"

"Mmph." Cait took another bite, topped off her cereal bowl, and trudged back toward the staircase.

"Me, too," Jamie echoed. As soon as Brooke left for work, she crept back up to her bedroom and dug through the profusion of clothes, books, and shoes spilling out of her suitcases until she found the crumpled ecru envelope she was searching for. Then she hurried back downstairs to the makeshift office space set up on a card table next to the fireplace and turned on the paper shredder. She ran her finger over the law office letterhead embossed on the upper left corner of envelope and then, without a moment's hesitation or any flicker of emotion, extracted the contents and fed them into gnashing metal teeth until her check for $250,000 was nothing more than confetti.

*T*wo hours later, Jamie awoke with a start to find her cheek plastered to the open pages of *10 Simple Steps to Becoming a World-Class Wedding Planner* and a thin rivulet of drool pooled in the book's spine.

"Oog." She rolled to the side and swiped at the page with her shirtsleeve. Studying in bed had always been her downfall; dull text and orange highlighters provided the perfect prelude to a catnap.

Coffee. She needed more coffee. Plus a more comprehensive how-to guide. At least four of the ten simple steps focused on creating and enforcing an ironclad client contract. She didn't need a manual to tell her to always get some money up front. Please. They might as well throw in sage little tidbits like *Don't sleep with the groom.* Jamie already knew how to protect herself; the whole point of becoming an event planner was to protect someone else's special day.

She headed to the kitchen, patting Mr. Wonderful on his winged cap on her way down the stairs. "Ahoy," she said when she saw Cait seated at the kitchen table. "Any coffee left? I need to double down on my caffeine consumption. I'm telling you, I should be writing this guide instead of reading it." She held up the book with a grimace. "Speaking of which, how's your writing going? Did you start chapter one yet?"

Cait stared down at her plate of apple wedges and cheddar cheese. "I've been at the computer all morning. Just taking a five-minute break."

Jamie nodded. "Well, let me know if I'm making too much noise or, you know, disturbing the creative cocoon in any way."

Cait shrugged one shoulder. "No, you're fine."

The ancient avocado green wall phone rang, making them both jump. Jamie picked up the receiver. "Hello?"

"Oh, thank goodness you're there, Jame, you have to help me!" Brooke's voice was a hiss of panic.

"What's wrong?"

"Hang on a second, I have to make sure no one hears this or I am fired, do you hear me? *Fired!*" There was a lot of rustling, then Brooke came back on the line. "The college is

hosting a 150th anniversary celebration the day after tomorrow and all the trustees and muckety-mucks are invited and
I'm in charge of the cake—I'm always in charge of the
cake—and I thought I called the baker weeks ago, I could
have sworn, but somehow, between everything with Arden
and the funeral and the inheritance and buying the house ..."

"There's no cake," Jamie finished for her.

Cait looked up from her apple with raised eyebrows.

"Exactly," Brooke said. "I just called the baker and asked
if she could pull something together on short notice, and she
actually laughed at me! She says there's nothing she can do.
I can't believe it, she's never said no before. And the college
has been such a loyal customer for the past few years."

"Jeez," Jamie said. "What a—"

"I know! That's the problem with trying to do business in
this smug little town: no competition. What am I going to
do? I can't show up to this with a grocery store cake!"

"Brooke. Settle down," Jamie said. "Seriously, breathe.
You don't want to get the vapors and pass out."

Cait's eyebrows inched higher and higher as she craned to
overhear Brooke's end of the conversation.

"I can't believe I dropped the ball like this." Brooke emitted
a tiny squeak of despair. "They're going to fire me, and I can't
blame them one bit. I'm going to have to rush order something
from Albany for half the quality and twice the price."

"No, you're not." Jamie turned to Cait and gestured that
she needed a pen and paper. "It's all about confidence, remember? Just put on your game face and maintain. Everything's going to be fine."

"But how? We only have two days. What are you going
to do?"

"I'm going to do what any self-respecting English major would do: pull something out of my ass. Isn't that why you called me?"

"Well, I—" Brooke stopped gasping for breath. "Yes."

"Okay, then. Leave everything to me." Jamie hung up the phone, whereupon Cait immediately demanded, "Brooke's freaking out? What's going on?"

"Nothing a crackerjack event planner can't handle." Jamie tossed *10 Simple Steps* in the recycling bin and started to smile in spite of herself. "I do my best work under pressure, you know."

"Uh-oh." Cait's lips formed a perfect O. "I know that look. That look means trouble."

"You wound me." Jamie snatched up the phone again, punched in numerals she knew by heart, and waited through three rings for someone to pick up. "Hey, it's me. What are you doing right now?"

"Ovulating," Anna said with decidedly un-Anna-like dejection. "All by myself."

Jamie didn't miss a beat. "Great. Can you ovulate and bake at the same time?"

"Might as well be productive, even if I can't be *re*productive. Why? What's up?"

Chapter 7

"Old houses mended,
Cost little less than new before they're ended."
—Colley Cibber, *The Double Gallant*

Brooke could smell the cinnamon and vanilla a block away from Paradise Found. Her pace quickened as she rounded the corner on her half-mile walk from work. The first floor of the house was brightly lit and upbeat New Wave music emanated from the open windows. As she ran up the steps and opened the front door, she set aside her anxiety and indulged in a moment of nostalgia.

She was coming home again. All of the stress and second-guessing of the past few weeks would be worth it.

"Honey, I'm home!" Brooke called as she hung up her handbag and light twill coat on the hooks next to the door.

All she heard in response was "Our Lips Are Sealed" by the Go-Go's blasting out of the kitchen. When she got to the end of the hallway, she saw Anna and Jamie stationed at opposite counters with several large mixing bowls and open containers of flour, sugar, and spices on the table between them.

"Anna!" Brooke cried. "What are you doing here? What's all this?"

"This"—Anna barely glanced up from the food processor—"is bakery boot camp. And I'm your commanding officer. Get in here and grab an apron."

"Not so fast." Jamie stopped whisking a metal bowl full of cream and pointed upstairs. "The insurance inspector is here. I let him in hours ago; he's gotta be almost done."

"How does he look?" Brooke asked. "Lenient and lackadaisical or surly and stern?"

"Couldn't really say. I've been too busy trying to appease the sugarcoated slave driver here."

"Less talking, more whisking," Anna barked.

"Sir, yes, sir." Jamie redoubled her whipping efforts.

"Where's Cait?"

"Grocery store run," Anna said. "Your pantry is scandalously understocked. I need more milk, butter, eggs, cream of tartar—"

"What the hell's cream of tartar?" Jamie asked. "I've never even heard of that."

"Don't you worry." Anna smiled wickedly. "You're going to find out all about cream of tartar, right around two A.M. tonight when you're exhausted and begging for a nap and a cheeseburger."

"Do your worst. You'll never break me, McCauley!"

"I'll be right back," Brooke said. "Save me a sifter."

She dashed up to the second floor and peeked in the doorways until she located the insurance inspector in the bathroom adjoining Cait's bedroom. "Hi! How are you? I'm Brooke Asplind."

A stooped, lanky man wearing scuffed olive pants and a white polo shirt was hunched over a metal clipboard. His pale blue eyes looked weary beneath the brim of his navy cap. "You the buyer?"

"That I am." She flashed her brightest, flirtiest smile. "Pleased to meet you, sir." She waited for him to offer up his name along with a handshake, but he merely scratched his neck and thumbed through his paperwork.

"Says here that you're planning to occupy the house as your primary residence and operate a bed-and-breakfast with the extra bedrooms?"

"That's the plan," she said. "May I offer you something to drink? A cup of coffee or tea?"

"Nope." He scribbled away with his pen. "I'm finishing up."

She crossed her fingers. "Everything checked out all right, I hope?"

"Pretty much," he said. Her spirits soared.

Then he added, "With one notable exception."

"Oh dear. That sounds ominous."

"There's good news and bad news." The inspector clicked his pen with finality. "I'll talk you through it. The good news is the plumbing looks okay, the roof's fairly new, and the smoke alarms are functional. I checked the basement and the attic for asbestos, and you're all clear."

Brooke nibbled the inside of her cheek. "And the bad news?"

"Well, you got a few minor issues to address: The back

porch has a loose board, the toilet tank in the downstairs bathroom has a hairline crack and it's leaking water, and you need to modify at least one of the ground-floor bedrooms to comply with the Americans with Disabilities Act."

"Of course, that makes sense." She paused. "What does that entail, exactly?"

"Well, the room needs to be wheelchair accessible, so you'll have to widen the doorway, install grab bars in the shower, make sure there's knee clearance under the sink, maybe add a ramp to one of the porches..."

"Sounds doable." She started to relax. "Expensive, but doable."

"Yeah, I think you can even get a tax credit for that type of remodeling." He thumped his thumb against the clipboard. "Now here comes the bad news."

His tone was decidedly worrisome.

"Shall I rustle up some tissues and bourbon before you break it to me?" Brooke asked. "Because you seem a little—"

"Ma'am, there's no easy way to say this, so I'll just come right out with it: You've got knob-and-tube wiring."

She blinked. "I've got what?"

"Knob-and-tube wiring. Through the whole house."

"I don't exactly know what that is."

"I'll tell you what it is: a house fire waiting to happen. Your whole electrical system's outdated and potentially dangerous. Probably installed back in the 1930s or so. At least. No way can we insure this place. Especially if you're planning to have boarders."

"But I just closed escrow! No one said anything about 'outdated and potentially dangerous' during the home sale inspection. They said the electrical stuff looked fine!"

The inspector rubbed his chin. "Follow me." He led her

down to the basement, where he pointed out the electrical service box tucked back by the laundry room. "Here's the problem. The fuse box and the meter box look like they were upgraded in the 1960s or '70s. Whoever upgraded them also put in a new breaker box and spliced a few yards of Romex wiring to the old knob-and-tube wiring. Then they put up paneling over the studs in the basement and the first-floor joints, so you can't see the knob-and-tube system unless you know what to look for."

Brooke tried to appear as if she was following this explanation, but she hadn't comprehended a syllable after the words "breaker box."

"I see." Her mouth went dry. "And how much do you think replacing the wiring might cost?"

"A lot."

"Could you be more specific?"

"Well, it's a pretty big house, so your material costs are gonna add up, plus you'll need to pay by the hour for a contractor or two."

She steeled herself.

He adjusted the brim of his cap and threw out a dollar amount.

"*How* much?" She stumbled back against the cold concrete wall.

"It's just a ballpark figure," he said defensively.

"That's more than my down payment!" she cried. "This is outrageous. I will—I will *sue!*"

The inspector squinted one eye. "Who you planning to sue?"

"The college. The realtor. The home inspector. Somebody!"

"The home inspector's evaluation is limited by what he

can see. If he didn't rip open the paneling here, there's no way he coulda known the whole house wasn't up to code."

"But you figured it out!"

"Only because I took a plug out of an outlet upstairs to make sure it was properly grounded." He looked proud.

"How very thorough of you."

"It wasn't, by the way. Grounded. So as long as you're rewiring the house, you need to install GFCI outlets, too."

She clenched her hands together. "What am I going to do?"

"Way I see it, you've got two choices. One, you can bite the bullet and hire an electrician who really knows what he's doing."

"And sell a few vital organs on the black market to pay for it? No thanks. What's my other option?"

"You can hit the library and the hardware store and try to do it yourself."

And here she thought the seller's agent had been doing her a favor by expediting the title search and agreeing to a fourteen-day escrow. "I don't suppose this is the kind of thing one can master with a trip to Home Depot and a few hours on Google?"

"Not hardly." He chuckled. "If I were you, I'd pay an expert and get it done right the first time." He handed her a sheaf of flimsy pink carbon paper. "Your copy of the report."

"This is a nightmare. How am I—" She stopped short. "Hold on. You're saying this whole house could burst into flames at any moment? We could all burn in our beds with no warning?"

"Oh, you'd have plenty of warning, ma'am. The smoke detectors all work great. Have a nice evening."

ere's the master plan: I'm making five separate sheet cakes with white icing, and I'll pipe on the details with yellow and blue." Anna waved her wooden spoon over the cooling cake pans like a culinary clergywoman delivering a sacrament. "I'm thinking the college's Latin motto for the round cake and maybe the outlines of a few of the campus buildings on the square cakes. Like the student union, the president's house, the chapel..."

Jamie whistled in admiration. "You can freehand the chapel?"

"If I can freehand the Eiffel Tower, I can freehand the chapel," Anna assured her. "I just need a photo to work from. And then, for a little extra pizzazz, I thought I'd do a sampler of historical desserts. You know, like 150 years of pastry to celebrate 150 years of Thurwell."

"That's a very cool idea," Jamie said. "But I feel compelled to point out that we have less than thirty-six hours til the reception."

Anna put down the spoon and wiped her hands on a dish towel. "That's plenty of time if we all work together. I'll even whip up a batch of my famous caffeinated cupcakes if you're lucky."

"Always the overachiever," said Cait, who had returned from the store with a trunkload of baking staples. "Is there anything you can't do?"

"Get pregnant," Anna said matter-of-factly. "Have a happy marriage."

They all abandoned their respective tasks and focused on Anna.

"And please don't start with platitudes and consolation."

Anna leaned over to check the oven temperature. "I appreciate the sentiment, but I came here to get away from all that."

Brooke finally screwed up her courage and asked the obvious question. "So you and Jonas are having big problems?"

A crisp nod. "Affirmative."

"Do you think you'll work it out?"

"Unknown."

"Is there anything we can do to help?"

Anna finally stopped fussing with the stove, drew herself up to her full height of five foot two, and regarded each one of them in turn. Her brown eyes were clear and her voice was steady. "Thank you, but no. I can take care of myself."

Meaningful glances ricocheted around the kitchen. Jamie and Cait clearly wanted Brooke to drop the whole topic, but Brooke, for all her ladylike delicacy, had never been fazed by Anna's bluntness.

"Of course you can," she replied gently. "But if you want to talk—"

"I don't," Anna said. "Being here, with you guys in this house, is therapy enough. Now let's stop jibber-jabbing and get down to brass tacks. Or in this case, blue food coloring."

Everyone resumed working. Though the night outside grew chilly and dark, the kitchen stayed warm and cheery. They stirred and seasoned and sang along with the Go-Go's and Liz Phair and the Indigo Girls until the first light of dawn.

"This cake-decorating session is hereby adjourned for a nap," Anna declared. "I'm so tired I can't even pipe straight."

"I'll stay up and make another batch of buttercream," Jamie offered.

"No, we need a break. Especially our little magnolia here." Anna turned to Brooke. "You don't look well."

"You do seem a bit peaked," Cait agreed. "Ever since you came up from the basement. Everything go all right with the inspection?"

Brooke retreated to the sink to wash her hands. "Yes, for the most part. Just a few minor things here and there: fix a loose board on the porch, replace a toilet, that sort of thing."

She couldn't tell them about the wiring. Not now. Not while they were still in the process of bailing her out from her last careless mistake. If she were to break down and confess her mounting money woes, Anna and Caitlin would probably feel honor-bound to offer up their portions of Arden's inheritance. Jamie *definitely* would. Brooke had already accepted more than enough assistance. They might all be back in their college residence, but this time they were living in the real world, and the time had come to stand or fall on her own merit.

Thirty-six hours later, tired but triumphant, Brooke watched Anna and Jamie carry the cakes and confections out to Anna's Volvo. Jamie waved as she climbed into the front seat. "See you in a few hours!"

"Thanks again, ladies!" Brooke called back. "I'll be on-site to help you right after lunch."

But first she had to squeeze in a quick meeting with Hank Bexton, the local contractor recommended by all the guys in Brooke's office. Hank had sounded both authoritative and affable over the phone, and Brooke found herself daydreaming about a handsome, muscle-bound maintenance man, complete with chivalrous manners and washboard abs.

At first glance, Hank appeared to fit the bill. He was young and strapping, just over six feet tall with skin still tan

from the summer sun and a chiseled jawline. Brooke introduced herself with a renewed sense of hope.

"Paradise Found Bed-and-Breakfast, huh?" He nodded at
the sign hanging over the porch. "That's quite a name."

"Thank you. I'm hoping to open for business as soon as
the electrical issues are resolved." She summarized the insurance inspector's report.

He listened intently, then asked, "Mind if I poke around
by the breaker?"

She offered to lead the way, but he instructed her to wait
in the living room. A few minutes later, he tromped back up
from the basement, shaking his head in disbelief.

"Calling me was a good decision," he said. "It looks like
they let a band of chimpanzees loose behind that paneling.
I'm surprised you have any electricity at all."

"But you can fix it?" Brooke asked.

"Sure. It'll cost you, but I can fix it." He hooked his
thumbs in his belt loops and rocked back on his heels. "I'm
probably the only one in town who's got the know-how and
the tools."

She batted her eyelashes for all she was worth. "I don't
suppose there's any chance you could cut me a deal?"

He crossed his arms over his chest. "I think my rates are
fair and reasonable."

"Yes, but you see, I'm dealing with quite a lot of start-up
expenses here and—"

"That's the cost of doing business. Old houses like this?
It's not all gingerbread trim and flower boxes. There's a lot of
upkeep."

"I'm aware." She set her jaw. "And I'm not one to shy
away from hard work. In fact, that's what I'm proposing: I
can help you. Evenings, weekends, any time I'm not at my

day job, I can do whatever needs doing here. I'm a fast learner and very diligent."

He glanced at her immaculate manicure and one side of his mouth tugged upward in a smirk. "Yeah. I don't think so."

"All I'm asking for is a trial period." She let a trace of her lilting Southern accent creep into her voice. "Don't be fooled by the dimples and the blond hair."

Hank's smirk turned to a grin, and for a moment, she thought she had him. Then he winked at her and said, "Hey, have you heard this one: Why can't blondes put in lightbulbs? Give up? 'Cause they keep breaking them with the hammers."

Brooke frowned. "I *beg* your pardon."

"Wait, I've got another one. Even better. How many blondes does it take to change a lightbulb? Three—one to find a bulb, one to find a ladder, and one to find a man."

"You know, I don't think I'll be requiring your services, after all."

"Aw, relax. It's just a joke."

"Thank you and good-bye." She marched across the room and held open the front door.

"Are you serious?"

"Quite."

"But I'm the only one in town who can get this job done before winter. Look, I'm sorry I offended you, lady. But you've got no other options here."

"A true lady always has options. I may have a manicure, Mr. Bexton, but I'm not afraid to get my hands dirty."

Chapter
8

"My cake is dough."
—William Shakespeare, *The Taming of the Shrew*

My word, Jillian, just *look* at this! It's a work of art!"

"I agree. It seems a crime to cut it."

"Did you see the chapel over here? And the student union? These cakes should be in a museum."

"They've really outdone themselves this time. Do you think the college hired a new pâtissier?"

Jamie strolled into the crush of oohing and aahing trustees gathered around the cake. "Isn't it incredible?"

Everyone nodded. "Absolutely."

Anna hung back under an ivy-laden trellis and watched Jamie work the crowd. From the moment they'd arrived at the college president's home to set up the garden reception, Jamie had assumed full command of the troops. She had charmed the caterers and joked with the students working as waitstaff, and now, an hour into the anniversary bash, everyone deferred to her. Even the weather cooperated; the afternoon was mild and sunny with only a slight snap of autumn in the breeze. Anna had to grin as she watched her housemate turn what could have been a stodgy social obligation into a rollicking party. Some things never changed. Jamie doted on the elderly guests, bantered with the younger ones, and cajoled everybody into having the time of their lives.

Everybody except President Terrence Tait, that is, whose face reverted to a dour expression between animated bouts of glad-handing deans and trustees. Which was odd because, back when Anna had been a student, President Tait had been known for his humor and approachability. This afternoon, his negative energy tempered even Jamie's ebullience. The two of them flitted across the lawn, alternately spreading sunshine and storm clouds, their paths never quite intersecting.

Suddenly, Jamie grabbed Anna by the elbow and pulled her into the center of the throng.

"Allow me to introduce the brilliant and talented Anna McCauley. Former Thurwell student and future pastry chef."

A smattering of applause broke out. "You did this? All by yourself?" asked a white-haired woman in a purple patterned dress.

Anna shook her head. "God, no. I had lots of help. Including Jamie."

"Please." Jamie waved the comment away. "All I did was turn on the mixer and grease the pan. Don't be so modest,

Anna!" She gestured to the baked goods with a flourish. "We gave her two days, and not only did she whip up these incredible cakes, she put together an entire dessert retrospective! Check it out: 150 years' worth of delicacies on a silver platter."

"That is so clever," declared a postmodern flower child with long brown hair, a batik skirt, and the subtle but unmistakable air of wealth. "And it all looks delectable. Tell me, what are these over here?"

"Those are little slices of Election Cake. It's sort of like fruitcake; they used to bake it in New England on Election Day. Lots of butter and brandy." Anna overcame her reticence and started to enjoy the opportunity to share her passion for baking with an enthusiastic audience. "These are called ammonia cookies. Don't be alarmed, I wasn't pouring cleaning fluid into the dough! They're just peppermint sugar cookies made with baker's ammonia instead of baking soda. And here we have Victoria Sandwiches, which are basically layers of cream and strawberry jam between sponge cakes. Popular in Britain during Queen Victoria's reign."

The flower child took a nibble and closed her eyes in a display of culinary ecstasy. "These are heavenly. Do you have your own bakery?"

"No. I'm what you might call a dessert dilettante."

The older woman in the purple dress wagged her index finger. "Don't sell yourself short, young lady. I know a thing or two about baking. It's an art and a science."

"I suppose," Anna said.

Jamie slung her arm around Anna. "I always knew she was destined for greatness. We were housemates back in our college days. Both English majors."

"But you're baking cakes now?" one of the student waiters asked as he passed by with a tray of empty water glasses.

"Yep," Jamie said.

"And she's an event planner," Anna said. "We English majors are very versatile."

"Cool." The waiter nodded. "That gives me hope."

"Why? You're an English major, too?" Jamie motioned for him to pause so she could adjust his crooked black bow tie.

"Yeah, my parents keep harping on me to study something quote-unquote 'practical.'" He heaved a weary, put-upon sigh. "They want me to sell out to The Man and be a corporate bean counter or whatever. But I told 'em I'd rather be poor and authentic than rich and spiritually bankrupt."

"If I may offer a word of advice…" Jamie said.

Anna's cell phone rang and Jonas's name flashed on caller ID, so she turned away as Jamie launched into an arm-waving, frothy-mouthed rant on the many benefits of selling out to The Man.

"Look into law school!" Jamie exclaimed. "You'll thank me later."

Anna ducked under the trellis, flipped open the phone, and said hello with deliberate casualness.

"Hi." Jonas sounded even more guarded than she did. "How's it going up there?"

"Great, actually. The cakes turned out better than I expected and I decided to do a bunch of old-school pastries to commemorate the sesquicentennial anniversary theme." She went on in this vein for several minutes before she realized he wasn't responding. She broke off and asked, "Is everything okay?"

"Yeah." He coughed. "It's just—my boss wants to send me to Europe to review the production records at the new factory in Brussels."

"Really?" She brightened. "That's wonderful!"

"I didn't think you'd be in favor."

"Are you kidding me? Free trip to Europe? Of course I'm in favor. When do we leave?"

He paused. "That's the thing. *We* wouldn't be going. Only me."

"Is that the company's decision, or yours?"

"A little of both." Another pause. "I think you and I could use some time apart."

"Oh." Anna swallowed back her fear and frustration and asked, "How long will you be gone?"

"Not long. A few weeks, maybe two months."

"Two months!"

"I know," he said. "Two more ovulations you'll never get back."

"I didn't say that."

"You didn't have to." He sounded rushed and rehearsed, as if he'd been dreading this conversation all day. "Look, my boss has been hinting that I might be up for a promotion if this trip goes well, and I was thinking we could use the extra money to—"

"Try in vitro again?" She perked up.

"No. We're done with IVF. I told you, it's time to move on."

"I see." And with that, she put her emotions on autopilot and focused on getting to the end of this conversation without any more dashed hopes or hurt feelings. "Well, if you're worried about wasting *your* money, you shouldn't. I've already offered to use my inheritance from Arden to pay for all our future fertility treatments."

"That's not what that money is for. Her lawyer specifically said you're supposed to put it toward paying off debt and starting a new career, and I agree. With your freelance work drying up and everything that's going on between us right now, I think it's good you have a hobby."

She let that comment hang between them for a moment.

Too late, he realized his misstep. "I didn't mean that the way it sounded."

"Allow me to enlighten you about a few things," she said primly. "First of all, baking isn't a hobby, it's a science and an art form." He started to say something, but she cut him off. "Second, you were right about us needing a break. Go do whatever it is you need to do over in Brussels, and I'll hole up here for a while with the girls."

"And when I get back? Will we be okay?"

"Let's be honest, Jonas. We haven't been okay for a long time. A couple of months and a few time zones aren't going to make a hell of a lot of difference at this point."

"You're mad."

"Honestly, I'm not." And to her surprise, she realized this was the truth. Her anger had dulled into a steady, almost soothing numbness.

"Okay. I'll call you?"

She stared up at the thick green tangles of ivy. "If the spirit so moves you."

A few moments after Anna hung up, Jamie rushed over. Her cheeks were flushed beneath her freckles. "See that woman over there in the navy pantsuit and the pearls?" Jamie pointed out a genteel-looking lady with fabulous shoes and an elegant silver pageboy. "She wants me to coordinate her daughter's wedding next month. Just like that! We're meeting tomorrow morning to go over the details. I'm going to have a real client. I'm officially an event planner! This is so much easier than I thought it would be!"

Anna forced a smile. "That's great, Jame."

"And she wants you to do the cake. She says she'll pay whatever you charge."

"Sure. Of course. No problem."

"And I was thinking we could—" Jamie broke off mid-sentence when she noticed Anna's expression. "Oh boy. What happened to you?"

"Nothing."

"You lie."

"I lie," Anna admitted. "Do you think Brooke would mind if I moved up into one of her spare bedrooms for few months? I think my break with Jonas may be turning into a breakup."

Chapter
9

Cait leaned back in her chair and assessed the total lack
of progress she'd made that morning.

The blank computer screen and blinking cursor
seemed to demand she fill the space with something worthy
of her potential. Something insightful and moving. All these
years, while she studied and lectured and ducked-and-
covered through the front lines of departmental politics,
she'd sensed deep down that her real talent lay in writing
rather than researching. *If only*, had been her wistful refrain. *If
only* she could eke out the time and resources to apply herself
to her true calling.

Well, here she was, hunkered down in Henley House of

all places, with her laptop and the whole day stretching out in front of her, and nothing to do but write. Days and weeks and months ahead.

And nothing to do but write.

She chewed her lower lip and clicked open her Web browser to check email again. A flock of Canadian geese flew over the house, honking madly, and Cait realized that, though the breeze this afternoon was still warm, soon enough she would awaken to find frost on her windowsill. The nights would get longer, the tree branches would go bare, and another season of her life would be gone.

The cursor kept winking, ticking off the passing seconds with unrelenting precision.

Screw this. She switched off the computer and got to her feet, determined to salvage something of the day. Maybe a brisk walk through town would jump-start her creative juices.

She changed into dark jeans and a fitted green T-shirt, shoved her feet into flip-flops and then, without stopping to analyze her motives, ducked into the bathroom to scrunch a bit of shine wax into her long reddish-brown hair and swipe on a bit of lipstick and mascara.

Her mood improved dramatically as soon as she stepped outside. She turned her face up to the sun and wandered past houses and parks and the public library with no particular goal in mind, until she found herself turning right at the intersection of Birch Street and Highland Avenue, which just happened to be where Professor Gavin Clayburn had lived when she was an undergraduate.

Not that she'd *stalked* him or anything. God, no. She'd never been that unhinged, even in her hormonal heyday. But

Thurwell was a very small town, and since she hadn't had a car in college, she'd mostly gotten around on foot. She'd just happened to enjoy the scenery in Professor Clayburn's neighborhood.

Her pace slowed as she approached the white clapboard two-story house with green shutters and screened front porch. In the fading daylight, she could make out the name "Clayburn" on the mailbox. She paused for a moment, staring at the tidy lawn and the dark windows. Just as she turned around to head back toward the college campus, a classic wood-paneled Jeep rounded the corner and pulled in to the driveway of the white and green house.

Cait darted across the street and crouched behind a parked minivan. She held her breath as the teacher who'd played such a prominent role in her postadolescent fantasies emerged from the Jeep.

Wow. He looked even better than she remembered: broad shoulders, long limbs, and thick, dark hair falling over his forehead. Nary a trace of an Arthurian mullet. And somehow, his blue chambray shirt and subdued blazer only served to enhance his air of rugged masculinity. He looked commanding, capable.

He also looked irritated.

"Hey, you!" Professor Clayburn tossed his briefcase back into the car and pointed at her.

Cait gasped and instinctively glanced behind her.

"Yeah, you!" He charged into the street. "I see you. I know what you're doing!"

Panicking, Cait staggered backward. The side of her face slammed into the crossbar of a For Sale sign hanging in the yard behind her, and her line of vision exploded into a hundred popping flashbulbs. She dropped to her knees, cupping her cheek.

She heard footsteps pounding and then his voice as he crouched down beside her. "Are you okay?"

She blinked rapidly, trying to clear her head. "I . . . ouch."

"Sorry. I didn't mean to scare you."

She felt his fingers trail along her temple and pry her hand away from her face. Then he announced, "You're gonna have a black eye."

"I was just out for a walk," she stammered. "I wasn't, you know, *doing* anything."

"Of course not." Now he sounded as chagrined as she did. "This is all my fault. Again, I apologize. I thought you were one of my overzealous female students. Every now and then, one of them gets carried away and sort of, well, *stalking* sounds over the top, but—"

Cait's cheek ached when she smiled. "Actually, I find that easy to believe."

He froze, staring at her. "I know you."

"You used to."

"Hang on. Don't tell me." He snapped his fingers. "Irish Literature, right? Second row?"

"Ding, ding, ding. I took your Romantic Poetry seminar, too." She extended her right hand. "Caitlin Johnson. Graduated ten years ago. I'm surprised you remember me. I barely said a word in class."

"I remember your papers. Very insightful." He took her hand in his and guided her toward his house. "Okay, Miss Johnson, let's get some ice on that eye before it swells shut."

"Call me Cait," she said. " 'Miss Johnson' makes me feel about eighteen."

"Then you have to call me Gavin. 'Professor Clayburn' makes me feel about seventy-five, and I'm probably only seven or eight years older than you."

"Thirty-two," she confessed.

"Forty next month."

He ushered her up the front walk, through the sparsely decorated screened porch, and into a small white kitchen where every available surface—the table, the counters, even the stovetop—was littered with books.

She nodded toward the literature-laden burners. "I take it you're not much of a chef?"

"I gave up after I burned a can of soup. Guys like me are why sandwiches and pizza delivery were invented. My housekeeper has given up trying to organize the clutter. She just cleans around the piles now." He rummaged through the top shelf of his refrigerator and handed her a cold can of Foster's lager, which she promptly popped open and sipped.

He looked taken aback for a moment, then grinned. "I meant that for your eye, actually, but by all means, drink up."

"Oh." Heat flooded into her cheeks. "*Oh*. Right."

"I don't have any ice packs and I'm out of frozen vegetables, so a cold beer's the best I can do." He handed her another can for first-aid purposes, then rummaged through the cabinet next to the sink. "Now, before you chug the rest of that, take a quick water break and swallow these."

He tapped two white tablets out of a bottle.

She glanced at the label. "Excedrin Migraine? But I don't have a headache."

"The caffeine will help your blood vessels constrict to prevent swelling," he explained. "Tonight, you're going to want to keep your head elevated. Sleep with a few extra pillows and try not to put pressure on this side of your face. Keep putting cold compresses on it for the next day and a half, then switch to a heating pad or a hot-water bottle."

"You sure know a lot about black eyes. Are you an EMT in addition to being an English prof?"

"Nah, I played hockey in high school." He leaned back against the counter and gave her a long, assessing look.

Cait stared down at the floor as the shock wore off and self-consciousness set in. "So ..."

"So what brings you back to Thurwell?"

"I'm taking a sabbatical from my job," she hedged, still not meeting his gaze. "I'm an English professor, too, now. Shayland College in Connecticut."

"Well done." He sounded genuinely impressed, despite the fact that Shayland was ranked several tiers beneath Thurwell. "Then we're colleagues."

"No," she said, still smarting from the last time she'd been attracted to a man she considered one of her peers. "I'm taking a break from teaching. Doing a little writing."

"Poetry?"

She shook her head. "Novel."

"Ambitious."

"Not as ambitious as publishing a short story collection that's been favorably compared to *Dubliners*."

He laughed and rolled his eyes. "One short story collection, published years ago."

"Yeah, but what a collection. Are you working on anything new these days?"

"Not really. Just dabbling. Guess I burned out after one book. What's your novel about?"

As she scrambled to come up with a response, a thin ribbon of blood trickled down from the cut on her cheek onto her shirt. She had never been so grateful for an open wound in her life. "I'm bleeding. Do you mind if I go wash off a bit?"

"Of course. The guest bathroom's right upstairs, first door on the left. There should be clean towels under the sink and Band-Aids in the medicine cabinet."

She started up the stairs and he called after her, "Let me know if you need anything. Sorry about the mess."

What mess? His bathroom was as spartan as his kitchen—clean and serviceable, but without any wall art, ruffled shower curtains, or froufrou skin care products. The pile of white towels stacked beneath the sink smelled faintly of fabric softener. The hand soap was generic, still in the plastic pump bottle.

She leaned over the basin to splash her face with cold water, then patted her cut dry with tissue. She was studying her reflection in the mirror, debating whether she should apply butterfly Band-Aids, when she noticed the silver lock gleaming in the hallway.

The second story of Gavin's house had three doors in addition to the bathroom. One of these was ajar, and one was closed, but the third was secured from the outside with a formidable steel contraption that looked like a padlock on steroids.

Cait cast a long, speculative look at the door before returning downstairs, where Gavin was waiting with car keys in hand.

"Do you need stitches? I can drive you to the hospital."

"No, I'll be fine. It's just a scratch."

"You sure?" he asked. She nodded. "Then I'll drive you home."

"Oh, I can walk back."

"Absolutely not. It's getting dark, and you never know what might go down on the mean streets of Thurwell after night falls."

"How chivalrous." She knew it wasn't any of her business but had to ask. "Hey, I couldn't help noticing—what's with the mysterious locked door up there?"

He flashed her a rakish grin. "That would be Mr. Rochester's lunatic wife, of course."

She laughed and waited for him to elaborate, but he changed the subject immediately. "Listen, I'd like to take you to dinner sometime. We can go out, grab a bottle of wine, talk teaching, writing, hockey injuries. What do you say?"

For a moment, she just stared at him, flustered, every fiber of her being screaming, *Yes! Yes! A thousand times yes!* Somehow, this internal riot of enthusiasm translated to her blinking several times in succession and volleying back with, "Okay."

"Great. Does Friday night work? Say around seven?"

Yes! Yes! A thousand times yes! "Okay."

Cait unlocked the front door to Paradise Found and waved to Gavin, who put the Jeep into gear and pulled away from the curb. She had hoped to slip into the house and up to her room without an interrogation, but Jamie, Brooke, and Anna were all lounging around the living room eating pizza and waiting for her.

"Look who's finally back," Jamie said. "Grab a plate and make yourself comfortable. We have news. Big news!"

Cait closed the door and turned around, giving everyone a good look at her face.

Brooke raised her hand to her lips in dismay. "Caitlin!"

"Oh my God." Anna winced. "What happened to your eye?"

"Oh, that." Cait tried to look nonchalant. "I ran into Professor Clayburn."

Jamie's eyes were huge. "In the middle of a bar brawl?"

"Not exactly. He asked me out. We're going to dinner on Friday."

"What?"

"Good evening, ladies, I have to go write." She dashed up the stairs.

"Oh no, you don't!"

"Get back here right now, missy, and spill your guts! We demand every last detail!"

"Sorry," she called, high-fiving Mr. Wonderful with her index finger as she rounded the landing. "The muse calls, and I must answer!"

She locked the bedroom door behind her and opened her laptop with subversive glee. Forget the Great American Novel. Tonight she would just indulge in a little warm-up exercise:

Helena Barnett glanced up from the pages of her book as a thunderclap rattled the library windows and a bolt of lightning streaked across the night sky. She pushed her spectacles farther up on her nose and prepared to resume reading when another flash of lightning revealed a man racing a massive stallion up the drive through the tempestuous storm. The book slipped from her fingers as she blew out her candle and pressed her brow against the windowpane, her eyes searching through the dark for a second look.

Why would such a man be riding in such weather, at such a dark hour of the night, toward the quietest estate in the dullest county in all of Britain? What business could such a man have with her placid, even-tempered father?

Lightning flashed and she glimpsed the rider again. He was much closer now, and she could tell that he was well formed; tall and broad-shouldered beneath his greatcoat. Her pulse quickened and her mind raced in a bid to recover her composure. She snatched up the book that had tumbled down to the thick Brussels rug and furtively tucked the leather-bound volume into the folds of her white muslin nightdress. Her father had long ago resigned himself to the fact that Helena preferred libraries to ballrooms and fictional heroes to flesh-and-blood suitors. But if he ever discovered the nature of her late-night reading material—scandalous novels such as this copy of Laclos's Les Liaisons Dangereuses—he would certainly take away her pin money, and her beloved books along with it.

Over a distant roll of thunder, Helena heard the pounding of the front door's brass knocker. Curiosity overruled good sense, and she crept down to the shadowed stairway landing. There, she crouched behind the embroidered damask divan, a vantage point that afforded her an unobstructed view of the foyer below.

Her father, clad in his plaid silk dressing robe, was murmuring to a stranger who seemed to fill up the entryway with his commanding presence. Water pooled around the soles of his well-worn boots, and his dark hair was wind-whipped across the hard planes of his face. He appeared as unforgiving and fierce as the storm he'd ridden through.

He looked, in short, like one of the heroes from Helena's beloved books.

As her father continued to address him in hushed tones, the stranger raised his face until his eyes locked on Helena's. She shrank back with a gasp, but he seemed able to stare straight through the divan and her modest ruffled gown. His amber eyes belied his severe countenance—they were smoldering, the color of warm whiskey.

Unequal to the frank, assessing nature of his gaze, she turned and fled back up the stairs to the safety of her chamber and locked her door behind her. But sleep eluded her and the prospect of reading held no pleasure for her now. A single glance from that dark, sensual stranger evoked thoughts more scandalous than anything printed on the pages of a forbidden French novel.

———

By the next day, Helena was wild with curiosity. Her father had left the house before she'd come down for breakfast, and her many questions about the stranger's identity and intentions went unanswered. And now her investigation would have to wait until later, for even here in Surrey, there were teas to attend and razor-tongued social critiques to endure. Helena nibbled a strawberry and inwardly smiled at the spiteful old tabbies whispering around the refreshment table at the back of the salon:

—"Have you seen what Helena Barnett is wearing?"

—"How could I miss it? The fabric is rich enough, but that pattern! Nary a flower to be found. Not even a stripe. And the color—well! The whole ensemble makes widow's weeds appear the denier cri. Is it any wonder she's about to be on the shelf?"

—"About to be? I'd say she's firmly wedged in between bookends and gathering dust already!"

At twenty-seven years old, Helena was well aware that her opportunities for a suitable match were dwindling. The prospect of spinsterhood did not trouble her. Indeed, she rather enjoyed the idea of remaining "on the shelf," sealed and self-contained like one of the leather-bound volumes tucked away in the library. She took her leave as soon as good manners would allow, refused all offers of escorts and carriages, and breathed a sigh of relief as she set off on foot toward home.

She took her time meandering along the garden path flanked with low hedgerows and vibrant blooms. The breeze was warm and the sunlight glorious, so she took off her bonnet and gloves. A sprinkling of freckles made no difference, after all, to a confirmed spinster.

As had happened repeatedly over the course of the day, her musings turned to the man who'd arrived the night before. Her mind roiled with questions about who he was, why he had come—

Foliage rustled just behind her. She whirled around to find herself facing the man who'd consumed her thoughts. Without a word, he strode closer *until she had to crane her neck to meet his eyes. Disconcerted, she immediately reverted to her drawing-room decorum.*

"Forgive me, sir." She schooled her features into a tepid smile. "You gave me quite a start."

"Did I, then?" His bold gaze roamed over her, from her kidskin boots up to her uncovered red hair. Was his deep voice tinged with a Scottish burr?

The corners of his mouth settled into a frown. "Your attire is leavin' much to be desired."

Definitely a Scot. A towering, broad-shouldered—

His words finally registered. Helena had become accustomed to stinging remarks about her lack of fashion and imminent spinsterhood, but this man's bold appraisal shocked her far beyond anything she'd ever experienced in a ballroom. She disguised her discomfiture with tartness. "My propriety can easily be restored by putting on my bonnet and gloves. You, sir, however, appear to be inalterably lacking in the most basic tenets of civility." She lifted her chin. "And as long as we're unintroduced strangers brashly pointing out one another's flaws ... Your penchant for dramatic late-night entrances will go unappreciated in a simple town like mine. Perhaps a swashbuckling character such as you fancy yourself would be better suited for the London stage?"

His frown vanished and was replaced with a roguish smile. "Ah, you mistook my meaning. I merely meant to say that I prefer your revealing attire from last night."

Her cheeks heated. "It was a modest gown—"

"Aye, but a hallway sconce gifted me with a silhouette I'll no' soon forget."

Oh Lord! How much did he see when I hastened up the stairs?

"Let us be strangers no more," he continued, as if he hadn't just mortified her. "Helena Barnett, I am Ross MacCormick, charged with your younger brothers' education."

"*The new tutor? Then why the urgency to arrive?*" *And why had her father been so secretive?*

"*I take my commitment to academics very seriously.*"

"*You truly are to be their teacher? I fear they are doomed.*"

"*I teach many subjects, lass. Society etiquette is no' among them.*" *He captured her ungloved hand in his and bowed low. The heat of his skin against hers seemed scorching as he slowly but deliberately stroked his thumb against the soft underside of her wrist.*

She snatched her hand away. "*You are quite improper, sir.*"

His eyes laughed at her, but beneath the amusement, she saw a challenge. "*But I wager no' half so improper, Miss Barnett, as you.*"

Chapter 10

'm probably your dream client." Maureen Richmond smiled across the coffee shop booth at Jamie and took a sip of herbal tea. "I'm very decisive, I'm very clear about my expectations, and I live in Vermont, so I'll be out of your hair for the most part. But Sarah is my only child, and I've been thinking about her wedding for years. We both have. I want it to be a day she'll remember for the rest of her life. And of course, I'm willing to write the checks to turn our dream into a reality."

"Don't worry, Mrs. Richmond, I'll make sure it's a beautiful, memorable day. You don't have to write a bunch of checks to ensure that," Jamie said.

"Please call me Maureen." The older woman stirred her tea and set her spoon down on the thick white saucer. "I want it to be a beautiful, memorable day with the best champagne, the most delectable food, and the most breathtaking floral arrangements upstate New York has to offer."

"Then by all means, open the checkbook." Jamie laughed. After Maureen approached her yesterday at the garden reception, Jamie had suggested this early-morning meeting at Pranza, a homey little café on Pine Street. The décor tended toward checkered cotton tablecloths and worn red Naugahyde booths, but the menu catered to both vacationing foodies and hungover college kids, offering everything from organic goat cheese tartlets and fair-trade espresso to hash browns and grilled cheese. Maureen had ordered only a cup of tea, citing concerns about fitting into her mother-of-the-bride finery, but Jamie was chowing down on a generous platter of French toast.

"My daughter is currently living in Manhattan, and she's been working with a wedding coordinator in the city," Maureen continued. "They've already taken care of most of the major details: the invitations, the guest list, the wine and liquor."

"That's quite a feat, planning an Adirondack wedding from Manhattan."

"Yes." Maureen's lips thinned. "I begged Sarah to have the wedding in the city—so much more accessible for out-of-town guests, not to mention style reporters from the *Times*—but she insisted on having it here. And in November! What if there's a snowstorm? I tried to be agreeable when she said June was 'too cliché,' but what's wrong with September, for heaven's sake? October, even?"

"Thanksgiving weddings are very chic," Jamie said. "Clearly, your daughter is on the cutting edge."

"She's stubborn, just like her mother." Maureen shook her head and laughed. "I need you to act as the local, day-of coordinator. To make sure everything goes smoothly at the big event, the rehearsal dinner, and the bridesmaids' tea."

"Sounds simple enough. I take it your daughter is a Thurwell alum?"

"No, Barnard College," Maureen said with obvious pride.

"Oh." Jamie tried to politely suss out their connection to the college and the board of trustees. "Did you and your husband go to Thurwell?"

"No. Both of us had to work our way through the University of Vermont," Maureen said. "And then my husband, Henry, got into law school in Boston and we had to pull together a wedding in six weeks during summer break. We had absolutely no money, and our parents couldn't help us out, but we did the best we could. I went to a bridal salon and offered to buy whatever they had on sale. They sold me a ghastly gown that was four sizes too big, but my mother and I got out the sewing machine and altered it ourselves. We made the bridesmaids' dresses, too, out of upholstery fabric, of all things. Henry and I bought each other plain gold bands, and we had the whole shindig in his parents' backyard. I carried a bouquet of fresh wildflowers Henry picked in the meadow for me just before the ceremony."

Jamie rested her chin in her hands and imagined the heartfelt, homespun ceremony. "Aw. That sounds lovely."

"It was." Maureen touched the simple gold ring still adorning her left ring finger. "For me. But not for my daughter. Sarah's going to have only the best. We ordered her wedding gown and veil from Vera Wang six months ago. Her shoes are being flown over from Milan. And of course, we'd always envisioned Henry walking her down the aisle, but he passed away two years ago. She's asked me to do it in his stead. Isn't that sweet?"

"Very sweet. I can't wait to meet her."

"She's planning to drive up next weekend, so I'll be sure to arrange a meet and greet." Maureen dug through her handbag and pulled out a leather organizer bursting with folded papers, fabric swatches, and multicolored Post-its. "Now, let's see...your friend Anna has agreed to do the cake. Do you happen to have contact information for her?"

Jamie spelled Anna's name and recited her email address and phone number.

"Excellent. I'm so pleased to have found her. I can't begin to tell you the problems we've had finding a suitable cake. The pastry chefs in Manhattan refuse to deliver all the way out here, and the local caterers have been pressuring me to hire the local baker, who they claim is the only available option in Thurwell, and who I'm certain is not up to Anna's level." Maureen scribbled away in her organizer. "Now. As for accommodations. We're expecting a good number of out-of-town guests, and the inn we've selected in Saratoga Springs is already booked to capacity. Can you think of a suitable hotel to accommodate the overflow? Someplace charming, nothing corporate or cheap."

"As it happens, there's a cozy little B and B right here in Thurwell that's about to open its doors. Down comforters, scented soaps, afternoon scones, the whole deal. It's called Paradise Found Bed-and-Breakfast. As soon as we're done here, I'll tell the owner to clear her reservation books for the weekend of the wedding."

"That sounds perfect!" Maureen beamed. "You *are* a treasure."

"What can I say? You just have to know the right people."

"True, very true. Tell me, how many weddings have you planned?"

"Well, I was in charge of three in Los Angeles," Jamie said, omitting the tiny detail that she had been the bride-to-be in all three and never once made it down the aisle. "But this is my first one in the Adirondacks."

"A Hollywood wedding planner! No wonder you're so connected. And you did an excellent job managing the party yesterday afternoon." Maureen, true to her word, looked like she had made up her mind and felt entirely confident in her decision. "You're hired. Did you happen to bring your contract?"

"Yes, ma'am." Jamie produced the standardized form she had downloaded from the Internet last night and modified with the appropriate names and dates. "Two copies, one for each of us. I just need a signature and a deposit, and we're good to go."

Maureen signed the contract after only a perfunctory skim, then whipped out her checkbook. "It sounds like you'll do a wonderful job. I can't wait for you to meet Sarah; you two should get along famously." She flipped through the organizer and handed Jamie a series of business cards, along with the deposit check. "Here's my home number, cell number, email, contact information for Sarah and her coordinator in New York City.... Feel free to call any of us at any time, day or night. Are there any other questions I can answer for you now?"

"I don't think so," Jamie said, and then glanced back at her signed contract and realized what she'd left out. "Oh, wait. Just one, but an important one. I assume you've already booked the ceremony and reception venues? Because if not, I could always—"

"Oh, of course. That was the very first thing we arranged. How silly of me not to mention it. The wedding will be held at the college president's home. You seemed very comfortable there yesterday. It all works out splendidly, doesn't it?"

"I—" Jamie froze, her fork halfway to her mouth. "Really?"

Maureen nodded. "If the weather is warm, we'll try to have the ceremony in the garden; but in all likelihood, it'll be freezing and we'll hold the whole thing indoors."

"Wow." Jamie chose her next words very carefully. "How'd you finagle that? The administration is notorious for barring 'noncollegiate' events from campus."

"As you say, it's a matter of knowing the right people." Maureen winked. "Getting permission to hold the wedding at President Tait's house is easy when President Tait is the groom. You've met Terrence, I assume?"

I've been waiting for you," Brooke said when Jamie walked through Paradise Found's front door. She appeared to be all ready for work in pearl earrings and a baby blue button-down shirt, with her black leather satchel in hand. "I'm going, but I didn't want to ask you this over the phone."

"I can't talk right now," Jamie murmured. All she wanted to do was crawl into bed, burrow under the covers, and devote the rest of the day to a protracted panic attack.

Brooke blocked the path to the staircase. "I know something's going on."

Jamie rubbed the heel of her hand against her forehead. "I don't feel well."

"Look, you know you can tell me anything, right?"

Jamie didn't reply.

"Right?" Brooke prompted.

The two women stared at each other across the sun-filled foyer. Finally, Jamie said, "What now?"

"Arden's estate attorney just phoned. He said he's been leaving messages on your cell for the last few days and you haven't called him back." Brooke put one hand on her hip and waited until Jamie made eye contact. "Why haven't you deposited your inheritance check?"

Chapter
II

"'These are not the hands of a lady,' he said and tossed them into her lap. . . .
'You've been working with those hands. . . .'"
—Margaret Mitchell, *Gone With the Wind*

I *just forgot."*

That's what Jamie had claimed when Brooke first confronted her about the phone call from Arden's lawyer. And then, when Brooke had persisted in asking how anyone could "just forget" about $250,000, Jamie had reverted to *I just haven't gotten around to it*, which progressed to *I just don't feel like it*, until, at last, they'd ended up in a stalemate with Brooke reiterating "But why?" and Jamie buttonhooking around her and fleeing up the stairs.

Brooke picked up the pace on her walk to campus and wondered what her friend could possibly have to hide. Jamie had a big heart and a bigger mouth, and her total inability to keep secrets had become a group joke over the years. And she was almost as bad at holding on to money as she was at holding her tongue.

So what on earth had happened between Jamie and Arden that would compel Jamie to turn down a quarter of a million dollars? Their friendship had never suffered so much as a ripple of discord, at least as far as Brooke knew. But she planned to investigate further.

Right after she investigated how to replace knob-and-tube wiring.

"Hi." Brooke approached the circulation desk of the Thurwell College library. "I'm embarking on a few home improvement projects, and I'm searching for books on electrical wiring. Nothing too technical. I need something written for the layman. Where would I look for something like that?"

The pale, obviously sleep-deprived student working behind the desk glanced up from her textbook. "Electrical wiring?"

"Yes. A how-to manual along the lines of *Rewiring Your House for Total Imbeciles*. Something at that level."

The student adjusted her retro cat's-eye glasses and tapped away at the desktop computer. "I'll check the system, but I don't think we have anything like that. Now, if you need a compendium on electrical engineering . . ."

"Here's the deal." Brooke sighed. "I don't have what you'd call a hard-science background. I was an English major here ten years ago."

"Ohhh." The student nodded with newfound understanding. "You know who you should talk to?" She wound her long dark hair around her index finger. "Professor Rutkin."

Brooke had a sudden flashback to the one and only course she had ever dropped out of. "Of the physics department?"

"Yeah, some of those science profs know all about electrical stuff. Professor Rutkin always helps the theater geeks set up the stage lights. They did a wicked series of gels for *No Exit* last semester."

Brooke smiled. "Let me guess. Theater geek?"

"Card-carrying member." The student smiled back. "Hang on, I'll look up Rutkin's office number." She pulled up the college website and clicked through the faculty listings. "Oh, look, the physics department has office hours scheduled for this afternoon. You should drop by. They probably won't remember you after all these years though, huh?"

"Oh," Brooke said with a rueful laugh, "I think Professor Rutkin might."

*B*rooke bolstered her confidence with a five-minute pep talk in the ladies' room mirror before finally mustering the courage to approach Professor Rutkin's office door. The physics department was buried in the basement of Thurwell's science building, and the total absence of natural light, combined with scuffed green floor tiles and academic posters detailing student research projects, gave the hallway an atmosphere of cold, clinical detachment.

Abandon hope, all ye who enter here.

Departmental office hours notwithstanding, the area appeared deserted. Brooke could hear the hum of the fluorescent lights and the low drone of a vacuum running somewhere near the stairwell. She stepped back from the office door and reevaluated the wisdom of this plan. Why humiliate herself this way? She could call another contractor. Read a few books. Professor Rutkin probably wasn't even here.

"How many blondes does it take to change a lightbulb?"

Brooke curled her soft, manicured fingers into a fist and rapped on the door.

For a moment, she heard nothing. She exhaled in relief. Now she could go home free of guilt, secure in the knowledge that she'd performed what Arden would call "due diligence." Then a voice emanated from the other side of the door: "Come in."

Brooke turned the knob and pushed, revealing the interior of a typical faculty office: dusty chalkboard scrawled with indecipherable equations, framed posters of a geodesic dome and Marie Curie, and a desktop cluttered with papers, textbooks, and a potted green plant, which—given the absence of sunlight—had to be fake.

A regal, willowy woman with short blond hair and impeccable posture sat behind the desk, red pen in hand. She wore a navy cashmere turtleneck, a single gold bangle, and an air of implicit authority. When she glanced up from her grading, Brooke started stammering.

"Hi, I'm so sorry to interrupt. I saw that you were having office hours this afternoon, and even though I'm not a student—well, I was, once upon a time, but now I work here, in the alumni affairs office."

Dr. Cassandra Rutkin put down her pen and peered at Brooke over the top of her reading glasses. "How may I help you?"

"I enrolled in your Intro to Physics course about twelve

years ago." Brooke's entire face felt as though it was about to burst into flames.

"Brooke Asplind. Ah yes, I remember you."

Brooke closed her eyes for a second and prayed for a quick, merciful death. "You do?"

"More to the point, I remember your midterm exam. A teacher encounters that sort of thing only once in a career."

Brooke had known from the very beginning that Introductory Physics was going to be trouble. Symbolic logic and abstract spatial relationships had never been her forte, but Thurwell College required students to take a certain number of "distribution courses" to ensure their education included all aspects of the liberal arts, and that included the physical sciences. So Brooke had signed up for physics, hoping that she could squeak through and maintain her place on the dean's list with a little luck, a lot of hard work, and her God-given gift for using a smoke screen of fancy words to obscure the fact that she wasn't saying anything of substance.

Then came the midterm. Dr. Rutkin's teaching assistant had held a pre-exam review session, during which he let slip that the essay portion of the exam would require a thorough explanation of the laws of thermodynamics. Brooke devoted the forty-eight hours before the test to memorizing everything she could about the history and application of each law, along with the corresponding equations.

The moment she had the midterm in hand, Brooke had flipped to the final page, ready to disgorge all her knowledge of thermodynamics. There, to her horror, she found an open-ended theoretical question on electromagnetic force.

She had spent the next half hour staring down at the blank

page, hyperventilating and clutching her forehead. She didn't answer any of the multiple-choice questions. She didn't even glance at the short-answer computations. Finally, drenched in flop sweat and despair, she had started scratching away with her number 2 pencil: "I realize that this question has nothing to do with the laws of thermodynamics, but that's the only thing I can intelligently discuss so that's what I'm going to write about...."

She'd gotten the exam back via campus mail right after spring break. Written on the final page in a slanted, elegant penmanship was a curt pronouncement that Brooke could recite verbatim even twelve years later:

"Pathetic but bold. D+"

Brooke had gone straight to the registrar's office and dropped the class. And she'd managed to avoid all contact with the physics department faculty for the rest of her time at Thurwell.

Until now.

The professor was looking at her expectantly, and Brooke realized that Dr. Rutkin must have asked her a question. "I'm sorry, could you please repeat that?"

"I was saying that I admire your moxie in coming to see me today. My door is always open to any student, present or former. I assume that, after all this time, you're not just popping by to say hello?"

Brooke nodded. "You may have heard that the college sold Henley House? Well, I'm the sucker who bought it. I'm turning it into a bed-and-breakfast."

"That sounds lovely."

"Yes, it *sounds* lovely, but in actual fact, it is the opposite of lovely. I just found out I have knob-and-tube wiring."

Dr. Rutkin adjusted her eyeglasses. "That's a problem."

"Yes. And I'm trying to rewire it myself and, as I'm sure I don't have to tell you, I'm totally incompetent."

The older woman didn't argue or agree. She sat silently, her head tilted to one side, waiting for Brooke to finish.

Brooke clasped her hands in front of her. "Word in the theater crowd is that you're something of an expert in electrical wiring, and I could really use a few pointers. I've done some preliminary research online and ordered a few how-to manuals, but honestly, I'm getting tangled up in all the terminology. Circuit breakers, conduits, volts, amps—it's one thing to read about a theory and quite another to implement it."

"That it is." Professor Rutkin sat back in her chair. "And you're determined to do this by yourself?"

"It's really my only option." Brooke addressed the carpet. "I know, I know: pathetic but bold."

"Very bold," the professor agreed. "But not pathetic. Because this time you're going to do more than memorize and recite a few pages of theorems. This time you're going to have to master the principles at work behind the words."

"Well. About that. The fact is, I only have a few weeks, so I was kind of hoping for a shortcut."

"The scientific method wasn't built on shortcuts. It is, however, comprised of small, discrete steps. And your first step will be to the hardware store. Do you have a pen and paper?"

Brooke rummaged through her briefcase, then wrote down the long list of equipment the professor rattled off.

"All right, so once I buy all this, what then?" Brooke asked.

"Then call me and we'll take it from there. I'm going to give you my home number. Guard it with your life." The instructor passed a square of scrap paper across the desktop. "This is a chance for you to empower yourself, you know. Scientific literacy is the cornerstone of true education."

"Hmm," was Brooke's only response to that. She glanced up at the diploma hanging behind the desk. "You must have done your graduate work at a time when there weren't too many female physicists, right?"

"There aren't many *now*. But yes, I was considered something of an oddity."

"Did you ever get any . . . jokes?"

Professor Rutkin raised one eyebrow. "Jokes?"

"From your male colleagues. You know, how many blondes does it take to change a lightbulb, that sort of thing?"

"As the only woman working in a lab full of sexually frustrated quark jockeys before the days of lawsuits and harassment policies? I had to contend with a lot more than blonde jokes. But I believe that Eleanor Roosevelt was correct in saying that no one can make you feel inferior without your consent. If you want something badly enough, other people's censure doesn't matter." Her expression went from steely to impish. "Besides, we have a different version of that joke around here. How many physicists does it take to change a lightbulb?"

Brooke shrugged. "I give up."

"Two: one to do it, and one to renormalize the wave function." Her green eyes sparkled when she laughed. "Get it?"

Brooke smiled weakly. "Hilarious."

A string of bells tinkled when Brooke pushed open the door to the hardware store five minutes before closing time. Rather than trying to navigate the long aisles jam-packed with equipment, she walked right up to the counter and produced Professor Rutkin's list.

A tall, lanky man in his twenties looked up from his magazine. He wore a plaid flannel shirt and a watch with a scratched face and band, but his strong, smooth hands and sensual lips provided a startling contrast to his utilitarian, outdoorsy clothing. "Hi there. Can I help you?"

Brooke, who was not in the habit of scoping out younger men's lips, tried to stay on task. "I hope so. I'm going to need, let's see . . . a thirty-two-circuit breaker box, at least five boxes of Romex wire, a few rolls of electrical tape, a voltage tester, a pair of leather gloves, a wire stripper, a pair of electrical pliers, a utility knife, a set of screwdrivers, a hammer, the sturdiest power drill you have, a set of drill bits, a set of speed bores, and, oh yes, some fishline if you stock it. Please."

"That's quite an order." The employee closed his periodical, a glossy publication called *Outdoor Photographer* that Brooke had never heard of. "Mind if I take that for a second?" He held out his hand.

She relinquished the piece of notebook paper, careful not to cast any more inappropriate glances at his hands. Or his lips. Or his intriguing gray eyes—*damn it.*

He disappeared into the aisles and eventually reemerged pushing a shopping cart full of home improvement equipment. "You must be working on a big project."

"I'm just starting one. Trying to, anyway." She waited for the rush of total empowerment that Professor Rutkin had assured her was on the way. "I may be back in a few days to return all this if things don't go well."

"That's fine."

"But, if things do go well, I'll be back to buy more

wiring." She tried to project confidence. "A lot more. An entire house's worth of wiring."

"That'll work, too." He ducked back behind the counter and started to ring up her purchases. He paused before calculating the total and sales tax. "I assume you qualify for the contractor rate?"

"I really look like a contractor?" She couldn't have felt more flattered if he'd asked if she was a model.

He shrugged. "You do if you want the contractor rate."

"Oh." She stopped congratulating herself. "Then yes."

He tapped a few keys on the register. "Name?"

"Brooke Asplind." She dug her credit card out of her wallet and confessed, "But honestly, I'm not an electrician or an engineer or anything like that. I don't even know how to use half this stuff." She glanced over at his reading material. "Are you a professional photographer?"

"Only in my own mind." His laugh was rich and deep. "I wanted to be, back in school. Thought I was the next Ansel Adams."

"Fine arts major?"

"Worse. Philosophy." He spread his arms out to encompass his realm of drywall and crowbars and PVC pipes. "See where four years of Aristotle and Descartes'll get you?" He held out his right hand. "I'm Everett."

She hesitated for a fraction of a second before sliding her palm against his. His touch was warm and strong and sure . . . *don't go there!* "You must be new in town. I don't think I've seen you around."

He grinned. "I get the feeling you don't spend much time in the hardware store."

"I've been living in Thurwell for over ten years and this is my first time in here," she admitted. "I just bought a house.

Gave up a perfectly nice apartment with a perfectly nice landlord I could call whenever something needed fixing." She sighed. "It seemed like such a good idea at the time. Here's hoping I don't electrocute myself."

"You'll do fine." He rubbed the fine layer of stubble on his jawline. "But just in case, I'll keep an eye out for you. People in the middle of these home improvement projects always come back—sometimes two or three times a day." He started packing all her supplies into brown paper bags and large cardboard cartons. "If you aren't back for more wiring and duct tape in the next forty-eight hours, I'll send out a search party."

"That's very gentlemanly of you." She desperately wanted to slip him her number but lost her nerve at the last moment. "See you in forty-eight hours or less."

Everett didn't glance up from the box he was filling, but she could tell he was smiling again. "Looking forward to it."

Chapter 12

"One of the most time-consuming things is to have an enemy."
—E. B. White, *A Report in January*

"How can I put this tactfully?" Anna scowled down at the tin of sunken chocolate cupcakes. "This oven sucks. For serious."

"Well, don't tell Brooke that," Cait said. "She's got enough home improvement projects already." She nodded toward the cellar door through which Brooke had descended an hour ago, armed with a flashlight, a pair of pliers, and an expression of grim determination. "Do you have any idea what she's doing down there?"

"None whatsoever. I asked, and she gave me this convoluted lecture about wiring, complete with diagrams, but I have to admit, I didn't follow at all."

"Me, neither. I think the gist of it is, the electrical system in this place is FUBAR."

"As is this oven." Anna tossed the cupcake tin into the kitchen sink. "I think our big baking marathon the other day must have killed it once and for all. The thing's gotta be twenty years old. Jamie's client is coming this weekend, and I need to provide her with some cake samples that don't taste like excrement."

"Please. Nothing you bake could ever taste like excrement."

"Oh really?" Anna peeled the foil liner off one of the cakes. "Care to sample?"

Cait took a big bite, then made a face and spat into the sink. "This oven sucks."

"It does?" Brooke peeked out from the cellar doorway. "Since when?"

Anna stared for a second, trying to figure out why Brooke looked so different, and then realized that Brooke was wearing a baseball cap for possibly the first time ever. Her golden hair was pulled through the back in a ponytail.

Brooke threw them a sassy smile. "What are you looking at?"

"You're a Dodgers fan?" Anna asked.

"Jamie is. I appropriated this from the top of her dresser. Do you think she'll mind?"

"Hell no." Jamie strolled in from the living room with a mug of coffee in one hand and the latest issue of *Modern Bride* in the other. "I can't stand the Dodgers. I'm a Yankees fan."

Cait frowned. "Then why...?"

"Ex-boyfriend's," Jamie said. "And now Brooke's. Wear it in good health, sugarplum."

Brooke plucked a strand of cobweb off her shirtsleeve and returned to the topic at hand. "So my oven sucks?"

"Blame Anna," Cait said. "She worked it to death."

"Well, put it on the list of things I need to repair," Brooke said.

"No, no, don't worry about it." Anna shot Cait a look, which Cait pretended not to notice. "This is not your problem."

"My house, my oven, my problem," Brooke insisted, then added sardonically, "Welcome to Paradise Found."

"Seriously, don't sweat it," Anna urged. "I won't be monopolizing all your counter and fridge space much longer." She prepared to break the big news. "I got a call from the English department this morning. They heard about the historical dessert tray I did for the anniversary bash, and they want me to bake for a faculty reception next week. I told them I'd do a literary theme: Jane Austen almond cake, Tristram Shandy sticky pudding, Beowulf mead, that kind of thing."

"What?" Cait whapped her playfully on the arm. "I'm so excited for you! But how dare you hold out on me all afternoon."

"Anna, that's amazing," Brooke chimed in. "Today, the English department, tomorrow the world!"

"I see big things ahead for you," Jamie predicted. "Like a Food Network series. A bestselling cookbook. Your own line of outrageously overpriced pots and pans."

"That's a great idea," Cait said. "She could inscribe the bottom of each with an inspiring literary quote."

"'Food for Thought' by Anna McCauley," Brooke suggested.

"Whoa, whoa, whoa." Anna laughed. "There are a few

minor details to take care of before I roll out my culinary cottage industry. Right now, I'm just looking into renting some commercial kitchen space. I need industrial-grade equipment and space to store all my supplies. Where I'm going to find all that in a town this size, I have no idea."

"I know the perfect place," Brooke said. "Pranza, that little café on Pine Street. They're only open for breakfast and lunch. I bet they'd let you use the back room at night. My coworker's cousin is engaged to the owner. Want me to give him a call?"

Anna joined Cait and Jamie in a moment of silent admiration for the blonde in the baseball cap. Then Jamie shook her head. "Is there anything you can't do?"

"It's amazing what one can accomplish with determination, duct tape, and good manners." Brooke waved her pliers at them and headed down the hall. "They call me the Stealth Magnolia."

"…So that about covers it. All the bowls are in the bottom cabinet, and the spoons and spatulas are in those drawers." Seth Becker, Brooke's restaurant connection, concluded Anna's tour of Pranza's kitchen space. "All I ask is that you clean up after yourself and remember to turn on the dishwasher so that the opening crew can get started on time in the morning."

"No problem," Anna assured him. "I really appreciate you leasing the space and equipment to me."

"Sorry I can only give you three nights a week, but if you like working here, and you're willing to outbid the other baker who leases the space, you can increase your hours next month."

"I'm gone five minutes and you're already renting the place out from under me? For shame, Seth!"

Seth whirled around to face the back door. "Trish? What are you doing here? I thought you went home for the night."

"Can't find my car keys." A tall, stalwart woman with broad shoulders and a thick auburn braid hanging halfway down her back strode into the kitchen. She started yanking open drawers and shoving aside sheet pans until she snatched up a ring of keys. "Got 'em."

Then she turned her full attention to Anna. Her gaze was unflinching and more than a little hostile. "So you're the one."

Anna blinked at her. "The one what?"

"I'll leave you two to get acquainted," Seth murmured and slipped out of the kitchen.

The Amazon in the spotless white chef jacket didn't acknowledge his departure. She kept staring down Anna with those fierce brown eyes. "The one who decided she could waltz right in and snatch up all my kitchen time. Not to mention my business."

"Um." Anna straightened her collar and forced herself to maintain eye contact. "Have we met?"

"Not officially, but I've heard all about you. I'm Trish Selway." Her voice rose. "The baker."

"Ah yes." Anna nodded as the pieces started coming together. "The baker who wouldn't do the college anniversary cake."

"Not wouldn't." Trish bristled. *"Couldn't."*

"Okay." Anna shrugged and opened up the carton of supplies she'd brought over from Brooke's place. "Fine. Whatever. I don't need all the details. I'm just going to set up my space and—"

"Help yourself to more of my customers?"

"Excuse me?"

"You heard me. I take a few weeks off work because my morning sickness makes me puke every time I smell vinegar or even look at raw eggs, and you zoom in and start poaching my most important clients."

Under any other circumstances, Anna would have delivered to this harpy the smackdown she so richly deserved, but the words "morning sickness" derailed her. "You're pregnant?"

"Four months along." Trish placed a protective hand over her belly. "Aren't you ashamed to be taking work away from a woman who's going to have a child to support?"

For a split second, Anna did feel ashamed. Then she caught a gleam of triumph in Trish's eyes and something inside her rebelled. "No. No, I am not. I'm a damn good baker and fertility—yours or mine—has nothing to do with this."

"A damn good baker? Give me a break." Trish snickered. "You're just another legacy kid using her connections to get ahead."

"Keep telling yourself that," Anna said. "Whatever makes you feel better."

"How long have you been in town? A week? Two weeks?"

"Almost a week," Anna admitted.

"And the college already booked you for a major event." Trish put her index finger to her chin in mock contemplation. "Hmm. What a coincidence."

"Coincidence or not, my food was so good that I'm already booking other events."

"*College* events?" Trish pressed.

"That's really none of your business."

"Yeah, that's what I thought. Let me guess. You woke up

one morning, decided it would be fun to play pastry chef, got your Thurwell sorority sisters to make a few calls for you, and all of a sudden, you're the Ace of Cakes. You know, some of us have to actually earn our referrals."

"First of all, Thurwell doesn't have a Greek system," Anna said. "And secondly, if you hadn't been turning down business, you wouldn't be in this position, so don't blame me."

Trish paused. "I'm going to ask nicely, with cream and sugar on top: Put down your spatula, get off my turf, and we'll save ourselves a whole lot of drama."

"According to the rental agreement I just signed, it's *my* turf now," Anna retorted. "Three nights a week, anyway. And I have a lot of work to do, so I'm going to have to ask you to get out of my kitchen."

"Fine. Have it your way. Don't say I didn't warn you." Trish pivoted and made for the door, but not before tossing back over her shoulder, "Legacy."

"Loon," Anna muttered.

Slam.

Chapter
13

"Writing only leads to more writing."
—Colette, *The Blue Lantern*

There." Brooke finished applying foundation and dusted Cait's face with translucent powder. "You can hardly even see the bruising."

"Masterful work. You're like Mary Cassatt with a makeup brush." Cait checked herself out in the bathroom mirror. "I look so much more alluring without the black eye." She leaned over the sink basin to examine a red smudge beside her eyebrow. "What is that? Am I bleeding?"

"No, I am." Brooke turned on the faucet and ran her right hand under the tap. "Sorry. One of my cuts must have re-opened." She pressed a folded square of toilet paper against her index finger. "Will you please check the medicine cabinet and see if we have any Band-Aids left?"

Cait obligingly opened the mirrored door and scanned the shelves. "I don't see any in here."

"Dang." Brooke removed the tiny tissue compress and examined her raw skin and ripped cuticle. "I must have used the last one yesterday."

"I think I have some in the travel kit I keep in my suitcase," Anna said. "But what on earth are you doing to yourself that requires a whole box of bandages?"

Brooke shrugged. "Wiring."

"*Here* you all are." Jamie's tanned, freckled face appeared in the doorway. "What are we doing?"

Cait scented a faint trace of cigarette smoke. Evidently, Anna did, too, because she made a big show of wrinkling her nose and asking, "Has someone been smoking?"

"Not I." Jamie crossed her arms and leaned against the doorframe.

"Really." Anna pursed her lips. "Because you smell like an ashtray."

"Must be my new shampoo."

"Huh. I didn't realize Marlboro had put out a line of hair care products."

"Oh yeah. It's all the rage."

"And is your mouthwash also by Philip Morris?"

"Ladies." Cait stepped in between them and called for a cease-fire. "I hate to interrupt, but could we please focus for a minute while I decide what I'm wearing?"

Anna glanced at Cait's plum-colored top, dangly turquoise earrings, and a dark denim pencil skirt. "You decided half an hour ago. You look fine."

"But I don't want to look fine." Cait ran her hands through her hair. "I want to look, you know, *fiine.*"

Jamie grinned. "Oh right; it's your big date with the loin-stirring man of letters. How could I forget?"

"You've had a lot on your mind lately," Brooke said. Her voice held an ominous undertone, but Cait had no idea what she was hinting at. "Have you called them back yet?"

"Called who back?" Anna asked.

"Never mind, it's not important," Jamie said hurriedly. "What is important is that Cait look as ravishing as possible. And I hate to say this, but that outfit's all wrong." Jamie shook her head. "Your neckline should be about three inches lower and your hemline should be about six inches higher."

"Don't you think that's a little desperate?" Cait said. "It's bad enough that I'm his former student. I want him to see me as a grown woman now, not some shameless teenybopper falling all over myself to get his attention."

"Most guys actually prefer the shameless teenyboppers," Jamie said. "Take my word for it. I have a no-fail halter dress. Guaranteed to get your man into bed every time. Want to borrow it?"

"No!" Anna and Brooke cried in unison.

"We're going for understated sophistication," Brooke added.

"In Thurwell, New York?" Jamie laughed. "Good luck with that." She turned back to Cait. "At least wear red lipstick with your wimple and your chastity belt."

Cait turned to Brooke for approval. Brooke sifted through the contents of her makeup bag and pulled out a tube of lip color. "Well. I suppose a nice shade of cranberry would be permissible."

"Thank you, Mother Superior." Jamie said. "I won't even waste my breath arguing for a padded bra and another coat of mascara."

Cait frowned down at her cleavage. "I could be talked into a padded bra."

"Stop trying to hussy her up," Anna scolded Jamie. "She's not that kind of girl."

Cait applied the red lipstick and said nothing. Her recent forays into literary lasciviousness had forced her to admit that she no longer knew exactly what kind of girl she was. Up until a few weeks ago, she had prided herself on being a scholar and a serious writer, but now that she was facing the blank page every morning, she found herself preoccupied with topics that she suspected her colleagues would dismiss as shallow and frivolous. Like falling in love. And romantic conflicts.

And sex. Lots of sex.

She gnawed on the inside of her cheek as doubt started to set in. "This is so weird."

"What are you talking about?" Jamie said. "It's your dream date with your dream man. Over ten years in the making."

"But think about it, you guys, it's *Professor Clayburn.* I know he's technically my peer now, but I spent all those years thinking of him as an authority figure. Totally off-limits."

"Forbidden," Brooke said with a little shiver.

Anna fanned her face with her hand. "It's gonna be hot."

Cait paced between the sink and the shower. "What if he kisses me at the end of the night?" Then a horrible thought struck. "What if he doesn't?"

"Stop obsessing." Anna leaned out into the hall and glanced out the window. "A car just pulled up out front."

"You look beautiful." Brooke bestowed one last pouf of the powder puff. "Do us proud."

"Yeah, you're living the fantasy of every English major who's ever undressed him with her eyes while he lectured about Seamus Heaney," Jamie said. "Have fun. Be safe."

"Don't do anything Jamie wouldn't do," Anna said.

Cait laughed and hurried out the door with her handbag. Through the darkening twilight, she could see Gavin getting out of the driver's side of his Jeep. He'd swapped his professorial blazer for khakis and a hunter green polo shirt that made his coffee-brown eyes appear even darker. He smiled when he saw her, then came around the car to open the passenger door.

Cait didn't even get a chance to say hello before she heard giggles emanating from the porch behind her.

"Caitlin." Gavin pressed her hand between both of his. "Nice to see you again. You look—"

Whatever he'd been about to say was lost amid another outbreak of female laughter and one high-pitched catcall.

Gavin laughed, too, low and deep. "Your chaperones, I presume?"

Cait covered her eyes with her free hand. "I'm so mortified right now."

"Don't be." He helped her into the seat. "Some of those chaperones look familiar."

"That would be because most of them took at least one class from you back in the day."

"And you're all having a private reunion weekend at Henley House?"

"Something like that. I'll explain over dinner."

Gavin waved to the trio on the porch. "I'll have her back by midnight, ladies!"

"Take your time!" Anna called back.

"We won't wait up!" Jamie yelled.

"Liars," Cait said as Gavin buckled up next to her. "They're going to pounce on me the second I walk back through that door and interrogate me in flagrant violation of the Geneva Convention."

Gavin started the car. "Well, then, we better make sure you've got something juicy to report."

"Is Italian okay for dinner?" Gavin asked as the Jeep pulled away from the curb. "The options around here are limited, as you know."

"Absolutely," Cait said. "Sounds perfect."

"And I hope you don't mind a quick stop back on campus. I left my wallet at the library. One of the student workers called my cell on the way over here."

"Left your wallet?" Cait relaxed enough to flirt a little. "A likely story. Admit it: You just want to get me down to Archivist's Alley."

He looked puzzled. "Archivist's Alley?"

"Yeah. You know, the archivist's office down in the basement by the geology texts and the map room?"

"What happens down there?"

"Everything."

"And by everything, you're referring to . . ."

"Snogging. Scamming. Canoodling. You name it." She shook her head. "How is it possible that you've been at Thurwell for over a decade and this is the first you're hearing about Archivist's Alley?"

"I'm asking myself that same question."

"Well, the students have good reason to keep it secret. You know, one faculty member finds out, he tells another faculty member, then word leaks to the dean and next thing you know, they're cracking down and expecting everyone to use the library for studying and sleeping instead of drinking and carousing."

He shot her a sidelong glance. "You used to booze it up in the basement of the library?"

"Well, not me personally," Cait admitted. "I was always too paranoid about getting caught. But some of my chaperones back there at Henley House? They could tell you a few stories."

"Interesting."

"Come on, don't tell me the instructors don't have their own secret hideaways for angsting and assignations."

"Nope." He shook his head. "Not that I know of, anyway."

"Really? At Shayland, the English profs pass around a key that gives us access to the roof of the building. Any student caught up there faces disciplinary hearings, but you can always find a faculty member up there with a bottle of wine when the weather's nice." As she said this, Cait couldn't help thinking about Charles and the romantic interludes they'd shared up there, watching the moon rise and the stars come out. But French kissing alfresco was as far as they'd ever taken it; neither one of them had really gotten a thrill from exhibitionism.

"And you left that job *why*?"

Cait was scrambling to formulate a response when something bumped against her bare ankle. She reached down and pulled from beneath the seat a pair of paperback books. One was a dog-eared copy of *Great Expectations.* The other looked brand-new and featured a cover illustration of an eerily lit silver obelisk on the cover.

"Prevnon's Pantheon." Cait read the title aloud and glanced over at Gavin with surprise. "Is this yours?"

He grabbed the book out of her hand and tossed it over his shoulder into the backseat. "You never saw that."

"What? Your secret sci-fi novel?"

"It's not mine." He looked supremely embarrassed. "My brother must have left that here when he was in town last month."

"Sure, sure; that's what they all say."

"I'll give you a hundred bucks to change the subject."

"So you have a thing for Klingons and Vulcans," she teased. "I won't tell anyone. I think it's refreshing, to tell you the truth."

"Genre fiction has its place; I don't deny that." His rakish grin returned. "But come on. We're literature professors. Imagine if you went around telling your colleagues that you spend your free time reading, I don't know, *romance* novels. You'd never live it down."

"Mmm." Cait turned her face toward the window.

He parked the car in a reserved faculty space next to the library. "I'll make this quick," he promised. "Would you rather come in or wait out here?"

"I'll come in," she said. "It'll be a blast from the past."

He held the door and Cait stepped into the high-ceilinged vestibule of the library's main floor. The "Libe," as it was affectionately referred to, had been designed and built during the 1960s. The exterior featured a façade of arched cement columns that bore a striking resemblance to an old-timey floor radiator, but the inside felt airy and modern.

When Cait closed her eyes, she immediately recognized the scent of photocopy ink and stress permeating the walls.

She wandered over to examine a glass display case filled with college memorabilia from the past 150 years—old yearbooks, varsity jackets, even a propeller beanie in Thurwell's school colors—while Gavin spoke to the worker at the circulation desk. A few minutes later, he joined her, wallet in hand. "Problem solved."

Cait looked up at him and smiled. "I'm ready when you are."

He hesitated for half a second, then asked, "Can I talk you into a quick detour? I have to see Archivist's Alley."

"Right now?"

"Why not? It's Friday night; the whole building is deserted. At least we won't be disturbing anyone's drunken debauchery."

"Well." She feigned a crisis of conscience. "All right. But I refuse to be responsible for ruining a time-honored student tradition. You have to swear never to reveal what you're about to see to The Powers That Be."

"I swear on that propeller beanie." He placed one hand on the glass case and his other in the air. "I shall never knuckle under to the tyrannical overlords. Death before dishonor."

"Exactly. Long live the rebel alliance."

He blinked. "What?"

"You know, like in *Star Trek*."

"That's *Star Wars,* not *Star Trek*." He grabbed her hand and pulled her toward the elevator.

As Gavin had predicted, the basement was deserted at this hour on a Friday evening. The towering bookshelves down here were more closely spaced than on the upper floors, and there were no chairs or study carrels. The gray carpeting and exposed concrete walls added to the drab, utilitarian atmosphere.

"Follow me." Cait led the way through the maze of shelves and metal wall cabinets. "It's back in the corner."

The total silence seemed to amplify the rustle of their clothes and their muffled footfalls against the carpet.

"This would be a great setting for a slasher film," Gavin whispered. "The college should charge movie studios to come film down here."

"And I thought I had a wild imagination," Cait whispered back.

"Why are we whispering?"

"So the crazed serial killer won't hear us, obviously." She turned the corner and pointed out an orange metal door flanked by battered old filing cabinets. "Here we are."

Gavin held out his hands, clearly disappointed. "This is it? Here I was expecting a hotbed of sin and hell-raising. But it looks so subdued."

"To the untrained eye, perhaps. But you see, it's the illusion of subduedness that makes it the ideal haven for hell-raising."

"True." He gave her a meaningful look. "That goes for people as well as places."

She felt her cheeks flood with heat.

"I have to admit, there is something about the smell of all these ancient reference volumes." He took a few steps into the shadowy cul-de-sac between the bookshelves and the wall and ran his hands along a tightly packed row of leather-bound volumes. "It's musty, but it's also kind of..."

"Sensual," she finished a bit breathlessly.

"Yeah. Sensual. And it's so cold down here, the covers are all smooth and cool."

She followed him in toward the archivist's office door. "That rippling noise when you flip through the pages."

"Maybe you have to be a book person to get it."

"I'm a book person," she said.

"So am I."

He turned around to face her, their eyes met, and suddenly, they were kissing. *Really* kissing. Not tentative, first-date bussing, but full-on, openmouthed making out like two freshmen gone wild with their first taste of freedom. His fingers curled into her hair and cradled the back of her neck. She pressed him up against the stacks of books and hooked her ankle around the back of his knee.

All of her senses went on high alert, along with several nerve endings she'd forgotten existed. She felt overwhelmed by the feel of his tongue and his scent and his skin against hers.

They broke apart for a moment, both of them panting and dazed, and Cait managed to murmur, "We should probably..."

Gavin cleared his throat and nodded. "Yeah, this isn't really..."

She attacked him again before he could finish. The intensity of her desire both thrilled and terrified her, but she was in no mood to overanalyze. The girl who'd been too cautious to misbehave in infamous Archivist's Alley all those years ago was about to make up for lost time. He kissed his way down her neck into the hollow of her throat, and she pulled back a bit to give him better access. Then she was digging her fingers into his back muscles and he was tugging up the hem of her shirt. His hand slid across her bare stomach and her whole body tensed in anticipation.

A high-pitched ding echoed through the silence, followed by the clanging of a metal cart rolling toward them.

Cait's eyes flew open. Gavin froze in mid-grope. As the clanging grew louder, they tried to compose themselves. He tucked in his shirt. She smoothed back her hair. They shared a conspiratorial grin and were just rounding the corner to make their escape when they found themselves face-to-face with a student worker preparing to reshelve a pile of books.

The student's gaze darted from the lipstick smear on Gavin's cheek to the bra strap peeking out from Cait's neckline. "Hey, Professor Clayburn."

"Hi, Jason," Gavin said. "How are you?"

Cait readjusted her bra as unobtrusively as possible.

"Fine." The student gave up trying to maintain any semblance of a poker face and gazed down at the carpet. "So, uh, see you in class Monday."

"See you in class." Gavin grabbed Cait's hand and started back through the labyrinth of bookshelves. They boarded the elevator in decorous silence, but burst out laughing as soon as the metal doors slid shut behind them.

"You're busted," Cait said. "Have fun teaching on Monday."

"Could be worse." Gavin shrugged. "I could have a visible hickey."

"The night's not over yet."

"Don't tempt me." He stopped laughing and shot her a look that could only be described as smoldering. "You still up for dinner?"

"I don't know," she said. "Most of the restaurants here

close so early, and all of the bars and pizza joints will be crawling with gossipy undergrads."

"We could go back to my place. I'll make dinner for you."

"That's a very tempting offer." Cait couldn't suppress a grin. "But aren't you the one who scorched a can of soup? I'll settle for a cold beer and good company."

"Done," he said. "And I promise I'll control myself, so long as you don't start in on the sound of flipping pages. Speaking of great literature, how's the novel coming along? Any chance you'll let me read what you've written so far?"

Chapter 14

"The most dangerous food is wedding cake."
—James Thurber

The big white wedding isn't really for me. It's for my mom." Sarah Richmond had her mother's warm smile and forthright attitude. Standing just over five feet tall, the bride-to-be was a petite powerhouse with long dark brown hair, classic features, and an impressive multicarat diamond glittering on her left ring finger. "I'm more comfortable in Target cargo pants than in Vera Wang. If it were up to me, Terry and I would elope to Hawaii or Bermuda. After all, it's his second marriage."

"Mm-hmm." Jamie hunched lower over her legal pad and pretended to take notes. Sarah had arrived in Thurwell late Friday afternoon and had invited Jamie to President Tait's home for their first planning summit. The large, stately house was frequently used for entertaining, and the interior décor struck the perfect balance between scholarly and sumptuous. The public areas were done up in rich wood tones, traditional dark Colonial colors, and antique furniture. Jamie and Sarah sat by the living room fireplace in matching slate blue wing chairs. Golden sunlight dappled the woven Persian rug.

"But Mom's so excited about planning all the details and inviting all her friends to the social event of the season," Sarah said. "This is the happiest I've seen her since my dad died. So I figure, if it means this much to her and all I have to do is throw on a gown and a veil and walk down an aisle, why not let her do her thing?"

"Mm-hmm," Jamie repeated, this time managing to smile and nod. She had been fervently hoping that her client would arrive in full Bridezilla mode, breathing fire and threatening retribution for the slightest infraction.

Instead, Sarah was proving sweet, funny, and totally down-to-earth despite her privileged upbringing. Under different circumstances, Jamie would have tried to strike up a friendship.

"I just feel bad that I couldn't pull off a June wedding for her." Sarah lifted one eyebrow. "I assume you heard her whole spiel on the depravity of November nuptials?"

Jamie grinned. "The subject may have come up."

"Well, she'll have to make her peace with it." Sarah lowered her voice and confided, "Don't tell her this, but actually, I planned for June when Terry first proposed. But then..." Sarah's expression darkened. "Let's just say that didn't work out."

Jamie leaned forward and waited for details, but Sarah

took a deep breath and resumed smiling. "So just talk me through whatever you're thinking for the reception and ceremony, and then we'll move on to the good stuff: cake tasting." Sarah rubbed her hands together. "I can't wait."

"I called the baker this afternoon to reconfirm and she should be here in about fifteen minutes with the cake samples."

"Great. I hope one of them's chocolate."

"Knowing Anna, more than one will be chocolate."

"It must come in handy to have a built-in cake connection in your line of work. And you guys have known each other for ten years?"

"Thirteen, actually. We met during our sophomore year in college."

"And now you work together on weddings? That is so cool."

"Well, actually, this is our first co-effort," Jamie said. "But I can assure you she'll do an outstanding job."

"As long as it's chocolate, I'm a happy girl."

Jamie got to her feet and led the way past the staircase to the reception parlor at the back of the house. She pointed out the bay window toward the large, flat lawn. "Assuming the weather's decent, I was thinking we could do the ceremony outdoors. We'll bring in rows of white chairs and the officiant can stand right over there by the trellis. We can tent the whole thing and rent heat lamps. But if it's snowing, we should probably move everything inside." She headed to the front parlor. "We could theoretically fit all the guests in here if we cleared out the furniture. It'll be a tight squeeze, but it's doable. You two could say your vows right over there." She gestured in the direction of the piano without looking directly at the gleaming black Steinway.

"Forget the lawn; let's do that!" Sarah exclaimed. "It would be so fitting. That piano played a pivotal role in our romance."

Jamie knew without having to ask that Sarah was not referring to a sentimental serenade.

"All right, then, we'll do the ceremony here. Then cocktail hour in the dining room while they set up for dinner."

"Sounds good."

"Now. Do you have any thoughts on the bridesmaids' tea? Themes, food, décor preferences?"

"Honestly? If it were up to me, we'd do Texas Hold-'em and Teal Squeals," Sarah said. "But I'm sure whatever you put together will be lovely."

"A girls' poker party can be arranged," Jamie offered.

"Are you kidding me? My mom would have a heart attack. No, no, let's stick to cucumber sandwiches and silver teapots."

"It's your call. But I'll make sure you get a Teal Squeal in your teacup instead of Darjeeling."

Sarah looked surprised. "You've heard of a Teal Squeal?"

"Vodka, Blue Curaçao, pineapple, and ice," Jamie recited.

"I'm impressed."

"Former bartender."

"Really?" Sarah's smile turned mischievous. "So, for example, you could mix up a Lemon Drop right now?"

"Not just a Lemon Drop. The best damn Lemon Drop you ever had."

"Well, we've got a wet bar at our disposal right here. Let's cleanse our cake-tasting palate with a cocktail." Sarah opened the cabinet above the bar sink and pulled out a bottle of vodka. "I really shouldn't; I've been starving myself for months so I can look fashionably emaciated for the big day, but as long as I'm blowing my diet with the cake samples, I might as well go all out. Hit me."

"You're the bride; your wish is my command." Jamie put aside her paperwork. "Let me go see if there are any fresh lemons in the kitchen."

"This is much more fun than obsessing over calligraphers and champagne flutes with my coordinator in Manhattan. Has anyone ever told you you're the best wedding planner ever?"

Jamie laughed. "Has anyone ever told *you* that you're the most low-maintenance bride ever?"

"I tell her that all the time," said a booming male voice from the doorway.

Sarah's eyes lit up. "Oh hi, honey."

"My love." President Terrence Tait strode across the room and kissed Sarah on the forehead. Jamie looked out the window. "How's the wedding planning going?"

"You made it just in time for cocktail hour." Sarah went up on tiptoe and kissed his cheek. "Remember I told you my mom finally found a local wedding planner? This is Jamie Burton."

Terrence extended his right hand. "Pleased to meet you."

Jamie held off as long as she could, then skimmed her palm against his in the fastest handshake in history.

"She was a student here, actually," Sarah continued, oblivious to the thickening tension. "Like ten years ago."

Terry hesitated for a moment, then smiled and shrugged. "Can't place the name, I'm afraid. My apologies, but so many students have passed through over the years."

Jamie shot him a murderous glare over Sarah's head. "Don't worry about it."

"The baker will be here in a few minutes with the cake

samples, but it turns out that Jamie here used to be a bartender, so of course I'm taking full advantage. Do you happen to have any fresh lemons, honey?"

"I'll check on that right now." Terrence shrugged off his suit jacket as he headed back toward the kitchen. From the back, his frame still looked young, strong, and fit. Jamie made sure to focus on his graying hair rather than his athletic ass.

Sarah caught Jamie staring and said, "I know what you're thinking."

"Oh, I doubt that."

"He's old enough to be my dad, right? But let me tell you, I have dated my way through every loser, user, and emotional abuser in the greater tristate area. Each relationship was worse than the last."

"I can relate," Jamie said.

"And then one night, fresh off another agonizing breakup, I came up here for a spa weekend to lick my wounds and I met Terry. You just get to a point where you start to appreciate stability, you know? I'd had it with all the drama."

"Uh-huh."

"And you probably can't think of him this way, since he's just a buttoned-up administrator to you, but he's romantic. He really pursued me." Sarah glanced down at her engagement ring. "The man was relentless!" She noticed Jamie's expression and started laughing again. "Okay, I'll shut up now. Give me a minute to pull myself together in the powder room, and when I get back, we'll have drinks and cake and I promise to stop gushing like a human Hallmark card." She hurried off toward the bathroom.

Jamie closed her eyes and forced herself to think optimistic, life-affirming thoughts. Maybe the Terrence Tait that

Sarah knew was nothing like the Terrence Tait that Jamie knew. Over a decade had passed. Maybe people really could change.

She felt a hand slide along the curve of her hip.

"What the hell?" Her eyes flew open and she found herself staring into the amused eyes of President Tait. "Don't touch me. Don't even look at me!"

"Time's been good to you, Jamie. You're even more beautiful now than you were at twenty-one." He gave her a thorough once-over as he deposited a trio of ripe lemons and a paring knife on the wet bar.

"Save the bullshit flattery for your committee meetings and your fund-raisers." Jamie ground her molars together. "Oh, and P.S.: The furrowed brow just now was overkill. As was blatantly ignoring me at the trustee reception last week. I know you remember me."

"Of course I remember you. How could I forget? Specifically, I remember the time you and I were sitting right there on that piano bench—"

"Knock it off! This is completely inappropriate." She snatched up a lemon and the knife and started hacking away with more force than necessary.

"I agree. That's why we should make amends and start fresh."

"With your hand on my ass?"

"Don't be such a Puritan," he chided. "You've been living in Miami and Los Angeles, haven't you? I'm surprised you're so uptight."

Her jaw dropped. "How do you know where I live?"

"Alumni contact database."

"Stalker much?"

"Efficient networker," he corrected. "It's my job to stay in touch with our graduates and make sure they continue to think back fondly on their Thurwell days."

"Just stay away from me." She dumped some ice into a silver cocktail shaker, then added a splash of vodka. "I don't find you charming anymore. I find you repulsive. You're engaged, and if this afternoon is any indication, your fiancée is about a billion times too good for you. Behave yourself."

"If memory serves, I'm not the only one prone to bad behavior."

Jamie slammed down the cocktail shaker and grabbed his lapel. "You listen to me. What happened with you, me, and Arden? No one is ever going to find out about that. *Ever.*"

He stopped trying to banter and got serious. "I heard about Arden. I'm sorry. I know you two were close."

"Stop that!" She gave him a little shake, then forced herself to let go before she throttled him. "Stop pretending you're a human being."

"As opposed to what?"

"As opposed to a sick, twisted, manipulative, two-faced, bottom-feeding incubus." She seized the lemon halves and squeezed until her hands ached.

His face settled back into a smirk of detachment. "Go ahead and vilify me if it eases your conscience. But we both know it takes two to tango. Or, in our case, defile a piano bench."

She gaped at him. "What is *wrong* with you?"

"What's wrong with you?" he countered. "You're the one who insinuated herself into the role of planning her lover's wedding to another woman. Talk about sick."

"Lover. Ha." She tossed her hair. "Let's get one thing straight: I might have had sex with you, but I never loved you."

He braced his hand on the fireplace mantel and said nothing.

"And, just for the record, I had no idea you were the groom when I agreed to this fiasco. I'm only doing this because I signed a contract and I'm a woman of my word."

"If you say so."

"Don't do this to me. Don't do it to her." Jamie took a slow breath and softened her tone. "Prove me wrong. Turn yourself into the man she thinks she's marrying. Fake it till you make it. Whatever."

He opened his mouth to respond, but she drowned out his voice with the ice-filled martini shaker. She realized she'd been reduced to pleading, but she didn't care. It wasn't like she had any dignity left to salvage.

She had lied when she said she'd never loved him. Which made her situation, both past and present, even more reprehensible.

Some people might say that a twenty-one-year-old student in her position was too naïve to understand what she was getting into, but Jamie had known exactly what she was doing. As much as she wanted to blame Terrence for taking advantage of her, *she* was the one who had initiated the flirtation. She had known it was wrong to dally with a married man. But the truth was, she hadn't cared about wrong or right. She'd gotten off on the heady sense of power and the aphrodisiac of secrecy. She'd been a headstrong, selfish little bitch.

And Arden had paid the price in the end.

When Jamie finally let up with the cocktail shaker, Terrence was studying her thoughtfully. "This means a lot to you," he said.

"No. It means a lot to *her*." Jamie jerked her head toward the doorway as Sarah returned from the bathroom.

"What did I miss?" Sarah asked.

Jamie handed over a frosty glass garnished with a curl of lemon rind. "Drink up and prepare to be amazed."

Sarah reached over to touch her glass against Jamie's and Terrence's. "Here's to love."

By the time Anna arrived ten minutes later, Jamie and Terrence had retreated to opposite corners of the room and Sarah was too buzzed to notice.

"Dude! This really *is* the best Lemon Drop I've ever had in my life! It should be in, like, a martini museum!" She put down her drink and engulfed Anna in a big hug. "Hiii!"

"Um, hi there." Anna patted Sarah's shoulder in an unsuccessful bid to free herself. "I'm Anna McCauley, and I come bearing cake."

"You'll have to excuse her exuberance," Terrence said. "She's a bit tipsy at the moment."

Anna glanced over at the half-consumed Lemon Drops, then shook her head at Jamie.

"Don't you even look my way." Jamie held up her hand. "She begged me to make them and they're not even strong."

"I can vouch for that," Terry said. Somehow, his coming to her defense made Jamie resent him even more. "My future wife has many virtues, but she's never been able to hold her liquor."

"It's true." Sarah giggled. "I'm a lightweight. Half-a-drink drunk."

Terrence put a steadying arm around her and kissed her on the temple.

"Okay." Jamie clapped her hands together and tried to regain some semblance of control. "Let's get a piece of cake into her before her blood turns to ethanol."

Anna pushed aside the knickknacks on the coffee table and set down a platter of samples. "Spice cake, red velvet, chocolate, lemon, coconut, vanilla almond. Have at."

Sarah bit into the white-frosted vanilla almond cake. Her eyes got huge. "Oh my God. I know I said I love chocolate, but this is seriously the best thing I've ever had in my life. Better than that Lemon Drop, even. Vanilla almond cake it is!" She turned to Terrence. "You do like vanilla, don't you?"

"I live for vanilla," Terrence assured her.

"Fantastic! And it's super traditional, so my mom will approve. This whole thing is working out perfectly." Sarah pounded back the remainder of her Lemon Drop, then beamed up at Terrence. "I love you."

"I love you right back."

Jamie's entire being screamed for a cigarette.

"Congratulations," Anna whispered to Jamie. "You're a smashing success as a wedding consultant."

"Don't jinx me," Jamie muttered. "It's still early days."

"Are you kidding me? Look at these two—you couldn't screw this up if you tried."

Chapter
15

"There ought to be a room in every house to swear in."
—Mark Twain

S on of a bitch!" Brooke threw down her cordless drill in disgust.

Anna, who had been trailing Brooke from outlet to outlet with a metal-caged utility light to better illuminate the tangles of wire within the living room walls, did a double take. "Do my ears deceive me, or did our delicate Stealth Magnolia just utter an obscenity?"

Jamie paused the TV midway through a recorded episode of *My Big Amazing Renovation* (Brooke's request). "Yeah, I thought that went against your personal code of gentility."

"That code doesn't apply in the presence of power tools," Brooke shot back before unleashing a fresh torrent of profanity. "This is the second drill bit that's snapped this week. These beams must be made out of petrified hickory. Or titanium." The other explanation, of course, was that she'd gotten careless while listening to HGTV and started drilling at a slight angle. But why blame herself when this stupid house was such an easy target? "It's been over a week and I've barely finished rewiring one room. At this rate, it'll be years before I get this place up to code."

"Don't even joke about that," Anna said. "We need to be up and running in time for Jamie's wedding."

"I'm not getting married," Jamie pointed out.

"You know what I mean. Just think about all the revenue and word of mouth that weekend's going to generate."

"Assuming the wedding's still on," Jamie said.

"Of course the wedding will still be on." Anna gave Jamie an exasperated look. "Why wouldn't it be? You are so pessimistic sometimes."

"I'm just saying, sometimes things happen after people get engaged. Exhibit A: me, me, and me."

"You think they might call it off?" Brooke couldn't hide her dismay. "Really? Should I not count on any reservations that weekend?"

"Don't worry," Anna said. "I've met the happy couple and I can assure you, they are almost obnoxiously in love."

"As in love as Cait and Professor Clayburn?" Brooke asked.

They all looked over at Cait, but she was lost in thought, scribbling in the margins of a catalog that had arrived in the mail.

"Hey. Johnson. Look alive."

Cait's head snapped up. "What'd I miss?"

"Are you working on your book?"

"Kind of. I just had an idea for a scene and I don't want to forget it."

"Look at you! You're such an *artiste!*"

Cait flushed. "Well...,"

"Communing with your muse while the rest of us watch TV and make inflammatory comments about you and Professor Clayburn. We should be ashamed."

"Oh my God. First of all, his name is Gavin. Secondly, we had one date."

"In Archivist's Alley." All three of them chorused, "Oooh..."

"We ate dinner afterward," Cait sputtered. "Conversation and camaraderie."

"Camaraderie. Uh-huh. Is that what they're calling it these days?"

"For the last time, you salacious gossip hounds, I did not spend the night with him. I was home before one, as you're well aware."

"Just because you didn't spend the night with him doesn't mean you didn't, ahem, *sleep* with him, so to speak," Brooke pointed out.

"Are you going out with him again?" Anna asked.

"Yes," Cait said. "But I'm not telling you where or when."

"Spoilsport." Jamie propped her slippered feet up on the coffee table. "Well, do me a favor and keep me in mind when you find yourself in need of a wedding planner."

"And I'll do your wedding cake," Anna said. "I can see it now: three-tier, white-on-white, piped with Elizabeth Barrett Browning verses. Or maybe John Donne, or Christina Rossetti."

"Can we please stop speculating on my personal life and get back to securing a roof over our heads?" Cait turned to

Brooke. "How can we help? Anna, want me take over as light holder?"

"No, I can't do any more until I replace this." Brooke held up the truncated drill bit. "Thankfully, they come with a lifetime warranty."

"And it gives you an excuse to go back to the hardware store," Anna teased.

"Yeah," Jamie said. "Give our best to your secret crush behind the counter."

"I never said I have a crush on him!"

"Honey, you didn't have to. I've never seen anyone so excited over the prospect of running out to get more electrical tape."

"I don't know enough about him to have a crush," Brooke insisted. "All I know is that he's well-read and well-mannered." Her composure cracked a little and she confided, "He gave me the contractor rate."

"Don't let him take advantage," Cait said. "Just because a man gives you the contractor rate doesn't mean you have to, ahem, *sleep* with him, so to speak."

Anna's cell phone rang on the windowsill and Brooke snatched it up, grateful for the distraction. She glanced at the name displayed on the caller ID screen and reported, "It's Jonas."

Anna's expression darkened. "Let it go to voice mail." Her tone did not invite questions, so Brooke replaced the phone on the table, and they all listened to the ringtone playing Counting Crows' "Anna Begins."

They all let a few more beats pass in silence, then Cait asked, "When's he coming back?"

Anna unplugged the utility light and began to wind up the cord. "I'm not sure."

"Are you guys going to work things out?"

"I would prefer not to talk about this, if you don't mind." She deflected their concerned glances with the closed, nonchalant type of smile she generally reserved for strangers.

Brooke did what she could to take the focus away from Anna. "Can I ask you guys for advice? And not get harassed like Cait?"

"Good luck with that," Cait said.

"Is this about the hardware store Adonis?" Jamie asked.

"Yes." Brooke tucked her hair back behind her ear. "We've been chatting every time I go over there, and he's sweet and attentive and always asking me about my progress, but he hasn't actually asked me out."

"Okay." Jamie nodded. "So what's your question?"

"How do I make him ask me out?"

"*Make* him?"

"Entice him. Whatever. I know he's interested. I have unerring instincts for this sort of thing."

Jamie shrugged. "Then ask him out."

"What? No!"

"Why not?" Anna asked.

"Because! I can't do that! I've never made the first move in my life."

"Then I'd say you're overdue."

"Yeah, you've never opened a B and B, either. Or rewired a house from top to bottom." Cait helped herself to a handful of popcorn. "Just like I've never written a book. We're all dog-paddling in uncharted waters here."

"Arden would definitely want you to ask him out," Anna said.

Cait nodded solemnly. "I'm pretty sure it was her dying wish."

"You guys are terrible." Brooke acted scandalized for two seconds, then got back to business. "Well, what do I say, exactly? I can't just come out with 'Wanna go catch a movie?'"

"Why not?"

"Because I'm a slave to subtlety."

"Ooh, I know." Anna raised her hand like they were back in Freshman Comp. "He's all about tools and construction, right? Why don't you ask him to come over here sometime and consult on the wiring job?"

"Yeah. Ask him to come over and hold the light."

"So to speak."

They all cracked up.

Brooke crossed her arms. "Must you always lower the tone?"

More giggling.

She waited for them to simmer down, then asked, "So if I ask him for his opinion with the wiring, you don't think that makes me look like a dumb blonde? The helpless damsel in distress?"

"Hardly." Cait made a sweeping gesture to encompass all the wires protruding from holes drilled in the drywall. "He'll probably be blown away by the progress you've already made."

"I *am* turning out to be quite handy, if I do say so myself." Brooke pocketed the broken drill bit and winked. "Okay, I'll do it. Right after I do my makeup. I'll be the hottest thing that hardware store has ever seen."

Cheers and applause all around.

Brooke deliberately timed her trip so that she'd arrive at the hardware store just before closing. Her plan was simple: The store would be deserted, Everett would be smitten by her charm and beauty, and they would live happily ever after in their lovingly refurbished home.

What could possibly go wrong?

"Hey there, stranger." Everett glanced up with a welcoming smile when Brooke walked through the door. He looked woodsy and rugged—even his sweat was probably pine-scented—and her stomach went all fluttery. "Haven't seen you in, what? Two days?"

"Two days," she confirmed, encouraged that he'd noticed her absence.

"Which means the project's going either really well or really poorly." He paused expectantly. "So which is it?"

"Somewhere in between, actually." She reached into her pocket and pulled out the broken drill bit. "I need another replacement, I'm afraid."

"Already?" He whistled. "You know, I've been working here on and off since I was in high school, and I've never had anyone bring a bit back more than once. What the heck are you drilling?"

"Wood." Brooke glowered. "Ancient, ornery wood that refuses to surrender without plenty of collateral damage." She forced her features back into an expression of come-hither coquettishness. "So does that lifetime warranty still apply?"

"It does, but tell you what. Let me save us both some time and trouble." He walked over to the power tool accessories. "I'm going to upgrade you to the industrial-grade bit brace. More precision, fewer broken bits. In theory."

"Sounds good." Brooke followed him back toward the cash register and prepared to make her move. "So, listen, I was wondering—"

"No charge," he assured her, making a note in the transaction ledger next to the register. "It's the least I can do for my favorite contractor."

"Why, thank you, Everett. That's sweet. As I was saying, I'm starting to run the wires and clamp the cables, but I'm worried I may end up overloading the circuit and I was thinking...well, I was hoping that you might be able to..." She took a deep breath and produced a business card on which she'd written her home number. "Come over to my house. And take a look at what I've done so far."

His mouth twitched and then he smiled at her, but not in the way she'd been hoping for. No, this was definitely more of an unnerved, stalling-for-time kind of smile. "I, uh...I..."

She could feel her own smile flickering. "I could really use an expert opinion."

The door chimes rang on the other side of the store and a gruff male voice said, "Oh good, you're still open." A flannel-clad man strode up to the counter and planted himself directly in front of Everett. "I need a forty-pound bag of resurfacer, ASAP."

"Yes, sir, right over there." Everett pointed toward an aisle. Then he glanced down at the business card, turned back to Brooke, and shook his head. "Oh man. I wish I could."

"Oh." Her voice came out high and pinched. "Okay." She backed toward the exit.

"I mean, it's not that I don't want to, but I can't."

"No need to explain." Brooke practically ran out the door, dived into her car, and waited until she was a mile away from the scene before pulling over in front of the bowling alley, covering her face with her hands, and dying a million deaths in the glow of a flashing neon Strike! sign.

Ten minutes later, she returned to Paradise Found with her head held high and her industrial drill bit in hand. Anna, Cait, and Jamie were still camped out in the living room, eagerly awaiting her report.

"Well?" Cait prompted as soon as Brooke crossed the threshold.

"What'd he say?" Jamie demanded.

Brooke crumpled up the brown paper shopping bag. "Let me put it this way: I'm gonna have to find a new hardware store."

She ignored all the questions and exclamations of outrage, retreated to her bedroom, and called the only person who could possibly assuage her burning sense of incompetence. "Hi, Professor Rutkin? It's me again. Is this too late to call?...Oh good.... Yes, my science education is continuing apace. There are certain things in this world that I'm never going to understand, but I'll figure out electrical circuitry or die trying. Do you think I might be able to drop by during your office hours tomorrow?"

Chapter
16

"War cannot be avoided; it can only be postponed
to the other's advantage."
—Niccolo Machiavelli, *The Prince*

O oh, a retro fifties cocktail party sounds fabulous,"
Anna said into her cell phone as she parked her car
in the lot behind Pranza and gathered up her coat
along with a trio of bags filled with refrigerated ingredients.
"And honestly, there's no need to apologize about the late
notice. I have the whole night to bake in a professional
kitchen. I'll just run back to the grocery store and then get
started. This is going to be fun. Don't you worry, I'll ferret
out some outrageous old-school recipes."

As she made her way past the dumpsters toward the
restaurant's back door, Anna sifted through her coat pocket

for the key and tried to allay her newest client's concerns about "not wanting to hurt anybody's feelings."

"Absolutely.... No problem.... I'm the height of discretion. I won't breathe a word of this to Trish Selway, believe me.... Right. Just give me your address and I'll deliver everything tomorrow morning."

Anna pushed the door open with her shoulder, clamped a pen cap between her teeth, and jotted down the customer's contact information on her hand as she entered Pranza's prep kitchen. "Seventeen Conifer Drive... fifth house on the left... red door. Okay, got it. I'll give you a call if I have any other questions. Thanks so much for taking a chance on me, Mrs. Elquest. You won't be sorry!"

She clicked off the phone and shook her head. Brooke hadn't been kidding when she said there was only one baker in this tiny town. Every single person who had called Anna over the past week—and the inquiries had been increasing as word started to get out about the Thurwell anniversary cakes—had either started or finished the conversation with a variation of "Please don't tell Trish Selway I called."

The rubber mat beneath her feet shifted, and Anna whirled around to find herself inches away from Trish, whose surly scowl and flared nostrils indicated that she'd been eavesdropping.

Anna staggered back against the steel door of the massive walk-in refrigerator and struggled to regain her composure. Or at least the power of speech.

"Was that Belinda Elquest?" Trish's eyes narrowed to tiny slits.

"What the hell are you still doing here?" Anna knelt down to retrieve the pen she'd dropped, but she didn't take her gaze off the other woman.

"You said 'Mrs. Elquest.' I heard you." Trish seized Anna's hand and examined the address scribbled on her skin. "I can't believe this."

"*I* can't believe you're lying in wait for me again." Anna snatched back her hand and stuffed it into her coat pocket. "The terms of our arrangement are crystal clear: From nine o'clock on, this kitchen is mine. Be gone."

Trish ignored this and kept right on seething. "I don't know who's worse: you, for luring away my loyal clients, or Belinda, that two-faced traitor, for calling you. I made her high school graduation cake, her wedding cake, her baby shower cake. I gave my all for that chick—blood, sweat, and the best frickin' buttercream of all time—and this is the thanks I get?"

"Did you ever stop to think that your attitude might have something to do with the mass desertion?" Anna said. "Besides, I don't have to 'lure' anyone; I'm getting the orders because I'm the superior baker."

Trish snorted. "You're a hack!"

"Is that so? What was it Mrs. Elquest was saying about the dessert tray I did for the college reception? Oh yeah— she said I'm the confectionary equivalent of a ninja." Anna flashed her most insincere smile. "On that note, I'm off to make a grocery run."

"Good riddance." Trish's scowl deepened. She rubbed her forehead and produced a tiny blue foil packet from her shirt pocket.

Anna glanced at the label. "Is that ibuprofen?"

"Yeah. So? You planning on stealing that, too?"

"You can't have ibuprofen." The words were out of her mouth before Anna could stop them, a reflex honed from years of paging through *What to Expect When You're Expecting.*

"Not if you're pregnant. You can only have acetaminophen, and only in extreme cases."

"Gee, the Bug and I really appreciate your concern," Trish said with an exaggerated eye roll. "But maybe you should have thought of all that before you gave me a splitting headache, you snooty—"

Anna frowned. "Did you just refer to your unborn child as a bug?"

"Not just a bug," Trish corrected. "*The* Bug."

"That's horrible!"

"Why? Haven't you ever seen an ultrasound picture? It looks like a blurry little bug."

"Well, you could at least call it something cute: the bean, the peanut, even the Gummi Bear."

"Gag. When *you* get pregnant, you can use whatever vomitous little nickname floats your boat. But I'm sticking with the Bug. Mind your own business for once."

"Fine." Anna bristled. "Call the kid whatever you want. Ingest whatever you want. I have ingredients to buy and cakes to bake, and you better not be here when I get back, or I'll call Seth and take your kitchen time along with what's left of your client base."

She pivoted on her heel, stalked back out into the alley, and let the heavy door swing shut behind her with a satisfying slam.

When Anna returned from the grocery store forty-five minutes later, she was relieved to find the restaurant kitchen vacant and a whole night of baking-induced Zen stretching out before her. She plugged in her mp3 player's portable speakers, queued up the *Pulp Fiction* soundtrack, and prepared to improvise a sophisticated version of the first '50s dessert on her catering list: Coca-Cola cake with buttercream frosting. The scent of sugar and cocoa and the familiar clatter of her metal measuring cups soothed her. So many things in her life had gone wrong lately, but a good recipe was always guaranteed to turn out well, provided you followed the directions.

After she measured out her dry ingredients and sifted together the flour, baking soda, and salt, she filled a white stoneware crock with room-temperature butter and locked the huge stainless steel bowl into the base of the industrial-grade Hobart mixer.

That's when she realized that the mixer's attachments were nowhere to be found. During Seth's introductory tour of the kitchen, he'd mentioned that the mixer accessories were all stored in a metal drawer beneath the counter, but Anna searched and came up empty. Then she searched the drawers above and below—still nothing.

She was rooting through the contents of the condiment supply cartons, figuring that someone might have absent-mindedly stashed the beater attachment in there, when her phone rang again. Jonas's name flashed up on caller ID. Again.

For the first time in days, she picked up. "Hello?"

"Hi." He sounded a bit startled. "Finally. I was about to call our mobile provider and ask if you'd canceled your service."

"No," she said shortly. "I've been busy."

"You've been avoiding me."

"You're the one who took off for another continent," she pointed out.

"I didn't have a choice, Anna. I have. To work." She could practically hear him gritting his teeth.

She forced herself to relax the muscles knotting in her neck and shoulders. "You know what? I don't have time to fight with you right now. I have work to do. I have deadlines."

"What's up?" He sounded heartened by the prospect of problem solving.

She gave him a thirty-second summary of the night's events. "...and honestly, what is the point of signing a lease and paying all that money to use this space if I'm going to be constantly harassed by the world's bitterest townie and I can't even count on having the proper equipment? This is bullshit, Jonas! Bullshit!"

"Calm down," Jonas said. "You're getting way too emotional."

"Of course I'm emotional! I'm tired, I'm exasperated, I miss you, I have no idea what's happening between us, I've got a client depending on me, and the clock is ticking, and—"

"Anna. Ease up." His voice got slower and calmer, the aural equivalent of Xanax. "One thing at a time. Don't freak out about what's going to happen twelve hours from now. Just concentrate on what you're baking tonight."

"That'd be a lot easier to do if I could get my hands on the fucking mixer attachment!"

"Ohhh-kay. I hate to do this, but I'm going to remind you that you ovulated thirteen days ago." He cleared his throat. "Which means that right now, you may be kind of, uh, irrational."

She sucked in her breath. "I *know* you did not just play the PMS card."

"Sorry, I take it back." He waited a beat, and then,

mistaking her enraged silence for forgiveness, forged ahead. "But you asked what I would do in this situation, and I'm telling you, if it were me, I'd stop ranting and raving and start doing something productive. Starting with finding an alternative mixer."

"Of course." She threw up her hands. "It's so simple. Why didn't I think of that?"

"I'm picking up on your sarcasm."

"Well, I'm picking up on your condescension. The whole point of leasing this space is so I have industrial-grade equipment. Where am I supposed to come up with another Hobart mixer in the middle of the night up here in the Adirondacks?"

"What about the one you brought from home?"

"Jonas, I'm supposed to be feeding fifty people. It's going to take forever to do everything that needs to be done with a single-batch mixer."

"All the more reason to get started right away."

She closed her eyes and curled her fingers around the edge of the counter. "I'm so glad we had this talk."

"Me, too." She could hear faint strains of music in the background on his end of the line. "So I was thinking about you today," he said.

"Oh?"

"Yeah. You're going to ovulate again pretty soon."

Anna's eyes popped open.

"And we're on different continents," he continued, with what sounded like optimism.

"Where exactly are you going with this?" she asked.

"Well. Isn't it kind of a relief?"

"Not to me. Why would you say that?"

"Because the pressure's off." He forced a chuckle. "We don't have to, you know—"

"Have sex? Have a baby? Have a future?"

"Force anything."

Anna picked up her measuring cups and held on to them tightly, until the rims dug into her palm and the thick metal walls began to warm against her skin.

"We're spending time together because we want to," Jonas continued. "Not because your basal body temperature dictates that we have to. See? Progress."

Anna wanted to ask him a million questions. Most of all, she wanted to ask him when he had stopped thinking of her as the love of his life and started thinking of her as a problem to be handled.

How much of this is my fault? When did we stop listening to each other?

All she said was, "I'm glad you want to spend time with me. On separate continents."

"That can't stand in our way. We could have phone sex."

That caught her off guard. "No, we can't."

"Not right now, obviously," he said. "You're on deadline. But once you finish up with everything there, you could call me back and we—"

Anna hung up on him, set the oven timer, and allowed herself exactly five minutes to sob into a linen napkin. She thought about their wedding night, when she had also wept, not from joy but because the emotional strain of spending a five-hour reception trying to head off conflicts between Jonas's divorced parents and Anna's divorced parents and a seemingly endless parade of easily offended step-relatives and in-laws had left them too drained to do anything but lie motionless in the huge four-poster bed in their honeymoon suite.

"Families suck." The down pillow under her head had rustled as she gazed at her brand-new husband. "Individually, everyone's fine, but as a group, they suck."

"Yeah, they do," Jonas had agreed. He was still wearing his rented tuxedo, looking simultaneously suave and vulnerable. "But that's the whole point of getting married, right? We get to start our own family. Speaking of which, we better get crackin'. How many kids did I promise you? Four? Five?"

"Let's start with one." She'd laughed. "Tomorrow. I don't think I have the energy to try for a wedding night baby."

He'd reached over and stroked her cheek. "How about a hot shower and a foot rub?"

She kicked off her high heels and wiggled her toes, which had lost all feeling right around the cake cutting. "This is already the happiest marriage of all time. And don't worry. We'll make up for lost time on the honeymoon."

"You're worth the wait." He trailed his hand along her neck, bare shoulder, and arm until he laced his fingers with hers. "Always have been, always will be."

They'd rested together in silence for a few minutes, their bodies relaxing into each other. Then Anna had mustered the energy to raise her head and prop herself up on her elbows.

"Promise me we'll never be like that." She'd squeezed his hand. "Promise me that our kids will not have to spend their weddings worrying about whether we're going to start brawling over stupid crap that happened fifteen years ago."

"I promise." He squeezed back. "We'll always be on the same team, no matter what."

"But life can surprise you." She thought about how all the

fractured, feuding families downstairs had started in rapturous honeymoons. "Marriage is tough."

He pulled her back down and wrapped her in his arms. "We're tougher."

The oven timer dinged. Anna wiped her eyes, splashed cool water onto her cheeks, and called in the family she'd created for herself, the sisters who'd stuck by and supported her during the toughest times of all.

C oca-Cola cake?" Jamie peered dubiously at Anna's recipe notes. "With actual soda in it? No offense, but that sounds kind of—"

"Iffy," Caitlin finished for her.

"It's a Southern classic," Brooke said. "Don't you people ever go to church potlucks?"

Anna ignored the commentary and guided each of her friends to the individual prep stations she'd set up. "I'm using gourmet dark cocoa imported from France and making the marshmallows from scratch. That's what the cream of tartar and the gelatin are for."

"You're making marshmallows from scratch?" Jamie asked.

"*You're* making marshmallows from scratch," Anna corrected her. "It's easy once you get the knack of spreading it on the marble slab. We'll do the cake first, and then, while that's cooling, we'll tackle the velvet Jell-O salad, the bread-and-butter pudding, and the Fruit Fool." She laughed at their expressions. "Hey, it's an authentic 1950s cocktail theme. The heyday of Wonder Bread and fruit cocktail. Our job is to take these ingredients and elevate them to an unprecedented level of playful refinement."

Cait and Brooke exchanged a look.

"Tell me what to do and I'll do it," Jamie said. "But the refinement part's all on you."

"Fair enough," Anna said. "I really appreciate you guys coming in to save my ass yet again. This is probably going to take all night, so I apologize in advance."

"Don't worry about it," Cait said. "We live for all-nighters."

"I'm just so frustrated about not being able to use the Hobart mixer," Anna said. "It would cut my work time in half. I know the beaters are supposed to be stored right here in this drawer, and I've torn this whole place apart looking for them. Now we're all going to be inconvenienced because of someone else's carelessness." She paused, her mouth hanging open. "Unless..."

"Unless what?"

Anna's mouth snapped shut. "I smell sabotage."

Two minutes later, they had located the local phone book in the back office and Anna was dialing Trish Selway's home number.

"Hi, Trish, it's Anna McCauley. Listen, I know it's late, but I was wondering if there's any chance you might have misplaced the mixer attachments while you were working tonight. Accidentally, of course."

"Who is this?" Trish mumbled.

"Anna. The other baker at Pranza."

A stifled yawn on the other end of the connection. "What time is it?"

"Listen, I'm sorry to disturb you, but I can't seem to locate the flat paddle attachment for the Hobart mixer."

There was a long pause, and when Trish finally replied, her voice dripped with schadenfreude. "Really? Hmm. That's too bad."

"I knew it!" Anna raised her fist in vindication.

"Knew what?" Trish asked.

"Don't play innocent with me. You made off with it while I was at the grocery store, didn't you? Have you no shame?"

"I have no idea what you're talking about."

"Come off it. Save yourself a world of hurt and just tell me where you hid it."

"Are you kidding me? You call me up, at home, in the middle of the night, to accuse me of—what are you accusing me of, again?"

"Concealing essential kitchen equipment with malice aforethought. You can't stand the thought of having competition, so you're sabotaging me!"

"Wow. Do you have any idea how insane you sound?"

"Oh right." Anna pounded her fist on the metal countertop. "*I'm* the insane one."

"You're the one rousting a pregnant woman at midnight and having hysterics," Trish pointed out. "Leave me alone, you psycho. The Bug and I need our sleep."

Click. Anna listened to the dial tone for a minute, then slowly turned around to face her friends.

"Good for you," Jamie said. "You really gave her what for."

"Yeah, she won't screw with you again," Cait said.

"She claims she has no idea what I'm talking about." Anna chuffed. "She called me a psycho."

"The nerve!"

Brooke, Cait, and Jamie turned to one another, exclaiming their assent with increasing force and frequency until Anna said, "Although."

The other three shut up.

"Now that I'm thinking this over, I have to admit that

there may be a teeny, tiny, very remote possibility that I jumped the gun here." Anna ran her index finger along the countertop. "I mean, you have to agree that these are not the actions of a rational woman. Calling up my competitor in the middle of the night and flat-out accusing her of theft and sabotage? Am I losing my grip on reality?"

"Of course not." Brooke cleared her throat delicately. "I will say, however, that you do seem to be wound a little tightly today. Forgive me for asking, but is it possible that you're PMS-ing?"

Anna burst out laughing.

"What?" Brooke asked, flushing pink.

"Nothing." Anna gasped for breath. "Everything. Let's get to work."

And they did, working magic with marshmallows and maraschino cherries until after dawn, when Trish Selway swept through the door. She drew up short when she saw Anna. "What are you still doing here?"

"We've all been slaving away for the last twelve hours." Anna tapped her whisk against the rim of her metal mixing bowl. "What are you doing here?"

"I have a breakfast meeting with Seth." Trish thinned her lips. "Not that it's any of your business."

"Well, I'm glad to hear that Seth is on his way. I have a lot to discuss with him, starting with the mysterious and oh-so-conveniently timed disappearance of the Hobart beater."

"Oh my God, you're still on that?" Trish marched over to the metal drawer, bent down to rummage through the utensils, and yanked out the flat paddle. "Is this what you're bitching about? This beater right here?"

"How the hell...?" Anna could feel the blood rushing out of her face. "I looked through that drawer twenty times!

That was not in there." She appealed to Cait, Brooke, and Jamie. "That was not in there."

"Sure. It just materialized out of thin air." Trish tossed it on the counter with a clang as she strode toward the dining area. "Sucks for your friends they had to stay up all night for no reason. Still want to talk to Seth, you paranoid legacy lunatic?"

"I am mortified." Anna couldn't look away from at the paddle still rocking gently on the counter. "I'm also PMS-ing. And blind. And a self-destructive maniac."

"But the good news is, you make excellent pancakes." Jamie gave her a consolatory clap on the back. "Now who wants breakfast? No mixer required."

Chapter
17

"He who never made a mistake never made a discovery."
—Samuel Smiles, *Self-Help*

*H*elena waited until she was certain that MacCormick had taken her brothers outside to the grounds for a botany lesson before she made her way to the last room at the end of the hall and tested the doorknob. As before, it was locked, but this time, she had come prepared. She produced the housekeeper's key ring and let herself in.

Inside MacCormick's chamber, she found nothing out of the ordinary. But she simply knew something was amiss with him. Over the last three weeks, he'd always seemed to be around her; nary an hour passed that she didn't feel that amber gaze upon her.

The clothes in the garderobe were of finer quality than befitted a mere tutor, but a cursory inventory of the desk drawers yielded no secret missives, only books—classical Roman works that she'd never read but had heard of.

Specifically, she had heard from her parents, her tutors, her society peers, that she must never compromise her virtue by reading them.

Naturally, nothing could now prevent her from poring over the pages.

Her eyes widened as she came upon a section with graphic illustrations of gods cavorting and fornicating. Knees gone weak, she sank onto the edge of MacCormick's bed. She devoured the pages with such fervor and concentration that she didn't hear MacCormick enter the chamber until the door slammed behind him.

His hands were clenched, his expression inscrutable as he spied the book's depictions that had riveted her so completely. Helena slammed the cover closed as she leapt from the bed. "I was only—I didn't mean—"

He saved her the trouble of stumbling over excuses. Without warning, his rough hand wrapped around the nape of her neck. He drew her closer and his lips descended upon hers.

She raised her hand to push him away, but his lips were so firm, and he moved them so shamelessly over hers. With each second, her body grew warmer until passion overpowered her propriety. She clutched his linen shirtfront, silently demanding more.

When at last he broke away, he rested his forehead against hers and murmured, his voice low and thick, "Ye've no need to read that, lass. I'll gladly demonstrate anything within those pages."

"Cait?" There was a soft knock at the door. "You in there?"

Caitlin looked up from her keyboard with a mixture of alarm and annoyance. She'd woken up this morning with an idea for a scene and had been on a roll ever since.

"Uh, just a second." She hunched closer to the computer screen, reread the sentence she'd just written, and closed the file before getting to her feet to unlock the door.

Anna stood in the hallway with a smudge of flour on her nose and a big cardboard box in her hands. Her expression was sheepish. "Sorry. I didn't mean to wake you."

"Oh, you didn't," Cait assured her. "I've been up for hours." Anna glanced at Cait's robe, threadbare plaid boxers, and woolen kneesocks.

"I haven't showered or eaten or left the room yet," Cait elaborated. "I've been writing."

"You must be really inspired. Now I feel doubly bad for bothering you."

"Anna, listen to me. Stop feeling bad. About everything. We all adore you, and as it happens, I'm overdue for a break." She nodded at the white bakery box. "Let me guess: You got my psychic breakfast order and have arrived to deliver warm crullers?"

"Even better." Anna lifted the lid of the box to reveal rows of light, oblong sponge cakes. "Boudoir biscuits."

"Oooh, sounds fancy." Cait closed her eyes and breathed in the scent of vanilla and powdered sugar. "Sounds kind of sexy, actually. Is this some traditional French postcoital treat?"

Anna laughed. "Sounds like someone's still hot and bothered after her little escapade in Archivist's Alley. But no, basically, it's just another name for ladyfingers. I'm trying out recipes for a reception in the history department, and I figured boudoir biscuits sounded classier than the other traditional name: cats' tongues."

"Much classier."

"I promised Brooke I'd drop these off at her office before her staff meeting at noon, but I just got a call from a potential new client who wants to meet me over at Pranza, like, this second, and Jamie's nowhere to be found."

"Give me fifteen minutes to make myself presentable and I'll dash right over there." Cait flashed her most winning smile. "Any chance you'll send me off with homemade quiche and a freshly brewed latte?"

"No time," Anna said. "How about lukewarm coffee and a shower with no hot water left?"

"You girls are too good to me."

Cait had just turned her car through the wrought-iron gates flanking the college campus entrance when her phone rang. A little shiver of excitement ran through her when she recognized Gavin's number. "Hello?"

"I'm sitting here in my office, looking at all these stacks of books, thinking of you." His voice sparked a resurgence of all the deep, dark desires she'd had in the library basement.

She struggled to keep her tone sweet instead of sultry. "Really."

"Really." He laughed. "I'll never think of the library the same way again."

Forget the library; her mind was now officially in the gutter. She braked at a crosswalk to let a group of students pass, then decided to just pull over and devote her full attention to this conversation. Much safer for pedestrians everywhere. "Is that a good thing?"

"Definitely. So what are you up to?"

"I'm on campus, actually."

His voice dropped to a husky murmur. "Want to meet me in Archivist's Alley?"

Her hand tightened around the steering wheel. "Right now?"

He laughed again. "I'm kidding. I'm not *that* coarse."

"Oh." She licked her lips. "Right."

"Besides, it's probably glutted with students at this time of day. You know these damn kids. They think *they* invented rule breaking and rebellion."

"Upstart whippersnappers." She swallowed back a sigh. "Just as well. We've sullied the good name of the English department enough for one week."

"True. We have to pace ourselves. I'd love to see you if you have time, though. My next class isn't for another hour. Any chance I could talk you into meeting for coffee?"

Small talk and Sumatra versus full-contact snogging? Boooring.

Cait caught herself mid–eye roll. *Pull yourself together. You live for this crap: cerebral chitchat, critical analysis. . . . Ring any bells?*

She wondered if Arden's passing was the impetus for her overnight metamorphosis from sideline sitter to thrill seeker. If, maybe, on some level, all this frenzied passion was just a distraction so she wouldn't have to feel the huge empty space left by Arden's death.

Then her thoughts skittered away from grief and back toward the delicious possibility. *Time is a luxury.* And Cait was done wasting hers on pointless dithering.

"Coffee sounds wonderful," she told Gavin. "As they say in all those Irish novels, I could murder a latte. I'll swing by your office as soon as I finish my courier duties at the alumni affairs building."

"Great. My office is on the second floor, down by the—"

"I remember." Cait unzipped her bag and pulled out her travel brush and a tube of lipstick. "See you soon."

Ten minutes later, she made the scene at the Thurwell College English department, ignoring the stares from impossibly baby-faced underclassmen and inhaling that inimitable English department smell: floor wax and chalk dust laced with just a hint of cheap sherry.

"When did the lit crowd get so buxom and buff?" she asked when Gavin opened his office door. "It's like the cast of *Gossip Girl* out there."

He glanced out at the throngs of students, oblivious to the flurry of hair fluffing and hem hiking this set off among some of the young women. "Looks pretty much the same as when you and your partners in crime were students."

"No way." Cait shook her head. "We were much dorkier. When I was a freshman, we didn't have online shopping or Joe's Jeans or cell phones with texting capabilities. We had to make do with whatever we could scrounge from the J.Crew catalog and the Pine Street shops. One year, we all wore those truly unfortunate velvet chokers—"

"Uphill both ways in the snow," he finished for her.

"Exactly."

She stepped into his office and produced one of the ladyfingers she'd pilfered from Anna's bakery box. "Oh, here, I brought you something. Boudoir biscuits."

His eyebrows shot up.

"It's not as naughty as it sounds. Just glorified sponge cake. I thought we could share a little snack."

"No snacks." He shook his head, resolute. "This time we are going to go out in public, as planned. Like regular people on a regular date."

"Regular people?"

"That's right." He ran his fingers through his thick brown hair. "No more getting sidetracked with basement shenanigans."

"That's very sweet." She smiled. "But for the record, I thoroughly enjoyed our basement shenanigans."

"Yeah, but..." A tiny muscle flexed at the corner of his jawline. "I realize this sounds unbelievably cheesy, but you deserve to be courted. Wooed. Whatever."

Her smile turned from flirtatious to flustered. This was something she had never experienced with Charles or her other ex-boyfriends. She'd become adept at figuring out who they'd needed her to be and then cultivating the requisite qualities.

"The problem is, we seem to have a lot of..." Gavin paused for a moment, his expression pensive. "Chemistry."

She took a bite of pastry. "Agreed."

"And watching you nibble on something called a boudoir biscuit isn't helping."

"I'm ravenous." She glanced up at him through lowered eyelashes. "A girl's gotta eat."

"So we're going for coffee." He reached for the jacket hung on the back of his chair. "No shenanigans."

They almost made it. He had one hand on the door-knob when she raised her arms to put on her coat, revealing a thin strip of flannel peeking out above the waistline of her jeans.

He stopped in his tracks. "Are you wearing boxer shorts?"

"Yeah." Cait hastily tugged down her sweater. "I was in a hurry to get out of the house this morning. It's this stupid superstitious thing I do when I write. I swear I'm not always this frumpy. Erase the image from your mind."

"Hell no." He was still staring. "It's hot."

Two seconds later, the office door was locked and they were both pressed up against the bookshelf, kissing and groping and tearing off their clothes.

"We're supposed to be on a regular date," he murmured

into her open mouth. "I'm supposed to be wooing you, damn it."

"Congratulations." Buttons went flying as she wrestled with his shirt. "Consider me wooed."

She caught his lower lip between her teeth and sucked gently. He yanked off her sweater and kissed his way down to her bra straps.

"I never do stuff like this," he said.

"Me neither." She arched her back.

This time, there were no interruptions, no second thoughts, and no turning back. They sank down to the carpet, exploring each other inch by inch, escaping together into senseless sensuality.

W ell, that was..."

They lay absolutely still on the hard, scratchy carpet, staring up at the water-stained ceiling tiles. The sweat on their skin glistened in the sunlight pouring in through the window.

Cait rubbed her cheek against his chest. "Mmm."

His breath came in short, raspy bursts. "There are no words."

"That's what you say now." She trailed her index finger along the thin line of hair that started at his navel. "You know you're going to write an epic poem about this later. Probably win a Pulitzer."

He laughed. "I did have a few transcendental moments there."

"Me, too. And bonus, no black eyes this time." She winced as she shifted position. "Although I think I may have rug burn in some very delicate places."

He clapped a hand over his eyes and groaned. "I'm the worst wooer ever."

"Oh, I disagree."

"I'm supposed to give a lecture about Jonathan Swift in twenty minutes. I have nothing to say about Jonathan Swift. My mind is a complete blank."

"Here, have a boudoir biscuit." She rousted herself just long enough to snag the baked goods from the desktop. "It'll help you regain your strength."

His eyes widened as he bit into the biscuit. "Did you make this?"

"No, I can barely make toast. My housemate is the culinary wizard. Anna McCauley, remember her? She was an English major, too."

"She missed her calling."

"She's answering it now, actually." Cait filled him in on the restaurant-renting endeavor. "She thinks she's going to leave us after her catering career takes off, but she'll never escape. We're spoiled rotten now from all the cookies and cupcakes. We'll lock her up in the attic if we have to, along with a rolling pin and a Viking oven." As the word "lock" left her mouth, her thoughts returned to the mysterious steel padlock in Gavin's hallway. She was trying to decide the best way to broach that topic when he brushed a strand of hair back from her forehead and asked, "So what are your long-term plans? Are you going back to Connecticut after your sabbatical's over?"

She pulled back, letting more hair fall into her face. "Should we really be having this discussion while naked?"

"It doesn't have to be a *discussion*," he said. "No pop quiz, no essay portion. Just wondering."

"Right. Well." She fidgeted. "I haven't really thought about it. I'm just trying to live in the moment for a change."

"It's the book," he said knowingly. "Right now, you're not thinking past the next chapter, right?"

She flinched at the mention of the book. "Pretty much."

"How's it going?"

"Um, good."

"What's it about?"

"Oh, you know, lots of things." Cait gestured vaguely with both hands. "It's very involved."

"But what's the main plotline?" he persisted. "The over-arching theme?"

She located her sweater and pulled it over her head. "Don't you have to get ready to teach?"

"Nah, I have my notes ready."

A rap on the door startled them both. Gavin rocketed into a sitting position. Cait tucked her knees up under the hem of her sweater. They shared a look of pure panic.

Another knock at the door. "Gavin? Hey, G, you in there?"

Gavin paused midway through tugging on his pants. "Simon?"

"Yeah, man, it's me." *Pound, pound, pound.* "Open sesame."

"Who's Simon?" Cait hissed, praying that the student worker who'd interrupted them in Archivist's Alley wasn't about to ambush them again.

"The FedEx delivery guy," Gavin whispered back.

She frowned. "You're on a first-name basis with your FedEx guy?"

He shrugged and pulled on his shirt. "Small town."

"Whatever. I'll just wait over here." Cait wedged herself into the nook between the bookcase and the wall, where she wouldn't be visible from the doorway.

More knocking, even louder this time. "Gavin? Come on, I've got places to go and people to see."

Gavin gave Cait a reassuring peck on the cheek, then cracked open the door just enough to converse with the guy in the hallway. "Hey, what's up?"

"Got an overnighter for ya. Urgent."

"Thanks." Gavin cleared his throat. "You couldn't leave it on my porch like usual?"

"Not this time." The FedEx guy spoke in a gravelly drawl. "Signature required."

"Gotcha. Well, thanks for coming all the way out to the office. See you soon."

"Not too soon, I hope." A conspiratorial chortle. "You better not wake me up at midnight again."

"One time." Gavin's laugh sounded stilted. "That happened *once*."

"Yeah: once at midnight, once at one A.M., and once at three in the morning. I had to drag my ass out of bed with bronchitis, remember? My wife was pissed."

Cait forgot about staying out of view and craned her head toward the door to catch Gavin's response.

But all he said was, "And I appreciate you going the extra mile, Simon. Bronchitis and all."

"Yeah, yeah. You're lucky you're a good tipper, man."

"Speaking of which—" Gavin pulled his wallet out of his back pocket and handed over a few bills. "Next round of antibiotics is on me."

"You rock, G. Keep it real."

Cait pounced as soon as Gavin closed the office door. "What was that all about?"

He wouldn't make eye contact with her. "What?"

"You and your long-lost brother there. You call him to pick up deliveries at three in the morning?"

"Oh, that."

"Yeah, that." She waited.

He shoved his hands into his pockets. "It's a long story. Highly unusual circumstances."

"I'll bet."

There was a long pause, during which he focused his attention on the ceiling, the bookcase, and finally, his watch. "I'm going to be late for class." He stepped toward her, cupped her face in both his hands, and gave her a soft, lingering kiss. "You're amazing, you're beautiful, I can't wait to see you again."

"But—"

"Call you tonight."

He slipped out into the hallway and closed the door with a gentle click, leaving her confused and totally exposed in more ways than one.

Chapter
18

"The past is never dead. It's not even past."
—William Faulkner, *Requiem for a Nun*

S o that's it? That's all he said?" Jamie asked over dinner that night. Without anyone making a conscious
effort to organize group meals, the four housemates
had fallen into a rotation of cooking and cleanup. They ate
dinner together almost every night and kept the common
areas presentable, and each gave Brooke a generous weekly
"rent check" to help defray the remodeling expenses.

"Yeah, and it was bizarre, because he'd just told me, liter-
ally two minutes prior, that he'd already prepped for class."
Caitlin picked up her fork and prodded her portion of
Brooke's homemade cornbread and chili.

"He's up to something super shady," Jamie declared.

"You don't know that," Anna said. "Being BFF with his FedEx guy isn't exactly damning proof of wrongdoing."

"Yeah, but who summons the FedEx guy in the middle of the night? Multiple times? And then there's the locked door in his house." Cait put down her fork and sighed.

"Eat," Brooke commanded. "Here, have some more butter."

Cait slugged back her ice water and waved away the butter dish. "One thing's for sure, I'm done dating English professors."

Anna grinned. "You say that every time, but we all know the truth: Well-read men are your drug of choice."

"He's so funny and nice and smoking hot!" The water glasses rattled as Cait pounded the table. "Why does there always have to be a catch?"

"Maybe he's a drug dealer," Jamie suggested.

"Maybe he's an arms smuggler," Brooke said.

"Ooh, I know," Anna said. "Maybe, behind the locked door, he's stockpiling the corpses of all his ex-girlfriends."

"And shipping them off via FedEx at three A.M.?" Jamie snorted.

"You guys, this is serious." Cait dropped her forehead into her hands. "I really like him."

"Let's not jump to conclusions," Anna said. "Maybe there's a reasonable explanation for all of this. Something you'll joke about at your fiftieth wedding anniversary."

"Yeah, we'll pop the champagne and laugh and laugh about all that weapons trafficking."

"Don't forget the dead bodies," Jamie added helpfully.

Anna tapped her fork against the rim of her plate. "Okay, well, what about this? Maybe he's selling off internal organs to pay off gambling debts. You know, a spare kidney here, half a liver there."

Cait lifted her head. "I thought you were the one claiming there's a perfectly reasonable explanation."

Anna shrugged. "I said 'maybe.'"

"Look on the bright side," Brooke urged. "At least you didn't sleep with him yet."

Cait buried her face in her hands again. "Yeah. About that..."

Brooke gasped. *"What?!?"*

Anna shoved aside her plate. "When did this happen?"

"About six hours ago." Cait's voice was muffled. "In his office."

"You vixen!" Jamie hesitated only a fraction of a second before deciding that yes, the question really needed to be asked: "So? How was it?"

"Heart-stopping. Toe-curling. Mind-blowing." Cait let out a whimper of despair. *"Damn it!"*

"Well, look at the bright side." Brooke tried again. "At least you got to have your way with him before you figured out he was shysty and callous."

Anna patted Brooke's hand. "Still haven't heard from hardware store hunk?"

"No. And I never will. He wasn't that hunky anyway." She took a huge bite of biscuit. "Ugh, I'm such a liar. He was sex in a flannel shirt. What was I thinking, asking him out? I'm sure he already has a girlfriend who looks like Adriana Lima. And another one who looks like Gisele Bündchen. He probably has a whole harem of supermodels."

Anna laughed. "In the Adirondacks?"

"No one works a parka and a pair of snowshoes like Gisele."

Jamie looked around the table at her friends: Cait's Gibson Girl profile and long auburn hair, Brooke's delicate blond beauty, Anna's sparkling eyes and adorable apple cheeks. "What the hell, you guys? This is absurd. We're bold, brilliant, beautiful babes who've been overqualified for every job we've ever had. How can we all be having man problems?"

"Anna doesn't have man problems," Brooke said.

"Au contraire," Anna muttered.

Jamie ignored this nitpicky side argument. "Honestly, look at us. We're total catches. We should be fighting them off with our nail files."

"Maybe we're cursed," Cait suggested. "Maybe we need to make an offering."

Anna leaned forward, looking intrigued. "To whom?"

"Mr. Wonderful," Cait said. They all tipped back their chairs to glance down the hall toward the staircase.

"What do you think a metal winged statue would want?" Brooke asked.

"A metal winged Barbie to keep him company," Cait suggested.

"I'll weld one for him," Brooke said. "Right after I finish replacing the wiring in the dining room."

"You guys are ridiculous." Jamie said. "Nobody's cursed."

"Then how do you explain the bad luck?"

"We're just..." Jamie thought about everything that had happened in the past few months, about Arden and the inheritance check in the shredder and the wedding she was supposed to be planning. "Experiencing a burst of a karmic static. It's not bad luck; none of this is random. We're back together, living here in Henley House again. What are the odds? There's got to be a reason for all this."

Brooke gaped at her. "Do my ears deceive me, or did Jamie Burton actually use the word 'karma'?"

"I think living in L.A. has gone to your head," Anna said.

"Mock me if you must, but you'll see," Jamie told them. "I sense a great disturbance in the force."

Cait rolled her eyes. "Now you sound like Gavin."

Jamie, Brooke, and Anna waited for her to elaborate.

Big, drawn-out sigh. "I think he has a secret sci-fi habit, on top of everything else."

"No!" Anna clutched at her heart. "You knew this and you still had sex with him?"

"She can't help it," Jamie said. "The better the sex, the worse the judgment. I've been there."

"Well, how exactly are we supposed to restore karmic harmony and balance and all that?" Brooke folded her napkin and pushed back her chair. "I'm fed up with renovating. I'm ready for results."

"All in due time," Jamie assured them with typical bravado. "Wait for a sign."

"What kind of sign?" Anna asked.

Jamie gave them a Cheshire cat smile. "I'll know it when I see it."

*D*uck!"

When Brooke shoved her, Jamie stumbled off the sidewalk and into the path of oncoming traffic.

A mud-splattered pickup truck veered around her, beeping its horn and drenching her with a sheet of last night's rainfall that had collected in the gutter.

Jamie wiped off her face with her coat sleeve and started picking wet leaves out of her hair. "You know, if you want me dead, you don't have to try to make it look like an accident. Just give me a few cartons of cigarettes and I'll take it from there."

"Get down!" Brooke seized her wrist and yanked her into the doorway of the town's used-book store. "Jeff Thuesen is over there!"

Jamie's whole body went rigid. "Where?"

"There!" Brooke risked a quick glance back toward the street. "He's walking this way."

Jamie flattened herself back against the wall until she felt the uneven grooves of brick and mortar digging into her head. "What the hell is Arden's ex doing in Thurwell?"

"How should I know? Oh my gosh, here he comes." Brooke implored her with desperate blue eyes. "What now?"

"I don't know." Jamie curled her fingers against the brick, scrabbling for a firm handhold. Was it possible for a fast-living thirty-two-year-old to suffer a stress-induced heart attack?

"You always know what to do!" Brooke said. "Hurry! Unleash hell! Be mean!"

"I—" Jamie gazed helplessly back at Brooke for a minute. Then she caught a blur of movement in the corner of her vision, and raw panic took over. She wrenched out of Brooke's grasp and darted into the bookstore, where she cowered in the children's section until Brooke came looking for her a few minutes later.

"Are you all right?" Brooke's complexion was ashen. "What happened to you out there?"

Jamie peeked over the cover of *Frog and Toad Are Friends.* "Don't worry about me. The more important question is, what happened to *you?*"

Brooke planted both hands on her hips and went into full

rant mode. "I'll tell you exactly what happened. That sorry excuse for a man had the unmitigated gall to come right up and say hello, and I just turned up my nose." Her face shone with triumph. "I gave him the cut direct."

"The cut direct," Jamie marveled. "The *ton* will be scandalized."

"Don't make fun of me. You know I have a hard time with confrontation. But he deserved it, the jackass." Brooke scowled. "I *hate* him."

"Well, I'm sure he got the message."

"But he didn't! Instead of having the common decency to turn tail and slink away, he started following me and asked about you!"

Jamie's heart rate kicked back up into cardiac-arrest mode. "What did he say?"

"He said he heard you were in town and he wants to talk to you."

"Oh my God."

"I know! Ooh, my blood is just boiling!"

"So, um, what did you say?"

"Not a word." Brooke smirked. "I just whipped out a pen and wrote down your cell phone number for him."

"What?" Jamie waved *Frog and Toad* wildly. "Why?"

"Because you actually say all the clever retorts that other people only think of three days after they've finished the argument. I hope he calls you tonight at dinner, so we can all hear you give him a verbal flaying."

"This is not good," Jamie said faintly.

"First Arden's memorial service, now this." Brooke fumed. "He doesn't know who he's dealing with."

Neither do you. Jamie sank down into a worn blue beanbag next to the child-sized reading tables.

"Jamie?" Brooke's worried face hovered above her.

Jamie turned her face into the slightly sticky blue vinyl.

The beanbag rustled as Brooke settled in next to her. "Jamie."

"I'm fine. Just leave me alone."

"You're not fine, and I will not leave you alone." Brooke paused. "I know something happened between you and Arden. And Jeff, apparently."

"Brooke, please just—"

"That's why you won't cash your check or call Arden's lawyer back. You're feeling guilty about something, and I think I know what."

"No, you don't. Trust me."

"You slept with Jeff, didn't you?"

Jamie whipped her head around to stare at Brooke. "What?"

"That's why he and Arden broke up." Brooke nodded, her hands clasped and her posture as regal as her current seating situation would permit. "Am I right? It's okay; you can tell me."

Jamie felt like she'd been punched in the throat. "That's what you think of me? You think I'm the kind of woman who sluts it up with her friends' boyfriends?"

"Well." Brooke examined the crosshatch of scratches and scrapes on her hands. "How else do you explain the way you've been acting lately? The smoking, the hangdog looks, the malingering?"

Jamie let her head thunk back into the beanbag. "I would never do that to Arden. To any of you."

"You always could get any guy you wanted," Brooke said softly.

"Regardless of whether or not I could, I *wouldn't*. I don't have a lot of friends, Brooke. You guys are pretty much it. Men come and go, but…" She trailed off as a horrible thought occurred. "Have you talked to Cait and Anna about this? Do they think I'm an amoral skeezer, too?"

"No one thinks you're a skeezer."

"That's not an answer." Jamie crossed her arms, surprised by how much it still stung to be cast as the token Jezebel amid a trio of good girls. She'd never blended in with the preppy Thurwell College elite, but when she was younger, her in-your-face sexuality had imbued her with a sense of power and authority. People noticed her, listened to her. But as she got older, she'd started to wonder if she'd ever be able to move beyond her brash party-girl persona.

"Well?" Jamie demanded with a hard edge in her voice. "Have you talked to Cait and Anna about this?"

"No." Brooke remained calm and composed. "I'm talking to you about it. Because I love you and I'm worried about you."

"How can you say that and in the same breath accuse me of breaking up Arden's relationship with the guy she planned to marry?"

Brooke placed her hand on Jamie's shoulder. "Everyone makes mistakes."

"Well, I don't make that kind of mistake." Jamie stuck out her chin. "Not now, not ever."

"All right, I believe you. But please, tell me what *did* happen between you and Arden?"

"I can't."

"Why not?"

A pair of preschoolers wandered into the children's book section, trailed by two mothers and a bookstore employee.

The employee took one look at the drama unfolding in

the depths of the beanbag and cleared her throat. "Can I help you ladies find something?"

"No, thanks. We were just leaving." Jamie got to her feet and hauled up Brooke behind her.

"Wait, don't you want to check out the bridal magazines while you're here?" asked Brooke. "Last week, you said you had to get caught up on all the current wedding trends."

That was before Arden's ex came back to haunt me. Jamie had been waiting for a sign, and the reappearance of Jeff Thuesen was like a big, flashing neon directive: Cease and desist. "No bridal magazines. No bridal anything. I think I'm going to have to cut and run on this wedding planner gig."

Brooke gasped. "You can't just quit!"

Jamie threw her bag over her shoulder and headed for the exit. "Watch me."

"But it's your dream job!"

"Not anymore." She buttoned up her coat. "I'm going back to bartending. At least I'm good at that."

"But one of my coworkers just got engaged and I gave her your number. She wants to hire you."

"She can find someone else."

"But what about that poor bride? You can't back out now. You signed a contract!"

"Look, I tried, but it turns out my dream job? Not so dreamy." Jamie opened the door and braced for a gust of cold, wet wind. "I'm glad the B and B is working out for you, but not all of us can be so lucky."

Brooke stopped protesting and glanced back down at her battle-scarred fingers. "Yes. About that…"

Chapter 19

"*Our houses are such unwieldy property that we are often imprisoned rather than housed in them.*"
—Henry David Thoreau, *Walden*

I hate this house." Brooke set aside her hammer and chisel and swiped at her sweat-drenched forehead with the clean washcloth Anna offered. "I wish I'd never bought it."

"No, you don't." Anna crouched down on the tile bathroom floor next to her.

"Oh yes, I do. Paradise Found, my foot. This"—Brooke peered down into the jagged black hole where the toilet used to be—"is the ninth circle of hell."

"That does look pretty hellacious," Anna admitted. "Why are you messing with the toilet down here, anyway?"

Brooke sighed. "Because I have to replace it with one that doesn't leak."

"So now you're a master plumber in addition to an expert electrician?" Anna whistled. "I'm impressed."

"All I wanted was chintz and scones," Brooke said. "Mints on pillows and a leather-bound guest registry. I never planned to round out my education in the practical sciences."

"This will all be over soon," Anna said. "And then you can surround yourself with patchwork and popovers and never look back." She paused, eyeing the contents of the toolbox strewn across the floor. "I've never replaced a toilet, but I was not aware that the job required a hammer and chisel."

"It doesn't, usually." Brooke grimaced. "Unless, of course, the toilet in question happens to be bolted to a cracked flange."

Anna regarded her blankly. "What's a flange?"

"This thing right here." Brooke pointed with her chisel to the blackened metal ring encircling the hole in the floor. "It's cracked, so it has to be replaced. And it's cast iron, which makes it practically impossible to remove. Hence the hammer and chisel. And the obscenities."

"But it looks like you're almost done," Anna said hopefully.

"I'm almost done with the flange. But see that?" Brooke ran her fingers along the web of hairline cracks spreading out across the floor. "All that pounding on the flange took its toll. Now I have to replace this old tile, which I'll have to pry off with a putty knife. And I have no idea what's underneath the tile, but if it was installed wrong—and *everything* in this house was installed wrong—I'll end up with a gaping hole in the floor. It never ends. I'm like Sisyphus with a sewer line.

I've spent my entire weekend literally staring down the toilet and inuring myself to the stench." She sat back against the shower door. "Makes me long for the good old days when all I had to worry about was the prospect of knob-and-tube wiring spontaneously combusting."

"I still can't believe how quickly you rewired this place. What was that, three and a half weeks?"

"Twenty-seven days," Brooke said. "But who's counting?"

"I thought you'd be done after that."

"Look at this bathroom. I'll never be done."

"Take a break," Anna urged. "A warm brownie and a cold glass of milk will do you a world of good."

"No time for brownies. I have to drive all the way to the Home Depot in Glens Falls before it closes."

"There's always time for brownies. I just took them out of the oven. Double chocolate, with walnuts. Smell them?"

"My olfactory system stopped functioning a few hours ago. Thank heavens." Brooke wadded up a fistful of paper towels to plug the hole. She got to her feet, straightened her back, and gingerly stretched her arms over her head. "Ow." She winced as her joints popped. "Ow, ow, ow."

"What was *that*?" Anna asked.

"My knees, wrists, and spine."

"I better lace the next batch of brownies with Percocet."

"Please do." Brooke gimped out to the hallway and called up the staircase. "I'm off to Glens Falls. Anyone need anything?" She sniffed, narrowing her eyes. "Jamie, I know you're smoking up there. Knock it off."

Anna raised one eyebrow. "I thought your olfactory system stopped functioning."

"I can always smell trouble brewing." As Brooke buttoned up her coat, she noticed the grime embedded underneath her fingernails, grime that no amount of soap and scrubbing could eradicate. "This house is my albatross. Remember *The Rime of the Ancient Mariner*? Samuel Coleridge probably wrote that while he was chiseling away at a corroded old toilet flange."

"You're just frustrated." Anna nodded up toward Mr. Wonderful perched on the newel post. "Deep down, you love this place."

Brooke shook her head. "I loved the *idea* of it, before I knew what horrors lurked beneath the drywall and the floorboards and the toilets. This house is not as advertised."

Anna abandoned her pep talk, plunked down on the steps, and rested her chin in her hands. "That's exactly how I feel about my marriage right now."

But Brooke was on a roll. She started gesturing and pacing the carpet. "All I ask for is a cute little hideaway that hasn't sustained decades of internal structural damage. I don't want a fixer-upper; I don't want to spend all my free time fixing the previous owners' mistakes; I just want to move in and unpack. Is that really so much to ask?"

"Yes," Anna said. "Both with houses and with men."

Brooke stopped ranting and focused on her friend. "Don't say that. Jonas is such a nice guy."

Anna shrugged one shoulder. "If Jonas had an MLS listing, that's exactly what it would say: *such a nice guy, move-in condition*. It's not that simple, though. It's never that simple."

"Oh, Anna."

"Oh, Brookie."

"What are we going to do?"

"Just keep chipping away at our respective toilet holes, I guess." Anna exhaled slowly. "But for now, how about a brownie for the road?"

———

*F*or the past few years, Brooke had been holding out for a nice guy. She'd never understood Jamie's penchant for baggage-laden bad boys or Cait's weakness for authority figures with superiority complexes. Her idea of male perfection was steeped in Southern nostalgia: a gentleman, in every sense of the word.

There was only one problem. After years of false starts and disappointing dates, she was starting to doubt that gentlemen existed anymore. Or, if they did, they seemed drawn to wild, troubled beauties like Jamie, who was forever bemoaning how many of her male "buddies" had blurted out their undying love for her and ruined the friendship. "He's like my brother," Jamie would say. "I just don't like him that way. I need a challenge, you know?"

Brooke didn't see the appeal in trying to tame a man or bend him to her will. She wanted to get married and stay married and share a functional, healthy relationship with someone who took pride in being a husband and father. The right man would arrive at the right time, or so she had always told herself.

She was starting to have her doubts.

Brooke turned her car onto Pine Street and braked for a red light. The sweet aftertaste of brownie turned sour in her mouth. When the light turned green, she U-turned and headed back toward the quiet faculty neighborhood near campus.

I need answers," Brooke blurted out when Professor Rutkin opened the door.

Cassandra didn't seem surprised to find a frazzled former student pacing her front porch on a school night. She simply took a moment to adjust the collar of her black merino robe and sipped her mug of tea. "Miss Asplind. Lovely to see you."

"Hi, sorry, I know it's abominably rude to drop by without calling, but I was on my way to Home Depot, and—" Brooke shook her head in a vain bid for clarity. "I need help."

"Come in." This was more of a command than a request. The older woman ushered Brooke through the living room, which was furnished in sleek Danish furniture and exotic-looking pottery pieces, and into a small, utilitarian kitchen. She prepared a mug of chamomile tea from the kettle of water cooling on the stove burner and pressed the mug into Brooke's hand. "Now, what can I help you with?"

Brooke tried to decide where to begin. "Well, I suppose it's a crisis of confidence, or a crisis of faith. I've started to question some of the fundamental tenets of my personal belief system."

A tiny smile played on Dr. Rutkin's lips. "That sounds like a lot to take on in one evening."

"I'll say. My guest room toilet is ruining my life and I need to fix it. Oh, and I asked out this guy and he turned me down flat."

"Well, you've come to the wrong place, I'm afraid. I have little to no experience with plumbing, and as for men— you're better off asking someone else for advice."

Brooke nodded. "I suppose you're too sensible to waste your time with dating."

"What on earth would give you that idea?" Cassandra squinted back at her. "I'm a physicist, not a vestal virgin.

Don't buy into all those hackneyed white lab coat stereo-types. I have stories from the trenches that would peel the polish right off your toenails."

"I'm so sorry, I didn't mean—"

Cassandra's smile returned. "Don't think you literary types have a monopoly on romance. I just don't kiss and tell. Especially when the kissing may or may not involve other faculty members at this college."

Brooke sized her up for a moment. "You've got some really good dirt, don't you?"

Cassandra winked. "That's immaterial."

"Okay, but can you just tell me if you've heard anything scandalous about Professor Clayburn in the English depart-ment?"

Cassandra didn't respond, but Brooke thought she de-tected a split-second flinch. "What?" Brooke pressed. "Is he a player? An addict? A secret back-alley internal-organs dealer? Give me a hint. I won't reveal my source, I promise!"

"Miss Asplind." The brusque, professorial air was back. "I believe you said you wanted to discuss plumbing."

"I do, but I really need to know if Professor Clayburn is, you know, a shiftless libertine. Because one of my best friends is getting involved with him way quicker than she should, and I'm concerned that—"

Cassandra stared her down.

"Fine." Brooke sighed. "Just give me the lowdown on plumbing."

"Unfortunately, that's not my area of expertise," Cassan-dra admitted. "Wiring is much more my thing. But, actually, if you'd care to experiment in the spirit of scientific inquiry, I could use some help clearing out my bathroom sink. It's been draining slowly and making gurgling sounds. My neighbor recommended a handyman to repair it, but I found his attitude appalling."

Brooke's head snapped up. "Was his name Hank Bexton, by any chance?"

"Why, yes, I believe it was."

Brooke devolved into a frothy-mouthed, semicoherent diatribe punctuated by liberal use of the phrases "blonde jokes," "Samuel Coleridge," and "crescent wrench chauvinism."

Cassandra waited patiently, sipping her tea, until Brooke wound down. "Feel better?"

"Much." Brooke rolled up her sleeves. "Now lead the way to the sink. I'm sure I can tackle this. Let's see, I'm going to need a drain snake, a wrench set, and some leather work gloves."

The professor's expression barely changed, but she granted Brooke a quick, approving nod. "The student has become the teacher."

"I feel like the Karate Kid of physics." Brooke couldn't have felt prouder if she'd aced a midterm on the laws of thermodynamics. "Wax on, wax off."

Chapter
20

"If this were played upon the stage now,
I could condemn it as an improbable fiction."
—Shakespeare, *Twelfth Night*

*A*nna shifted her shopping basket from one hand to the other and stared up at the grocery shelf. Brooke had been right about Thurwell's only supermarket branching out over the past decade; in addition to organic produce and dairy products, it now stocked a small selection of gourmet European cocoa and exotic spices. Usually, Anna loved selecting ingredients almost as much as she loved baking, but today the sweet, rich scent of chocolate made her eyes sting and her heart ache.

She studied the fine print on the bright red chocolate wrapper: *Product of Belgium.* Which made her think of Brussels, which made her think of Jonas, which made her want to scarf down an entire bag of chocolate chips.

Maybe she should go with a French chocolate. Maybe Dutch. Or maybe not. The supermarket hadn't branched out *that* much; her choice seemed limited to rich Belgian decadence or the traditional American standbys.

"Excuse me, aren't you the lady who made that fabulous Coca-Cola cake?"

Anna snapped to attention. "Yes. Hi. Anna McCauley."

A short, stout woman bundled up in a red barn coat and multiple colorful winter scarves smiled at her. "I thought that was you. You probably don't remember me, but we met at Belinda Elquest's party. Kris Doyle." She extended her right hand.

"Of course I remember you, Kris," Anna fibbed, shaking hands. "It's wonderful to see you again. How are you?"

"I can't stop thinking about that cake." Kris kissed her fingers in appreciation. "You know, I'd never heard of making cake with soda pop, and when Belinda gave me a piece, I admit I was reluctant, but my word! You've really got talent."

Anna returned the Belgian chocolate to the shelf and tried to will herself into a cheery, convivial mood. "Thank you."

"I've been dying to know: Wherever did you find that recipe?"

"Oh, I collect vintage cookbooks."

"Really!" Kris put down her shopping basket and started to unwind her jumble of scarves. "Do you buy them on eBay?"

"Once in a while, but I've found some amazing stuff at garage sales and used-book stores. I love reading about all the different food fads that have come in and gone over the years."

"What a fascinating hobby."

"My husband got me started." *Why* was she talking about Jonas? Stupid Belgian chocolate. "He gave me a first edition of *The Joy of Cooking* for our first anniversary, and I used it to make a custard pie. I've been hooked on baking ever since."

"How sweet." Now Kris was taking off her coat and settling in for a nice long chat right here next to the sacks of flour. "You're lucky to have such a thoughtful husband."

Anna's thoughts flashed over to the last conversation she'd shared with him: reckless accusations of PMS followed by unsolicited phone sex propositions. "Yeah, he's a real prince."

"Do you two live here in town?"

Anna paused. "Not really. Well, I live here. For now."

Kris tilted her head, waiting for Anna to finish.

"I went to Thurwell." Anna smiled brightly, as if this explained everything. "Graduated ten years ago."

"And your husband?"

Anna pretended to misunderstand the question. "Oh, he went to Skidmore. We didn't meet until the end of senior year, actually. He sat next to me on the bus to the airport for spring break."

When Kris opened her mouth to interrogate her further, Anna cut her off with, "Anyway, I have a few cookbooks from the 1950s, and sometimes I'm religious about following the recipe to the letter, but for the Coca-Cola cake, I ended up playing around with the ingredients and adding a few little extras. I thought palatability was more important than historical authenticity."

"What sort of extras did you add?"

"Trade secret, I'm afraid. But if you give me your email address, I'd be happy to send you the original recipe and you can whip up your own variation."

Kris dug through her handbag and produced a business card. "How far in advance do you book up? My husband is the president of the local Civil War reenactment society, and I'm hosting the holiday dinner for all the members and their wives. Do you have any desserts that might do for that sort of event?"

"Oh, I'd love to do a Civil War buffet!" Anna clapped her hands together.

Kris looked impressed. "You've done them before?"

"No, but I've got loads of ideas. I could do an orange flummery, maybe a modified Spanish blancmange, a plum cake—oh, and I'll have to see if I can scrounge up some gooseberries. You know, it's funny you should ask me about this today. Just last night, I was reading about a really rich sponge cake called a Robert E. Lee cake."

Kris's eyes lit up. "You're hired. But you have to make the Robert E. Lee cake completely authentic. And don't give anyone else the recipe!" She rubbed her palms together with glee. "Oh, this will be the talk of the Civil War circuit. I pity next year's hostess."

Anna saw an opportunity for Henley House synergy and made her move. "You know, if you really want to wow your guests, I can research Civil War centerpieces and table settings. One of my best friends is an event planner, and I'm sure she'd work with me."

"That's not a bad idea." Kris nibbled her lower lip. "Oh, and then I'm hosting a baby shower for my niece. I'd love to serve one of your cakes. Something feminine, but not too cutesy."

Anna's spirits plummeted at the mention of the b-word. "I apologize, but I can't."

"But I haven't told you the date yet."

"Well, you see..." She exhaled slowly. "The thing is, I don't handle baby showers."

Kris looked startled. "Why on earth not?"

A voice cried out, "Hey! Kris! Hellooo!"

I'm saved! Anna took a step back and prepared to make her exit.

Trish Selway strode down the aisle and wedged herself directly between Kris and Anna. She gave Kris an air kiss and Anna a sharp, dangerous smile. "I thought that was you."

I'm screwed!

"Trish!" Kris's face went crimson. "Goodness, dear, I didn't even see you over there!"

"I'm getting harder and harder to miss these days." Trish patted her belly, which was obscured under a puffy down parka. "Second trimester in full effect."

"Second trimester already!" Kris exclaimed. "How are you feeling?"

"Much better, now that the morning sickness is gone. I'm back to business as usual," Trish said. "Speaking of which, did I just hear you say that you need a baby shower cake?"

Kris started weaving her fingers through her scarf fringe. "I...well...that is—"

"Look no further," Trish said. "I'm your girl."

Anna cleared her throat.

"Yes?" Trish towered over her. "You have something to say, Legacy?"

Anna used her wire shopping basket to stake out her personal space. When Trish tried to jostle her aside, Anna's handbag fell to the floor, spilling out her wallet, cell phone, and a tattered paperback volume of Shakespeare.

"Oops." Trish didn't even bother turning around to assess the damage. "I am so sorry. Must be that pregnancy klutziness."

"Oh, I had that in spades." Kris crouched down to help Anna gather up her belongings. "I spent the entire nine months covered in bumps and bruises. It was especially bad with my youngest." She picked up the paperback and glanced at the title. *"Twelfth Night?"*

"Yeah, it's my favorite of the comedies." Anna tucked the book into the interior pocket of her bag. "I like to read it every few years. It's such a funny, hopeful story, you know? Always cheers me up."

"Now, which one is that, again?" Kris furrowed her brow. "Is that the one with Uncle Toby and the yellow garters?"

"Exactly. And Sebastian and Viola."

"Viola. What a pretty name."

"I always thought so," Anna said. She and Kris were both kneeling, which excluded Trish entirely from the conversation. "In fact, I decided, way back in college, that if I ever had a daughter, I'd name her Viola."

"Viola," Kris repeated. "It's got a nice ring to it."

"And it's unusual without being ridiculous or impossible to spell."

"Viola?" Trish suddenly hunkered down alongside them. "What a coincidence. That's what I'm planning to name the Bug here, if it turns out to be a girl."

"You are not!" Anna said.

"Oh yes." Trish nodded solemnly.

Anna searched for an appropriately stinging response. She finally managed, "Nuh-uh."

"It's true." Trish smirked. "Viola is number one with a bullet on my baby name list. Has been for years. Ask anyone."

Anna stood up, offered her hand to Kris, and helped her newest client regain her footing. "You know what, Kris? I'd be honored to cater your niece's shower. Just let me know when and where, and I'll whip up something truly—"

"Too late," Trish interrupted. "You already turned down the job."

They both turned to appeal to Kris.

"I have to go." Kris pivoted and fled in a flurry of tartan wool.

"Email me!" Anna called after her. "Pleasure seeing you again!" Then she rounded on Trish. "What is wrong with you? Trying to poach my clients right in front of me!"

"Who's poaching?" Trish shot back. "You said no to the baby shower. I heard you with my own ears."

"So you're an eavesdropper *and* a poacher."

Trish squared her shoulders. "That's it, Legacy. I tried to be nice. I let you share my kitchen—"

"*Let* me?!?" Anna choked. "*Your* kitchen?"

"—and I let it slide when you called me up, all hysterical in the middle of the night, and accused me of stealing equipment that was right under your nose."

Anna's indignation faltered as she fought off a fresh wave of embarrassment over the Hobart mixer incident.

"But I'm through being nice," Trish announced.

"Then so am I."

They faced off in silence for a few seconds, posturing like parka-clad prizefighters.

"Tell you what," Anna finally said. "I'll give you the baby shower job if you step away from my baby name."

"I don't need you to 'give' me anything." Trish grabbed an armful of the Belgian chocolate bars Anna had been eyeing.

"Hey, I was looking at those!" Anna protested.

"Yeah, and I'm buying them." Trish swept her hand to the back of the shelf to make sure she'd gotten every available bar.

"You can't buy them all!"

"Watch me."

Anna gasped and reached into Trish's cart, but Trish slapped her fingers away.

"Back off, Grabby. That chocolate was on the shelf. That's fair game. Public domain." She shook her head. "God, you really are psycho, aren't you?"

"But I need it," Anna said.

Trish shrugged again. "Life's a bitch sometimes."

"I don't think 'life' is the bitch here." Anna wrapped her hands around the rim of the cart's basket while Trish secured the metal handle in a death grip. A brief scuffle ensued, punctuated with high-pitched yelps, until the store manager dashed over to break it up.

Gary (according to the small gold name tag pinned to his shirt pocket), a stocky, middle-aged man with nervous eyes and patchy stubble, made his way through the small crowd clustered at the end of the aisle and regarded Anna and Trish with evident trepidation before puffing out his chest and asking, "What seems to be the trouble here?"

Anna pointed at Trish. "She stole my chocolate!"

"Liar!" Trish retorted. "I got all of this right from the shelf."

Gary's gaze went back and forth between the two of them

for a moment. Finally, he addressed Anna. "Is that true? It was on the shelf?"

"Technically, yes," Anna admitted.

Damp sweat stains had started to appear in the armpit creases of Gary's white shirt. "I'm going to escort you to the checkout line," he told Trish. "And then I'm going to have to ask you both to leave the premises."

"We're *banned*?" Anna had to fight an overwhelming urge to laugh. She'd never been banned from anyplace, ever. She'd never even gotten detention in high school.

"Not banned," the manager said. "But I'm going to have to ask you to finish your shopping at another time. We can't allow this kind of behavior."

Anna lowered her face and humbled her tone. "Of course. I apologize, sir, and I promise this will never happen again."

When she glanced up again, she saw Trish making a face and mouthing the words "kiss ass."

She ignored Trish and asked Gary, "Before I go, is there any way you could check in the back and see if there are any more of those chocolate bars available?"

He used his shirt cuff to dab the sweat off his upper lip. "Whatever we have is on the shelf. A new shipment might be in next week."

"Guess you'll just have to use Nestlé's Toll House," Trish said. "But that shouldn't be a problem, you being the confectionary ninja and all."

"Checkout," Gary said hastily. "Let's go."

Trish tossed a wink back over her shoulder at Anna. "Until we meet again, Legacy."

sensed her complete surrender to him, he maneuvered himself between her legs.

"I should no' do this, but God help me, I want you so much," he grated.

"You promised to show me," she reminded him. "You promised me anything."

"I've something I dearly want to show you, something I've been imagining...."

His mouth roamed down her neck to her breasts. When he suckled one budding nipple between his lips, his tongue lashed over it, hot and wet, making her moan low. Her other breast received the same tender ministrations before he began kissing down her stomach.

Once he reached her navel and continued lower, she gasped. "What are you doing?"

"I'm preparing to be very improper with you."

As she felt the rasp of his beard nuzzling her inner thigh, she trembled with both surprise and anticipation.

"We're nearin' the point of no return, love." His voice sounded strained, his accent growing stronger with each word. His rough palms skimmed up over her belly to cup her breasts. He rubbed his thumbs over her nipples, which were still damp and aching from his kisses. "If you want to stop, tell me now."

Her arms fell over her head. "Let us reconvene on the matter of stopping—after you reveal your notion of improper."

Helena was in no way prepared for the shock of pleasure when he pressed his mouth to her sex. Her knees fell open wide. The second he delved his tongue, she helplessly arched her back, moaning his name.

Again and again, his tongue flicked and played, the sensations so exquisite, so maddening.... She threaded her fingers through his hair to draw him closer as she rocked her hips to his mouth. Just as the coiling tension within her threatened to release, he broke away.

"No!" she cried in frustration. "Please.... Why did you stop?"

Chapter 21

"Truth is tough."
—Oliver Wendell Holmes, Sr. *The Professor at the Breakfast Table*

*H*ow can you look at once so delicate and so decadent?" Mac-Cormick's gaze raked over Helena's unclothed body, his eyes full of heat, nearly palpable upon her flesh.

Even in the soft candlelight, she felt shy before him—she'd never been exposed like this, had never before been in a room with an unclothed man. But he gave her no time for a maiden's sensibilities.

His mouth met hers once more. When she drew a breath, she felt his tongue slip in between her lips. She'd read enough about kissing to know that she should meet him in kind. Once she did, he groaned against her, his grip on her waist tightening.

Deeper and harder he kissed her until any inhibitions that might have remained vanished. Nothing could stop her from having this man. As if he

He raised himself up on his knees, sliding his arms under her thighs.
With a devilish glint in his eyes, he said, "I've only just begun."

W ant to hear a secret?" Gavin murmured into Cait's
ear. They were entwined in his bed, naked and exhausted, listening to the chapel bell toll across campus. Pillows and clothes were scattered across the sun-dappled green
throw rug.

"Mmm." She tucked her head under his chin and breathed
in his scent along with the fragrance from the freshly laun-
dered sheets. "It's about time. Spill your guts, Clayburn."

"I think I'm addicted to you," he said. Cait couldn't see
his face, but she could hear the slow, wicked smile in his
voice. "Your taste, your smell, the way you do that thing with
your tongue."

"I have many hidden talents."

"Yes, you do. You're like . . ." He paused, thinking. "What
was that jacked-up opium derivative that Charles Dickens
and Wilkie Collins used to take?"

"Laudanum?"

"Yeah." He rubbed her back, starting at her shoulders
and kneading his way down her spine. "You're like a bottle of
laudanum in plaid boxer shorts."

She laughed. "That's the most romantic thing anyone's
ever said to me."

"I'm quoting directly from Shakespeare's sonnets," he
swore.

"And which sonnet would that be, Professor?"

"Uh, that would the little-known 'In Praise of
Hallucination-Inducing Hotties.'"

"I see."

"Shall I compare thee to a habit-forming controlled substance? Thou art more—"

"If you ever want me to do that thing with my tongue again, I'd quit while you're ahead."

"Shutting up now."

"Have you noticed we have a theme going?" She nodded at the wall of bookshelves opposite the window. "Literary love nests: libraries, English department offices—"

"*You* have a theme going," he corrected. "I was just trying to take you to lunch."

"That's what you said last time, and the time before that, and the time before that." She rolled to one side and stretched her arms out over her head. "I think we're going to have to accept the fact that we're never going to actually sit down to a meal in public together."

"What about right now?" He sat up, suddenly energized. "Now that we've gotten that out of our systems, let's get dressed and hit the town. You. Me. Clothes. It can happen."

She gazed up at him a moment, then asked, "But what if we get dressed and get out there and then, you know."

His gaze intensified. "What's on your mind?"

"Does it bother you that we don't actually know each other?" She reached up to brush back the fringe of dark hair over his forehead. "In the nonbiblical sense?"

"That's why we'd be going to dinner."

She nibbled her lower lip. "Yes, but..."

He settled in next to her. "I'm all yours. What would you like to know?"

So many questions sprang to mind: *What's barricaded behind your guest room door? Why are you calling your FedEx guy for urgent predawn pickups? What was your last girlfriend like and is she stashed under your floorboards?*

Cait decided she'd start with a softball and work her way up. "Where'd you grow up?"

"Portland, Maine."

"Favorite film of all time?" she asked.

"*Blade Runner.*"

"Never seen it."

"How can that be?" He shook his head. "Ridley Scott? Harrison Ford? Come on, it's a classic."

"I've seen *Indiana Jones,*" she said.

"Not the same thing. Not even remotely. That's it—we're watching *Blade Runner* on our next date. Along with your all-time favorite movie, which is?"

"Don't judge me." She covered her eyes. "*Dirty Dancing.*"

"That's going to be quite the double feature." He grinned. "See? This isn't so hard. Next question, Ms. Johnson?"

"Okay." She took a deep breath and lowered her voice with exaggerated suspense. "What's the deep, dark secret lurking behind that mysterious padlock in the hallway?"

He didn't miss a beat. "Would you believe Jimmy Hoffa?"

"No."

"Narnia?"

"Come on." She whapped him in the chest with a pillow. "I'm dying to know."

"Hold that thought." The mattress bowed as he leapt out of bed and headed for the adjoining master bathroom.

She lifted her head and called after him. "Gavin?"

"Back in a second." He closed the door.

Then she heard the shower turn on. So much for the Q&A portion of this rendezvous.

Somewhere in the depths of his pants pockets, a cell phone started ringing.

Cold, naked, and very confused, Cait gathered the rumpled white cotton sheet around her like a makeshift toga and knocked on the bathroom door. "Your cell's ringing."

No response. All she could hear was running water and the occasional splash. She knocked once more, then sat down on the edge of the bed and waited.

The cell phone stopped ringing. Two seconds later, the landline started. Since the phone on the nightstand was simple white plastic, there was no caller ID box, but Cait figured whoever was calling must really want to talk to Gavin.

She hammered on the bathroom door with the heel of her hand. "Gavin! Your phones keep ringing. Would you like me to pick up?"

His response was garbled, but she thought she heard him say, "Take a message."

So she picked up the receiver and tried to sound casual. Or at very least, clothed. "Hello?"

"Hello?" said a low, cultured, female voice.

Cait's eyebrows shot up.

"Hello?" repeated the other woman. "Who is this, please?"

"This is, um—" Cait coughed. "Gavin Clayburn's phone."

"Ah." An audible intake of breath. "I'll call back."

"Wait!" Cait cried, desperate for more clues. "I can take a message for him."

"No specific message. Just kindly let him know that Yvette called."

"I'll do that," Cait said, and the caller clicked off immediately.

By the time Gavin emerged from the bathroom, showered,

shaved, and smelling vaguely of aftershave, Cait's list of questions for him had multiplied exponentially.

"Who's Yvette?" She cocked her head and waited for him to assure her that *Yvette's my sister/cousin/incredible talking French poodle.*

Instead, his expression hovered halfway between horror and excitement. "Yvette called?"

"About five minutes ago. She sounded quite sultry on the phone. Is there anything I should know about?"

His gazed shifted. "What did she say?"

"Nothing. She refused to leave a message. Just wanted me to let you know she called."

Relief flooded into his eyes. "Okay, great. Thanks." He leaned over and kissed her hard. "You look devastating wrapped up in my sheet like that. We better get going before I lose all self-control again. I'll meet you downstairs."

Cait pulled away and yanked the sheet up to her chin. "Are you kidding me? That's it?"

He opened his closet and selected a simple white button-down shirt and a pressed pair of khakis. "What do you mean?"

As if on cue, the doorbell chimed. Gavin zipped up his pants and took a single step toward the hallway.

"Do not answer that," Cait commanded. "We're not done here."

He stopped in his tracks. "I'm listening."

"I don't need you to listen, I need you to talk. I have questions, burning questions, and it makes me very nervous that you keep changing the subject and deflecting me with humor and escaping into the shower whenever I—"

Ding-dong.

"Hey, G?" bellowed a voice from the front porch. "It's Simon, man. Got a delivery for you. Overnight express."

Cait threw up her hands. "What is the *deal* with you and your FedEx guy?"

"It's fine," Gavin said quietly. "He can leave it at the door."

But Simon was nothing if not persistent. "Hey! I need a signature here, buddy! I know you're home; your car's in the driveway."

Gavin shrugged in helpless frustration. "He needs a signature."

"I heard."

"I have to get that."

She sighed. "Of course you do."

He ran down the stairs and she collected her clothes, save her lucky plaid boxer shorts, which had somehow gotten lost in the frenzy of foreplay. She arrived on the landing just in time to glimpse Gavin sending off Simon with a bottle of water.

"See you soon," Gavin called. "Say hi to Heather for me."

"Will do." Simon climbed back into his truck and waved. "Thanks for the water."

Gavin turned, closed the front door, and stashed a bulky Tyvek envelope in the storage bench of the antique walnut hall tree.

"What's in the package?" she asked.

He closed the bench lid firmly. "Nothing."

She sat down on the stairs and rested her chin on her hand. "Gavin. What's going on? The padlock, the phone call, your deep and enduring bond with your FedEx courier. I have to tell you, I'm more than a little freaked out here."

He finally looked up at her, and she could tell that he was choosing his words very carefully. "I'm sorry. You're right. The last few weeks have been a little crazy."

"No kidding." She leaned against the banister.

"But it's got nothing to do with us."

She held her tongue and waited him out.

"I'll explain everything eventually, I promise, but for now you'll just have to take it on faith that I have very good reasons for all of this."

Cait pushed off the banister and sat up straight. "As I was saying earlier, we don't know each other that well yet. But here's something you should understand about me: I don't do secrets, and I don't tolerate subterfuge. My ex-boyfriend was big on both, and I'm not going down that road again."

"Is that why you left your teaching position?"

"That's part of it."

He nodded. "I hear you, loud and clear. But I'm asking you to realize that I'm not your ex-boyfriend. I'm asking you to trust me. Just for a little while. Can you do that?"

Cait crossed her arms and considered the consequences for a long moment before relenting. "I can try."

*Y*ou'll never guess who just called for you," Brooke said when Cait returned to Paradise Found.

Cait crossed her fingers. "Gavin?"

Brooke shook her head. "Cheerio Charles."

"You cannot be serious." But from the pained expression on Brooke's face, Cait knew this was no prank. "His timing couldn't be worse."

"He called on the main house line. He said, and I quote, 'The matter is urgent.'"

Cait tossed her purse onto the pile next to the glass-paned front door. "How does he even know I'm staying here?"

"I have no idea. He said you weren't picking up your cell."

"More like I permanently blocked his number." Cait trudged up the staircase, all too aware that she was going commando beneath her jeans. What had started out feeling cheeky was starting to chafe.

"Are you going to call him back?"

"I think I will. I've got a ton of pent-up hostility at the moment, and he's the perfect target. Give me two minutes to find out what he wants and then I'm at your disposal. I need a few hours of mindless physical labor to clear my head."

"Perfect. I could use a hand laying tile in the bathroom."

"Don't start without me." Cait marched up to her bedroom and dialed Charles's office number, half hoping he'd already gone home for the evening.

As soon as he picked up, she got right to the point. "It's me. How'd you find me, and what do you want?"

"The department secretary was kind enough to share the contact information you'd given her to forward on your mail and your final paycheck. And I must say—" He paused but couldn't hold himself back. "Paradise Found Bed-and-Breakfast? Really? *Paradise Found?* Milton is spinning in his grave."

"Did you call just to patronize me?" Cait chomped down on a pen cap.

His tone changed instantly from mocking to mollifying. "When you left, you may remember that I mentioned the dean suspected financial irregularities with the speaker fund and the department slush fund."

"Vividly." The pen cap was going to have permanent molar imprints.

"Yes." She heard him shuffling papers. "Well."

"Well, what?"

More paper shuffling, then a drawn-out sigh. "It appears that now the shadow of suspicion has fallen over me."

Cait spat the pen cap clear across the room. "It was *you!* I should have known. That's why you put me in charge of those accounts, isn't it? All the better to frame me!"

"No, no, no. Let's not fly off the handle here. First and foremost, you should know that there is no concrete proof of any wrongdoing." *Yet*, his tone clearly implied.

"But there was enough to justify strong-arming me out of my job."

"Be fair. You asked for a sabbatical."

"I see. So if I decide I want to come back next year, I'll be welcomed with open arms."

Dead silence.

"Yeah, that's what I thought. Thanks for calling. Bye now."

"Wait!" he cried.

She froze, her index finger hovering over the disconnect button.

"The dean has hired an auditor to investigate the allegations of financial mismanagement within the department," Charles said.

She drummed her fingers on the desktop. "Uh-huh."

"And it occurred to me that, since you don't work at Shayland anymore, it really doesn't matter if you misappropriated funds or not."

"Are you kidding me?" she sputtered. "*No.* Before you go any further, the answer is no. Hell no. Never gonna happen, not in this world or the next."

"I'm not asking you to lie," he wheedled. "But if the

auditor should happen to track you down, I'd appreciate it if you'd—"

"The auditor won't have to track me down; I'll call him myself as soon as we hang up." She searched for a new pen. "What's his number?"

He sniffed. "Don't be spiteful."

"I'm being ethical, not to mention practical. I may be on the job market again soon. What am I supposed to say when a potential employer asks for references from Shayland?"

"You're looking for another professorship already?" he asked. "Guess the novel's not going so well, hmm?"

"I will kill you," she hissed.

"In all sincerity, I know how difficult it is. Believe me. I've been toiling on my work-in-progress for the last five years."

For a moment, she was too stunned to be angry. "You're writing a novel? You never told me that."

"No offense, but it's a rather bleak, modernist narrative. Evocative of Kafka, I flatter myself." He chuckled. "Not really your cup of tea."

"Too literary for a lightweight like me, in other words?"

He shifted back into his patient, pedantic mode. "Must you turn everything into a battle, Caitlin?"

"You're the one who's trying to skim money off the colloquium fund and throw me under the bus!"

"Just to be clear, there are no actual monies missing at this point. If someone has indeed been, ahem, *borrowing* without administrative approbation, he or she has repaid the accounts in full."

"Well, that's very magnanimous of him or her. And just so you know, the novel is going swimmingly. It's brilliant. It's breathtaking. The *New York Times* reviewers are going to wet their pants over it. Suck on that, Kafka."

She hung up on him before he could utter another syllable and immediately dialed up the all-knowing oracle: "Hi,
Penny, I just got off the phone with the department chair.
He was about to give me the contact information for the auditor the department's working with, but he had a student
emergency to attend to. Is there any way you could track that
down for me?...Great, I knew you could help me out.
Thanks, Penny!"

Then she sat back in her chair and stared out the bedroom window. The view had barely changed since she had
lived in this house as a college senior—same maple tree,
same house next door, same chapel bell tower looming over
the rooftops—but everything else in her world had shifted
radically. The stakes were higher now, the dilemmas much
thornier. And so many of her assumptions about who'd she
be when she "grew up" had turned out to be laughably erro-
neous.

What she needed right now, more than anything, was to
sit down with Arden and have a lengthy heart-to-heart complete with laughing and crying and white wine chilled with
crushed ice (because, as Arden often said, "That's how they
do it at the poshest Connecticut boarding schools. Trust
me."). Cait was very close to Anna, Brooke, and Jamie, but
she and Arden had developed a special bond over the last few
years.

And now Arden was gone. Cait could alter everything else
in her life, from her career to her behavior, but she couldn't
change the fact that she would never be able to share anything
with her best friend again. There, ensconced in the same
room that had been her refuge all those years ago, Cait finally
allowed herself to absorb the full weight of her grief.

She put her head down on the desk and cried for the first

time since Arden's funeral. Gut-wrenching, body-wracking sobs. She cried until her cheeks went numb and her nose felt raw and her wellspring of fear and sorrow ran dry.

Then she washed her face, fixed herself a Chardonnay slushy in a ceramic coffee mug for old time's sake, and switched on her computer.

"Here's to you, babe." She hoisted her mug toward the setting sun. "No more excuses, no more extensions."

How did you get this scar?" Helena traced her finger along the line of pale, raised flesh that ran from MacCormick's shoulder to his stomach.

He shuttered his gaze. "An accident," he said. "When I was younger."

"It looks like a sword wound."

"Does it, then? And how would a tutor incur a sword wound?"

She rose up and tilted her head. "My question exactly. I can't shake the conviction that you're hiding something from me. Some dark secret——"

"Helena, I read about epic battles; I do no' fight them." His tone sharper, he added, "You search for intrigue where there is none. Likely because you've been reading too many of those bloody novels."

Like a shot, she reached for the haphazard pile of her garments, unable to cover her nudity fast enough——not only because his censorious words were like a blow, but because she knew he'd turned to insults to distract her from her questions.

She yanked her chemise over her head, then faced him. "How would such a rarefied man of letters know anything about what I read in my novels? I know you're hiding something. If you can't tell me the truth, I'll be forced to assume that you're out committing dastardly deeds each night."

His laugh mocked her. "You'd like me better as a highwayman, wouldn't you? Never underestimate the appeal of a rakish masked man to a lady of virtue."

"I will not be put off," she warned him as she gathered up her gown. *"I will discover your secret."*

With his brow creased in anger, he yanked on his trousers. *"You stubborn chit. Unlocking my door and ransacking my belongings is no' going to unearth any truths."*

Helena stared at the man to whom, just moments ago, she had offered up her body and her very soul. *How could she have let the fleeting pleasures of passion overrule her good judgment? "I, too, can lock myself away. I, too, can protect myself and my own interests."*

Threading his fingers through his hair, he exhaled a long breath. *"Can you no' just trust me?"*

"Can you not just tell me?" she countered. *His reply was silence. "You ask me for trust, yet offer none in return."*

Cait wrote for hours, until the first hint of dawn crept over the horizon. While she typed, she chipped away at her long-standing beliefs about who she ought to be and what made her worthy and what everyone else might say. So she wasn't going to be the second coming of Willa Cather. So the National Book Award committee wouldn't be pounding down her door. So what? At least now she could get down to work without all the self-inflicted guilt and second-guessing.

Next step: getting over Gavin. Her mind flashed back to the question he'd asked her yesterday: *Can you trust me?*

And she realized that the answer was no.

Chapter 22

"We are all apt to believe what the world believes about us."
—George Eliot, *The Mill on the Floss*

J amie? Hello? Are you ever going to answer me or should I call 911?"

Jamie's eyes popped open. Her mouth tasted sour and her bare feet were freezing. She rolled onto her side and saw the comforter on the carpet. Thirty-two years old and she still kicked off her covers.

"Jamie!" Anna's voice sounded a bit panicked, and Jamie wondered how many times her housemate had already called her. "Sarah Richmond just called and said she's running late for your meeting, but she'll be here in about an hour."

According to the digital clock on the desk, Jamie had

napped away the entire afternoon, but she felt more exhausted than when she'd first crawled into bed. "Mmmph."

"Hark! Do I hear signs of life?"

"Mmmph."

"It's about time. Dinner's ready."

Jamie grabbed the comforter and nestled back against the wall. "Go ahead and eat without me."

"Would you like me to keep your plate warm?"

"No thanks, that's okay. I'm not feeling very well."

"Still? Do you think maybe you should see a doctor?"

"I'm fine," Jamie insisted. "I appreciate your concern, but truly, I'm fine."

"If you say so." The floorboards creaked as Anna shifted her weight out in the hallway. "It's just, you know, you've been sequestered in there since Wednesday, and we're starting to get a *leetle* concerned."

"I'm just, uh, hungover."

"For forty-eight consecutive hours?"

"I had a *lot* to drink."

"Liar. I'll bring up some grilled cheese and soup and leave it outside your door. You don't have to talk to us if you don't want to, but you have to eat something."

Jamie tucked her cold toes into a warm fold in the blanket. "Yes, Mom."

"And if you want to chat or watch a marathon of those horrifying medical documentaries you love so much, we're all here for you."

"Yes, Mom."

Anna paused. "We love you, Jame."

"Yeah, yeah."

Jamie held her breath until she heard footsteps retreating

down the stairs, then relaxed and let her eyes flutter closed. To this day, she could never say the word "Mom" without a heavy dollop of sarcasm, probably because her own mother had prided herself on being the antithesis of maternal. Charlene Burton was a ballsy blonde with an infectious laugh and a keen capacity for enjoyment. She worked lots of different jobs and dated lots of different men, and the only constant in her life was her restlessness. Jamie had once sat down and figured out that they'd moved nine times between the day she started kindergarten and her high school graduation. Being the perennial new girl had taught her a lot about how to survive socially—she'd simply brazen her way into the popular cliques by showing no fear and "willing" herself cool.

Charlene treated her young daughter as an adult, and Jamie had been allowed to eat what she wanted, stay up reading until dawn, and dress herself as she pleased. Radical haircuts and multiple body piercings wouldn't have shocked her mother, so Jamie never bothered. As she drifted into the choppy waters of adolescence, Charlene made it clear that Jamie could experiment to her heart's content with cigarettes, beer, and boys, as long as she took responsibility for her own actions. "Don't ever say I didn't give you your freedom," Charlene would say. "I'm your mother, not your warden."

Jamie's father, Dale, had also been willing to grant Jamie lots of freedom, to the point that he barely made contact over the years. He and Charlene had never married, and though Charlene swore he'd been present at Jamie's first birthday party, when Jamie asked to see the photographs, Charlene brushed her off with, "Don't live in the past, honey." Dale got married to another woman when Jamie was four; he and his wife had a son and two daughters. Every December, the family sent Jamie a Christmas card along with a posed family snapshot. Dale's wife Melinda was the daughter of a fishing boat captain, and Dale joined up with the crew, spending weeks at a time out at sea. When the boat docked, Dale didn't have a lot of free time to call or write to Jamie. He had to make up for lost time with his "real family." (That's how Charlene had put it, anyway: "Munchkin, trust me, you don't want any part of that white picket fence bullshit. Sure, it looks swell in the Sears portrait studio, but wouldn't you rather be a woman of the world? We've got choices in life, you and me, just remember that.") Charlene didn't believe in sending holiday cards. She dismissed it as depressing and suburban, and the one year Jamie decided to do it herself, she got as far as buying foil-embossed cards and a book of stamps before realizing that she had no one to send to.

Jamie kept writing to her father, though. Not very often—she had *some* pride, after all—but she mailed him copies of her report cards at the end of every semester. She wanted him to see the columns of A's, to marvel at her mastery of words and numbers and abstract ideas. But he never commented on her GPA. "Don't have unrealistic expectations of your father," Charlene chided when Jamie sulked about this. "Honey, he probably has no idea what precalculus even is. School was never important to him." Jamie decided that school wasn't important to her, either. All you had to do was read and remember. That wasn't so hard.

Then, one sweltering Saturday in July when Jamie walked back to their current crappy rental house (Jersey shore) from her current crappy job (scooping ice cream for tourists) to shower and slather on too much makeup before heading out with her current crappy boyfriend (a college sophomore/tortured aspiring songwriter named Brent), she'd opened the mailbox to find a thin white envelope from her father. Enclosed was a newspaper clipping announcing a scholarship to some snooty college for "promising students who represent the first generation in their families to attend college." Her father had scribbled a note in the margin: *Thought of you.*

"That's it?" Jamie had said aloud, turning the scrap of newsprint over and over. But here was irrefutable proof that her father did think about her. So she spent the next six weeks before her senior year of high school working on her Thurwell College scholarship application. She lost patience with Brent's ballads of existential woe and dedicated all her spare time to writing and rewriting her application essay.

A few months later, she received the official approval from the scholarship committee: fifty percent tuition reimbursement, provided she kept her GPA high and her disciplinary record spotless. Her teachers were thrilled; her mother told everyone that "we Burton girls are brainy *and* beautiful, and don't you forget it." Jamie overnighted a copy of her acceptance letter to her father, but he never wrote back.

So she stopped contacting her dad and headed off to college, where she caught the attention of another very powerful man. She captivated him, Terry confessed. He couldn't stop thinking about her. She was irresistible. This time, she was going to win out over the "real family."

Except she didn't. Terry gradually stopped talking about leaving his wife, and then he stopped returning Jamie's calls, and when she tearfully asked him if he still loved her, he'd stroked her hair and said, "If anyone finds out about us, Jamie, anyone at all, I'll lose my job and you'll lose your scholarship. I can always find another job, but you... This is for your own good, sweetheart. This is for the best."

Six months later, Jamie graduated with a B.A. in English,

an impressive collection of student loans, and a secret that gnawed at her conscience for the next decade.

She heard Anna's voice at the door again. "I've got your tray and I'm leaving it right here by the door."

"Thank you."

"Oh, and please tell Sarah that I got the wedding cake topper her mom sent from Vermont."

"Will do."

"Although I have to tell you, I'm a little nervous to take it out of the box, let alone stick it on top of a layer cake. I get the impression her mom spent about a thousand bucks on it."

Jamie tried to muster enough energy to yell back. "Her mom thinks any wedding-related item worth less than a thousand bucks is tacky crap from the dollar store."

"Got it." Anna went quiet for so long that Jamie thought she might have left. But then she piped up with, "And Jame? Please let me know if there's anything I can do to get you out of seclusion and back to being our take-no-prisoners woman of the world."

Jamie sat bolt upright when she heard that phrase, which resonated all the way back to her childhood. Twenty years later, and here she was—another sassy, brassy woman of the world ready to give up and move on as soon as the going got rough. *Just like my mother.*

Galvanized, she swung her frigid feet onto the floor. "I'm up."

"Now this is the way to plan a wedding: doing shots in a bar with my event planner." Sarah Richmond slid into the wooden booth, her cabled cashmere sweater and diamond earrings striking a jarring contrast to the neon-lit ambiance of Thurwell's Pine Street Pub.

"*One* shot," Jamie reminded her. "And you better stick to half a shot, if our last planning session was any indication."

"What'll it be?" asked the waitress.

"Two shots of tequila," Jamie said.

"Patrón, if you have it," Sarah added. "We need the good stuff."

"And two huge glasses of water," Jamie said.

After the waitress returned, they clinked their glasses and threw back the shots. Sarah coughed and sputtered as she swallowed.

"You okay?" Jamie asked. "Raise your hand if you need the Heimlich maneuver."

"I'll be fine." Sarah dabbed at her mouth with a napkin. She didn't seem at all fazed by the hard rock blaring over the speaker system or the water-spotted silverware. "Wow, I needed that. I have had a *week*."

"Last-minute wedding stress getting to you?"

"Oh, no, the wedding's fine." Sarah dismissed this with a flip of her long, dark hair. "As I said, my mom's the one who's all worked up about who's RSVP'd and who hasn't and what the corsages are going to look like and are the napkins monogrammed in the right typeface."

"I can check on the cocktail napkins for her." Jamie whipped out her planning binder and prepared to jot this down.

"Don't worry about it. She's obsessed with my wedding being perfect, but it's never going to be perfect because my dad's not here, so she's channeling her energy into micro-managing the tiniest details." Sarah's smile was a bit lopsided.

"She just wants me to have everything she never did. I mean, you know how mothers are."

Jamie nodded politely and waited for the bride to continue.

"I need a shot of tequila because I just gave notice at my job today. The movers are coming to pack up my apartment next week, and I told my landlord that I won't be renewing my lease." Sarah laced her hands together and stretched her arms out over the table. "Yep. In two weeks' time, I'll be married and living in the sticks and unemployed for the first time since college."

Jamie chewed on the end of her straw. "You sound kind of ambivalent."

"It's just a lot of change all at once. New town, new people, new role. I never really pictured myself as the demure little faculty wife. It's going to be more work than I anticipated, all the traveling and entertaining and fund-raising. I had no idea what a hotbed of politics and scandal academia is."

"You don't know the half of it."

Sarah tucked her hands back under the table. "At least I'll have you to hang out with once I take up residence in The Manor. It's such a relief to know there are other uprooted city girls out here. We can go skiing, get mani/pedis, maybe we can even double-date. Me with Terry and you with all the men you must have lining up."

Jamie flagged down a passing server. "I'll have another shot of Patrón, please."

Sarah's eyes widened. "I can't keep up with that."

"I don't want you to," Jamie said. "I just want you to sit back for a second and try to keep an open mind. There's something I have to tell you."

"Uh-oh." Sarah laughed. "Sounds ominous. Dun, dun, *dunnn*."

Jamie remained deadly serious. "Here's the thing. I'm glad you're happy and I don't want to interfere with your relationship in any way, but..."

Sarah mirrored her grim expression. "Spit it out."

"You should know that, back in the day, Terry had a little bit of a reputation."

"Oh, that." Sarah looked relieved. "Yeah, his first marriage was miserable."

"Yes, but it was more than that." Her kingdom for a cigarette. "He kind of breached the sacred trust."

"Say no more." Sarah's tone was still friendly, but her eyes had darkened. "I see where you're going with this."

"You do?"

"You're talking about that student, the girl with the weird name. What was it? Arielle? Artemis?"

"Arden," Jamie said softly.

"Arden." Sarah lifted her chin. "I've been to a lot of college functions since Terry and I started dating. The trustees like to gossip and the alumni council members are even worse. So yes, I know he has some regrets in his past."

Jamie was startled to hear that term applied to her: a "regret." Such a gentle, tactful term for such a sordid act.

"That makes it sound like it was a minor mistake." Jamie leaned forward. "It was an affair with a twenty-year-old student, not an administrative oversight."

"It wasn't an affair, it was a vicious rumor." Sarah got more detached with every syllable. "If he had breached anything, he would have been fired immediately. I've heard Terry's side of the story, and that's all I need to know."

Jamie had to hear this. "What's Terry's version?"

Sarah stopped looking at her. "The whole thing is ancient history. I love him, I trust him, and I don't need to listen to any more unfounded speculation."

"But actually, you do. Because Arden was one of my best friends and—"

"Before you continue, let me ask you one question. Are you telling me all this for my sake? Or for yours?"

"Yours, of course." Jamie paused. "I thought you needed to know."

"In that case, thank you for your concern, but I'm a big girl. I can take care of myself." Sarah nodded crisply to indicate that the subject was closed.

Jamie was debating the wisdom of pressing her point when a voice behind them broke through the music and Friday night chatter. "Jamie Burton? Is that you?"

Jamie flinched before she even turned her head, because she knew who that voice belonged to.

"I've been trying to call you." Jeff Thuesen materialized at the side of the table. He looked very tall, very handsome, and very resolute.

"Oh," Jamie said. "I haven't been checking my voice mail."

"I asked Brooke for your number when I saw her a few weeks ago." Jeff braced his hands on the back of a chair and seemed ready to sit down and join them. "Did she tell you she ran into me?"

"She might have mentioned it."

He stared down at her, obviously waiting for her to ask why he'd been trying to get in touch. When it became equally obvious that she wasn't going to take the bait, he said, "I need to talk to you."

Jamie deflected with, "What are you doing out here in Thurwell, anyway? I thought you lived in Manhattan."

"Brooklyn, actually, but yeah, I work in the city. I'm here to interview candidates for one of my company's summer internships."

"Oh. Okay. Great."

"But I went to the memorial service, as I'm sure you're aware."

She feigned total innocence. "No. I didn't see you there. But it was so crowded, you know, and such a difficult day."

"It was." His hands opened and closed on the back of the chair. "Look. I know this is awkward, but I have some questions that I'm hoping you can answer for me."

"Listen, Jeff, I'd love to chat, but I'm right in the middle of something here."

"Hi." Sarah waved. "I'm Sarah Richmond. She's planning my wedding."

"Yeah? Congratulations." He turned right back to Jamie. "What about tomorrow?"

"No good. I'm booked solid. Meetings with the caterers, finalizing everything for the bridesmaids' tea."

"Next week, then." Jeff wasn't asking. "I'm coming back for the last round of interviews on Friday."

Jamie toyed with her earring. "I'd love to, but I'm just—"

"Next Friday, high noon," Sarah assured him. "She'll be here."

"I'll hold you to that," Jeff said. "See you next week."

"Bye!" Sarah trilled after him. Her exuberance vanished when she got a load of Jamie's expression. "Uh-oh."

"You have no idea what you just did to me."

"Set up a date for you with a hot guy?"

Jamie gave her a look. "First of all, you're walking down the aisle in two weeks, so you're not supposed to be scoping out hot guys."

Sarah laughed. "I'm engaged. I'm not blind."

"And second of all, it's not a date."

"It sure seems like a date. Hot guy, single woman, pre-arranged social meeting."

"Things aren't always what they first appear," Jamie said. "Which brings us back to the subject of Terry and his—"

"Stop." Sarah crossed her arms. "I like you, Jamie, and I want to continue to like you. So unless *you* slept with my fiancé, I'm not going to discuss this further."

"Will you kindly excuse me for a moment?" Jamie grabbed the emergency pack of cigarettes in her bag and stepped outside to light up. White tendrils of smoke unfurled into the chilly night air. Jamie shoved one hand into her jeans pocket and inhaled as deeply as she could, gulping down the warm, pungent fumes until her lungs burned and her hands stopped shaking.

When she returned to the table, Sarah was waiting for her with a peace offering of artichoke dip.

"Let's start over." Sarah handed her a napkin. "Why don't you dazzle me with all the details of the bridesmaids' tea?"

"Fair enough." Jamie cracked open her wedding-planning binder and recommitted to her long-standing policy of non-interference. "Let's talk tulle."

Chapter
23

*"No woman is so good or so bad, but that at any moment she is capable
of the most diabolical as well as of the most divine..."*
—Leopold von Sacher-Masoch, *Venus in Furs*

Anna used her chef's knife to slice open the cardboard box that Sarah Richmond's mother had sent, unspooled yards of bubble wrap to make sure that the porcelain bride-and-groom wedding cake topper (hand-painted, one-of-a-kind, heirloom-quality European craftsmanship, according to Mrs. Richmond) was still intact, then turned her attention back to the gelatinous mass of dough oozing slowly across the pan. She could master any cake or cookie, but breads were hit or miss. Her sole attempt at croissants had ended in charred, leaden triangles of flattened pastry and a wine-fueled tirade against the French.

"Hey, what's in the box?"

Anna dropped her knife with a clatter as she realized she was no longer alone in Pranza's kitchen. She whirled around to find Trish Selway standing right behind her.

"What's in the box?" Trish repeated.

"Stop sneaking up on me!" Anna had to tilt her head back to meet Trish's gaze. She backed up in an attempt to reclaim some personal space and said, "And go away. It's my night, free and clear. Check the schedule."

"Simmer down; I'm just here to put the finishing touches on a cake I had to leave in the walk-in. I'll be in and out in ten minutes. Seth already cleared it. Go ahead and call him if you have a problem." Trish switched her focus from the cardboard box to the baking sheet. "And what's this jacked-up yeasty mess supposed to be? Looks like epoxy in a pan."

"It's *brioche au fromage*," Anna said in her snottiest French accent.

Trish laughed out loud. "I know a brioche when I see one, and that? Is no brioche."

"Oh please. Like you could do any better."

"I absolutely could. It's bread, babycakes, not rocket science."

"I couldn't agree more. And since I'm following the recipe to the letter, I can only assume the instructions are flawed."

"Don't blame the recipe. It doesn't get more basic than brioche." Trish leaned over and skimmed the list of ingredients. "Just flour, eggs, butter, sugar, yeast, and Gruyère. But, you see, it's the simple classics like this that separate the true chefs from the poseurs with Williams-Sonoma catalogs and too much time on their hands."

Don't engage, don't engage. With the grocery store fracas fresh in her mind, Anna spun on her heel and stalked over toward the refrigerator. Then she heard an ominous utterance behind her:

"Oops."

She raced back to discover that a bottle of blueberry syrup had splashed across the vintage cookbook.

"Gosh, I'm sorry," Trish said with a simper. "Pregnancy has made me so klutzy."

Anna adopted Trish's earlier tone of condescension. "Don't blame the Bug. Between this pitiful attempt at sabotage and that stunt you pulled with the Hobart mixer, I now understand how truly insecure you are."

"The fact that you're still accusing me of taking that mixer attachment shows how delusional you are," Trish countered.

"I guess we both have our crosses to bear." Anna sectioned out the damaged pages of her cookbook, headed back to the sink, and tried to salvage the brioche recipe with a hot, damp dishcloth. But the text was irreparably obscured.

This whole thing with Trish was so petty. So high school. Scratch that—more like middle school. Anna reminded herself that she was a mature adult, with a home and a husband and lots of friends and a rich, multifaceted existence. She refused to debase herself by stooping to dirty tricks and passive-aggressive mind games.

Then she gazed down at the sticky, sodden cookbook that Jonas had given to her on the hot summer day they'd moved in to their house in Albany. She'd thrown together a simple tomato salad for dinner, and then they'd made love on the floor in the empty living room and giddily assured each other that they'd just created the first of the children who would eventually fill up the spare bedrooms.

Now her cookbook was trashed, her house was empty, and Jonas was on the other side of the ocean.

Suddenly, Anna was back in seventh grade.

When Anna returned to the prep area, Trish was chatting on her cell phone. "Hi, this is Trish Selway, calling about the cake delivery. . . . Yeah, I just want to double-check everything to make sure it's perfect. You want me to pipe 'Congratulations, Terrence' on the top in red, right? . . . No flowers, no scallops, no other decoration? . . . Okay. Got it. I'll be over to drop it off ASAP. See you in a few minutes."

Anna leaned back against the metal countertop and waited. When Trish ended the call, she asked, "Who's the cake for?" She figured there couldn't be too many Terrences running around Thurwell, New York. "Is it for the college president?"

"Mind your business, Legacy." Trish packed a pastry bag full of red icing and started piping.

For several minutes, the two bakers pointedly ignored each other and the tension thickened to the consistency of Anna's brioche dough.

Finally, Trish broke the silence. "Shouldn't you be trying to fix your slab of fancy French *merde* over there?"

Anna peeked over Trish's shoulder at the sheet cake, which now featured elegant red cursive across the smooth white icing. "Oh my God."

"What?"

Anna tittered behind her hand. "Nothing."

Trish flushed. *"What?"*

"Don't you worry. You'll find out soon enough." Certain that Trish was still watching her, Anna made a big show of digging out her cell phone from her coat pocket and retreating to the restaurant's dry-storage area. There, surrounded by huge metal cans and Lexan containers full of flour and sugar, she pretended to dial the phone and then, tamping down a momentary stirring of shame, pretended to be talking to Jamie.

She pitched her voice to be loud enough for Trish to overhear but hushed enough to sound as though she were trying to be secretive. "Hey, Jamie, it's me. Did you let Terrence's staff order a cake through that other baker?"

She paused for a moment to listen to her nonexistent conversation partner's nonexistent reply. The rest of the kitchen had gone totally, eerily still, which meant that Trish had to be listening in.

"Jamie, how could you?... Yeah, yeah. Well, it doesn't matter, anyway, because"—Anna lowered her voice even more—"she spelled his name wrong on the cake! Swear to God. She spelled Terrence with *e-n-c-e* when he spells it *a-n-c-e*. I know!... Of course I'm not going to tell her! Are you kidding me? Anyway, yeah, once she shows up with the typo cake, I doubt they'll be hiring her again." She strolled out of the pantry and feigned shock when she saw Trish scurrying away from her eavesdropping post around the corner.

"Oh, hello. You're still here?" Anna exclaimed.

"For about thirty more seconds." Trish leaned over the cake and picked up her pastry bag. "Then I'm out the door."

"Well, be extra careful not to trip, won't you?" Anna cooed. "I certainly wouldn't want you to drop that beautiful cake, what with all your pregnancy klutziness."

Trish folded down the lid of the large rectangular bakery box. Anna strained to catch a glimpse of the top of the cake. Sure enough, Trish had changed the spelling to "Terrance."

Mission accomplished. Revenge was a dish best served with buttercream frosting.

But instead of basking in smug satisfaction, Anna felt a twinge of remorse. She couldn't help envisioning the party host's reaction and Trish's public humiliation in front of an entire roomful of supercilious "legacies."

Her resolve splintered and she threw up her hands. "Wait," she said. "You need to change the spelling."

Trish snorted. "Oh please, I'm not falling for that. I know how to spell 'Terrance.' Just because I don't have some overpriced degree doesn't mean I'm illiterate."

"No, you were right the first time. It's an *e*, not an *a*. I made the whole thing up back there." Anna couldn't even look at her. "I wasn't really on the phone."

"Every time I think you can't possibly get any crazier, you prove me wrong. I bet your husband hides your chef knives before he goes to sleep, doesn't he?"

Anna started toward Trish. "Come on. I'll help you fix it."

"Stay away from me!"

"But I can't let you—"

"If you take one more step, the pepper spray comes out." Trish gripped the cake box tightly and edged toward the exit, glaring at Anna as she went. "When I want spelling tips, I'll ask for them."

*T*wenty minutes later, the kitchen door flew open and a blast of frigid winter wind blew in.

"You evil, lying, conniving *hag*."

In her haste to confront Anna, Trish hadn't bothered to scrape the freezing rain from her boot treads, and tiny ice crystals scattered across the tile.

"You're tracking slush all over the floor," Anna pointed out.

"You screwed me over on purpose." Trish threw down her coat and rolled up her sweater sleeves.

Anna had never been in a fistfight, and she had no intention of starting now. Especially with an opponent who was in her second trimester. She retreated to the other side of the counter, trying to put a few barriers between herself and the enraged Amazon in the Fair Isle sweater. "I will admit that things got out of hand, but I honestly tried—"

Trish held her body ramrod straight with her fists balled at her sides. "You can't stand that anyone from that college still hires me for anything. You think you deserve to have all my business handed to you on a silver platter."

"That's not true!" Anna cried.

"Well, let me tell you something: I was here first. And I'll still be here, long after you've given up on the pastry chef fantasy and moved on to basket weaving or beekeeping or whatever your next whim happens to be. I went to school for this. I work my ass off. This isn't some fun little side job for me. This is my *life*."

"Oh, spare me the guilt trip. You're the one who started this whole thing!" Anna nodded toward the blueberry syrup. "From the second I met you, you've been nothing but nasty, with the tricks and the threats and the 'Legacy' crap—"

"You *are* a legacy! What culinary credentials do you have, other than watching the Food Network?"

Anna had no response for this.

"I'm waiting. Do you have any professional training at all?"

"As you yourself said, just because I don't have a fancy degree doesn't mean I can't do a good job."

"Whatever." Trish wrinkled her nose in disgust. "You're

spoiled and self-entitled, and I hope you choke on that hot mess you call a brioche."

Anna opened her mouth to respond, but her words died on her lips when she noticed the dark red stain spreading at the juncture of Trish's light khaki trousers.

"Hey!" Trish's voice sounded far away. "You're not even listening to me!"

Anna stepped forward, her hand outstretched. "Are you all right?"

"What do you mean?"

Anna glanced at Trish's crotch as delicately as possible.

"What now?" Trish followed Anna's gaze and yanked at the plackets of her pants. She dabbed at the stain with a single paper napkin, then blinked down at the crimson smears on the napkin's crisp white surface.

After a few seconds, Trish looked back up, her expression completely blank. "Oh."

"Are you hurt?" Anna asked.

"No. I mean, my back hurts, but I thought that was from hauling around a ginormous slab of cake all day. Oh God. What do I do?"

Anna pointed to the bathroom door. "Go check it out. Call if you need help."

Two minutes later, Trish returned from the restroom. Her face had gone pallid. "It's not stopping. There's a lot of blood down there."

Anna grabbed her car keys. "Let's go. The clinic's only a few blocks away. This'll be faster than waiting for an ambulance."

Trish waved her off. "I can drive myself."

"Are you kidding me?"

"I'm fine, seriously, I'll just—" Trish took two steps toward the door and slipped on the melting slush she'd tracked in a few minutes ago. Her arms pinwheeled wildly as she started to fall, and Anna lunged across the kitchen to steady her.

"I'm not letting go." Anna clutched one of Trish's forearms with each hand. "Now shut the hell up, get in the car, and cross your legs until we get to the clinic."

*I*s there someone we should call?" Anna asked once they'd been whisked past the clinic's admitting desk and straight into the E.R.'s "GYN room." "Your husband?"

Trish folded her hands over her abdomen and kept her gaze fixed on the exam room ceiling. "My boyfriend is out of town and no, we definitely shouldn't call him yet."

"You want to wait until you know for sure," Anna said.

"Give me a break. I look like the Red Sea parted in my pants." Trish closed her eyes. "I think we already know for sure what's happened."

"Don't say that. You have to keep your hopes up until—"

"And on top of everything else, I ruined your car upholstery."

Anna blinked. "Are you honestly thinking about my upholstery right now?"

Trish curled her fingers into the starched bedsheets. "What is taking that ultrasound chick so long?"

According to the physician's assistant who'd performed Trish's intake assessment, the only on-call obstetrician was currently in surgery performing a C-section, which meant that Trish would first be checked by an ultrasound tech. But, due to the small hospital's limited resources, the ultrasound techs had already gone home for the night. So Anna and Trish were left to talk amongst themselves while they waited for the on-call tech to respond to her emergency page.

"Should be here momentarily," Anna said. "They said she only lived about ten minutes away."

"It's been eighteen minutes. I'm counting."

Right on cue, the ultrasound tech bustled in, wearing maroon scrubs and a harried expression.

"Hey." Trish raised one hand off the bed. "Sorry to drag you in after hours." She sounded meek; totally unlike the bully in the baking aisle.

"No problem. Sorry to take so long getting here, but the roads are getting a little dicey with all this freezing rain." The tech took a seat and switched on the monitor. "Ready when you are."

Trish tucked in the paper sheet around her hips and yanked up the hem of her flimsy cotton gown, exposing a bare, pale strip of belly. "I'm ready."

The tech squirted a dollop of clear gel onto Trish's abdomen, then produced the ultrasound wand and got to work. "Okay, lie still and try to relax."

A few faint bursts of static crackled through the silence. Then they heard the unmistakable pulse of a heartbeat. Trish's and Anna's gazes locked.

"Well, from what I can see, your little guy looks fine," the tech announced after a few minutes. "There's the heartbeat. He's moving, he's breathing. Look, he's sucking his thumb."

"Hold on." Trish lifted her head off the pillow and peered at the fuzzy image on the screen. "It's a he?"

"Mm-hmm." The tech nodded. "It definitely looks like a boy. Didn't they take a guess at your nuchal translucency screening?"

"I don't think I had that."

"Oh, well, they'll know for sure at your twenty-week ultrasound. I wouldn't paint the nursery blue just yet, but I'm hardly ever wrong."

Anna squinted at the blurry black-and-white blobs. "You can get all that from this? It looks like ... well, a bug."

"I told you so." Trish turned back to the tech. "So what's wrong? Why am I bleeding?"

"The OB will have to make the diagnosis," the tech said.

"Yeah, but hearing a heartbeat is good, right? Breathing is good. Thumb sucking's good."

"The doctor will be here shortly." The tech gathered up her notes and slipped out the door.

Trish let her head drop back down. "I'm starting to freak out."

"Don't freak out." Anna squeezed her hand. "I'm sure you'll both be fine."

"If everything were fine, she wouldn't be passing the buck and escaping as fast as she could."

"Don't think like that. We have to stay positive. Positive thoughts will yield positive results." Anna realized that she'd spoken these exact words to Jonas after every round of IVF, after every compulsory bout of preovulation sex, and look how that had turned out. But *this* time (and she always added that part, too) would be different.

"Ugh." Trish stuck out her tongue. "Don't you dare go Kumbaya on me now. I liked you better when you were ruthlessly sabotaging me."

"In that case," Anna said, "at least we know you're having a boy. Now you won't be able to steal my baby name."

"This whole thing is crazy." Trish rubbed her forehead. "I didn't exactly plan to get pregnant. When I saw those two blue lines on the test, I sat down on the bathroom floor and cried. I went to the drugstore and bought like eight different kinds of tests, hoping there'd been a mistake, but they all came back positive. Blue line, blue line, blue line—bam, bam, bam. Total sucker punch. I wasn't ready to be somebody's mom. I'm *still* not. There's a reason Mother Nature made pregnancy last nine months. That's how long I thought I'd need to come to grips with the reality of the situation. But if the Bug and I can make it through tonight, we can make it through anything." She glanced at Anna, then lowered her gaze. "Sorry. I probably shouldn't say any of this to you."

"Why not?"

"Because of your, you know, situation."

"Infertility?" Anna half smiled. "You can say it out loud; the truth doesn't offend me. How did you hear about that, anyway?"

"I didn't. But I knew something was up when Kris Doyle asked you to do the baby shower cake. The look on your face said it all."

"Well, you're right. My husband and I have been trying for years, and nothing." Anna settled back in her seat and fiddled with the buttons on her jacket. "The doctors can't find anything wrong with us. 'Unexplained infertility.' We don't get to know why we can't conceive; we just have to accept it."

"That sucks."

"Big-time."

"Yeah, but if you did get pregnant, you wouldn't curl up in the bathtub and cry." Trish started to shred the paper towel she'd used to wipe off the ultrasound gel. "Normal women don't cry when they find out they're pregnant."

"I've never been accused of being a normal woman," Anna said.

"You know what I mean. You'd be all misty-eyed and glowing. And your husband would probably tag along to every single doctor's appointment and both of you would team up to decorate the perfect nursery with organic everything from Pottery Barn Kids."

Anna raised one eyebrow. "You have some interesting ideas about my life."

"Well, you have the designer label education and the yuppie car, so I figured Pottery Barn is your natural habitat." Trish sounded more wistful than snide. "But I shouldn't rush to judgment; maybe you're more into Crate and Barrel?"

The door opened and a physician in blue scrubs walked in. She looked athletic and startlingly young, although the stethoscope around her neck added to her air of capability.

"Hi, I'm Dr. Lafosse." She offered her hand to Trish. "Sorry to keep you waiting. How are you feeling?"

Trish managed a weak smile. "I've been better."

The doctor scanned the medical chart. "Your baby looks good. Strong vitals, no sign of distress." She washed her hands at the sink, pulled on latex gloves, and settled herself on the stool at the foot of the bed. "May I?"

Anna flipped through a dog-eared celebrity tabloid while Dr. Lafosse performed a brief internal examination on Trish. After several long, silent minutes, the OB wheeled back the stool and jotted down some notes.

"Well, the bleeding seems to have subsided, which is an encouraging sign. Have you noticed any spotting over the last few days, or did this come on suddenly?"

"No spotting at all," Trish replied. "Everything was fine until an hour ago."

"Any abdominal pain? Back pain?"

"My back has been a little achy, but I chalked it up to dragging baking equipment around."

The doctor nodded and kept writing. "Any contractions?"

"I don't think so, but I've never been pregnant before, so I don't really know what they feel like."

"With any luck, you're going to find out in just a few more months."

The exam table shifted as Trish's body relaxed. "So I'm really going to be okay? And the baby, too?"

"I'm optimistic." The doctor nodded. "As far as I can tell, we're dealing with a Class One partial placental abruption. What that means, basically, is that a small section of the placenta separated from the uterus, you started bleeding and, in your case, a clot formed and stopped the bleeding. Although." Dr. Lafosse frowned down at the chart. "We don't usually see it this early in a pregnancy. How sure are you of your due date?"

"Not very. This baby is kind of a surprise."

"Well, don't worry; we'll figure it out." More rapid-fire note taking. "We're going to do some blood work and double-check the fetal measurements on the ultrasound."

"What made the placenta start to tear away?" Trish asked.

"I wish I had an answer for that, but honestly, most of the time there's no obvious cause," the doctor said. "There are a few factors that can elevate your risk: smoking, drug use, episodes of high blood pressure. But in the majority of cases, it's just a fluke."

"None of that applies to me," Trish said.

Anna held up her palm. "Wait. High blood pressure?"

"Yes." The doctor pushed back a section of hair that had started to come loose from her ponytail. "But we don't need to worry about that. Your friend shows no signs of preeclampsia—"

"She was kind of worked up right before she started bleeding. We were having an argument." Heat rushed into Anna's face. "This is my fault."

"Don't flatter yourself," Trish said. "I wasn't that worked up."

"You were yelling at me. You were ready to kick my ass."

"I can do that without breaking a sweat."

"Your placenta is messed up—you could have lost your baby—because I conned you into putting a typo on a cake." Anna buried her face in her hands. "I'm going to hell."

"If you're going to hell, then I'll see you there in the baking supply aisle. Jeez, Legacy, don't be so melodramatic. This had nothing to with anything that happened in the kitchen tonight."

But Anna knew the truth. "I'm bad baby karma."

"The Bug's still kicking," Trish pointed out. "You're good baby karma."

The doctor clicked her pen and reclaimed control of the conversation. "We're going to keep you here for a few more hours for observation and then you can go home," she told Trish. "But you're going to have to stay on bed rest."

Trish's forehead creased. "For how long?"

"Until you deliver the baby," Dr. Lafosse announced, then glanced down at her pager and rushed for the door.

"There's no way!" Trish cried. "I don't *do* bed rest! I can't lounge around eating bonbons and watching TV for the next four months. I have bills to pay. I have events I'm already contracted to cater."

"I'll do them," Anna volunteered.

"*No.*" Trish looked murderous. "No way, no how."

"It seems to me you don't have much of a choice."

"I'll figure out a way to bake in bed," Trish said. "We are not friends, and I'm not your charity case. Besides, I have my own special recipes and techniques for everything that I make."

Anna smiled sweetly. "Then you're going to have to give me very detailed instructions."

"Aha! See? You just want to steal my secrets!"

"And you say *I'm* melodramatic?"

Trish swiveled the upper half of her body until all Anna could see was the thick auburn waves at the back of her head. "I work alone and I like it that way."

"Well, you know what they say: A baby changes everything."

"*Security!*"

They both started laughing.

After a moment, Anna said, "If it makes you feel any better, I will admit that I do love going to Williams-Sonoma."

"Actually, it does." Trish released her death grip on the hospital sheet. "And if it makes you feel any better, I was lying when I said I had nothing to do with the missing mixer attachment. I totally took it to mess with you. I had it tucked inside my coat, and I put it back the next morning when I opened the drawer."

Anna leaned back and exhaled. "That's such a relief."

"It is?"

"Yeah, I was starting to worry I really was going insane."

"I didn't used to be like this," Trish said softly. "I used to be tough and confident and fearless."

Anna rested her palm on her flat stomach. "Me, too."

"And now look at us."

"Disgraceful," Anna agreed.

"So how do we stop acting this way?"

"I think we just did." Anna cleared her throat. "By the way, don't worry about the typo cake. I'll smooth things over with the college president."

"How?"

"I'm Legacy, remember? I have connections."

"Tell you what. I'll teach you how to make a proper brioche." Trish grinned. "Check it out. The Bug's bringing people together already."

"He's destined for greatness," Anna said. "If he can accomplish all this in utero, imagine what he'll be capable of in thirty years."

"My boy's gonna broker peace in the Middle East." Trish froze and sucked in her breath. "Oh. Except I should probably warn you, I did one more tiny little thing to screw you over. Sorry in advance."

Anna rubbed her temples. "Oh Lord, what now?"

"I may have taken a few artistic liberties with that china cake topper you had in the kitchen."

Anna's breath caught. "What kind of artistic liberties?"

"Let's just hope the bride's a Groucho Marx fan."

Chapter 24

"In literature, as in love, we are astonished at what is chosen by others."
—André Maurois

he florist dropped off yet another delivery for you." Anna peered through the half-open door to Cait's bedroom. "Lots of lilies this time. Really gorgeous."

Cait glanced up from the stack of pages in front of her, wrinkled her nose, and quoted, "'Lilies that fester smell far worse than weeds.'"

"Now, now. Let's not drag the Bard into this."

Cait popped a red grape into her mouth from the snack bowl next to her keyboard and chewed contemplatively before announcing, "One good thing about being single: It frees up a lot of time to write."

Anna leaned against the doorframe. "You're not even going to *talk* to him?"

"I have talked to him. I've begged and pleaded and nagged and cajoled, and he still won't tell me the truth about anything." Cait devoured the last remaining grape. "So fine. We're done."

"But he's calling you and texting you and sending you flowers. Surely that means something?"

"Yeah, it means he wants to keep having kinky sex in unusual places."

Anna shot forward and closed the door behind her. "Like how kinky are we talking here?"

"Let's just say I didn't know I had it in me."

"Good for you. You're maturing, you're embracing your sexuality, you're—okay, I have to ask, have you brought in third parties and/or livestock?"

"Anna!"

"What about whips and chains?"

"No." Cait mulled this over for a moment. "Although I'm intrigued by the accessory possibilities there. A dominatrix outfit would be the perfect excuse to buy black leather thigh-high stiletto boots."

"They'd go perfectly with your down parka."

"Exactly." She sighed. "But for now, it's back to my usual wellies and Uggs."

"That's such a shame. I've never seen this side of you: the brainiac bad girl. And you seemed, I don't know. Happy? Hopeful?"

"I may be hopeful, but I'm not delusional." Cait recounted Charles's latest shenanigans. "And I've known Charles for years. I loved him, or thought I did. But I'm starting to realize that I didn't know him at all. I spent an hour on the phone this

morning with the dean discussing how he's the Bernie Ma-
doff of Shayland College. So, with Gavin, who flat-out *admits*
that he's hiding things, I'm going to do myself a favor and
not get emotionally involved." *Or, at least, not any more than I al-*
ready am.

"But Professor Clayburn always seemed so forthright and
principled," Anna said. "You don't think there's any chance
there could be a good explanation for all his bizarre behavior?"

Cait shrugged with a nonchalance she didn't feel. "Anything's possible, I guess. But since he refuses to explain, I have
to err on the side of breaking up with him."

"But all these bouquets—"

"Let me ask you something. If Jonas sent you flowers
right now, would all be forgiven? He wouldn't have to say
anything or do anything to demonstrate his eternal devotion
other than cough up a few lilies?"

Anna paused. "I see your point. Well, if you need a break,
we're all in the kitchen trying to scrub down walls that have
accumulated twenty years of college kids' cooking."

Cait waited until she heard Anna's footsteps on the stairs,
then took off her reading glasses and put down the green pen
she'd been using to mark up the printout of her latest chapter. Her nerves were frayed and her concentration was shot,
all because of some stupid lilies. She had to admire Gavin's
persistence. A solid week of unreturned calls and emails
hadn't deterred him in the least. If anything, he'd ramped up
his relentless campaign to "woo" her. She was surprised he
hadn't sent over an antique bottle of laudanum yet.

Well. Such ardent wooing with such murky motives could
only lead to trouble. She'd read enough Jane Austen to know
that.

A rapid-fire litany of obscenities interrupted Cait's brooding. She hurried downstairs to find her housemates covered in sweat and smudges of white paint.

"I'm ready to go Caligula on this kitchen," Brooke said in response to Cait's questioning glance. "The walls are filthy. Even the primer won't stick. It's literally coming off in sheets. I need to wash this whole room down in trisodium phosphate and I don't have time to drive all the way out to the Home Depot in Glens Falls. I hate this house!"

"I'll run to the hardware store on Pine Street," Cait offered.

"No!" Brooke threw down her sponge. "I have my pride! I'm not about to give any more business to a man who—"

The phone rang, cutting off Brooke. Anna answered, did a lot of noncommittal mm-hmming, hung up, and announced, "That was the guy from the appliance store calling to say they're sending someone over tomorrow afternoon with the new oven and refrigerator. So we better be done painting before then. I'm afraid it comes down to a choice between pride and practicality."

"Don't worry," Cait assured Brooke. "Just give me a detailed list of what to buy. He'll never know you sent me. I'll wear sunglasses. I'll be totally incognito."

Brooke snatched up a paper and pen and started scribbling. The last thing Cait heard on her way out the front door was a howl of frustration and the now-familiar refrain:

"I hate this house!"

Here you go. All the trisodium phosphate a girl could ever want, plus trim brushes, rollers, and a metal paint tray for each of us." Twenty minutes later, Cait handed over a pair of bulky brown paper bags.

Brooke didn't even open the bags before asking, "So? Was Everett there?"

"Not unless Everett's a grizzled old pepaw," Cait said. "The guy behind the counter was about a hundred years old with eyebrows that could be trimmed into topiary. Not really your type."

"Hmph. Everett was probably in the back room with Gisele and the rest of his supermodel harem."

"Yes, that certainly is the most logical explanation." Cait broke off as she noticed Anna and Jamie whispering and nudging each other. "What's going on?"

Anna announced, "You have a gentleman caller."

"Who?" Cait's jaw dropped. *"Gavin?"*

"He showed up on our doorstep about two minutes after you left for the hardware store. He offered to help with the paint job, but we sent him upstairs to wait for you."

Adrenaline surged through her. "Upstairs? Upstairs as in my bedroom?"

Jamie nodded. "We had to send him up there so we could talk about him down here."

Cait raced down the hall and took the stairs two at a time. When she skidded into her room, she found Gavin seated on her desk chair. Her manuscript was literally right under his nose.

When he saw her, he held up her plaid boxer shorts. "You left these in my bedroom. I thought you'd want them back."

She froze in the doorway, paralyzed by equally powerful urges to charge forward and to whirl around and flee. "I do, thank you."

He nodded at the pages. "Is this the book you're working on?"

The sight of him glancing, however fleetingly, at her work sent her into a panic. But to her surprise, the moment of panic was followed by a rush of relief. "Yes," she said. "Did you read it?"

He looked insulted. "Of course not."

"Are you lying?"

"No." He stood up and started toward her. "I meant it when I said you can trust me. I don't lie, Cait."

"Neither do I, so let me tell you what I'm working on here." She widened her stance and looked him right in the eye. "It's a romance novel, Gavin. A juicy, steamy, historical romance with a kick-ass Victorian heroine and a rough-hewn Scot with a rap sheet as long as his kilt. There's lots of action and intrigue and love scenes that practically burn a hole through the page. And—hold on to your Hemingway—there's going to be a happy ending."

He sat back down. "I see."

"I, Caitlin Johnson, am a romance novelist." She put her hand on her hip, then added, "Well, I suppose more accurately, I'm an *aspiring* romance novelist. That's the truth. That's who I am. Judge away; I can take it."

"You seem a wee bit defensive."

"Maybe I am. But we can't all write Kafkaesque narratives and Joycean short stories."

He placed her boxer shorts on top of her desk and held out his hand to her. "Come with me."

"Where are we going?"

"You're going to boldly go where no Thurwell College English major has gone before."

$\mathcal{A}$ re you sure you want me to unlock this?" Gavin asked. "Because once the door is open, there's no turning back."

Cait eyed the padlocked door in the hallway with increasing trepidation. "With a lead-in like that, how can I say no?"

He jangled his key ring and glanced back at her. "I'm giving you fair warning. Not even my housekeeper's allowed in here. What you're about to see may disturb you. Viewer discretion is advised."

"Thanks for the legal disclaimer. Now open up."

"Just remember, you asked for it." He slid a key into the thick steel lock and twisted until the shackle released with a gentle snick. Then he stepped aside to grant her access. "Have at it."

Cait pushed open the door, and peered into a large, shadowy room that contained...a huge mess.

"I'm confused." She blinked as her vision adjusted to the dim light. The furniture consisted of a huge wooden desk that looked like it'd been swiped from the set of a 1950s Hollywood detective film, an equally massive wooden chair, a small refrigerator, a printer, and towering stacks of paper on every available surface. She stepped inside and studied the series of framed posters on the wall above the desk. The artwork featured sleek silver rocket modules and exploding stars. "What are we looking at?"

He hung back in the doorway. "My home office."

"Why are there giant pictures of spacecraft everywhere?" And then she recognized the image of a silver obelisk set against a black background. "Hey, that was on the cover of that book you had in your car on our first date. Remember?"

"Vividly." He walked over to a built-in bookshelf that had obviously once been a closet and produced a copy of the novel.

"*Prevnon's Pantheon.*" Cait studied the cover art and noted the author's name: G. C. Grayson. Was this going where she thought it was going? She glanced over at Gavin for confirmation, but he had turned away from her and was staring out the window into the backyard.

She took a closer look at the desktop: an open dictionary, a pack of red pencils, a bottle of correction fluid. "What are those for?"

"Proofreading my galleys."

"You're G. C. Grayson."

He nodded but didn't move from his post at the window.

So she crossed the room to the bookshelf and trailed her finger along the spines of the paperbacks, many of which were duplicates. The novels were neatly grouped by title and, presumably, publication date. "Wow, you've written a lot of books."

"Eight." He glanced at the piles of paper atop the printer. "I'm putting the finishing touches on nine and ten."

She studied the accolades printed under the book's title. "According to this, you're a bestseller. Why haven't I heard of you?"

When he finally turned to address her directly, his smile was subversive. "Perhaps because sci-fi isn't considered an essential part of the canon?"

She burst out laughing. "Oh please. I'm spending my days with a rough-hewn Scot. Don't 'canon' me." She struggled to reconcile this new revelation with all of her previous assumptions about him. "How long have you been writing sci-fi?"

"I've been writing it since I was in high school. Publishing for about ten years. I sold my first novel shortly after I started teaching here." He extracted another paperback from the bookshelf and handed it to her.

She pressed the two books between her palms. "Why G. C. Grayson?"

"Grayson was my mom's maiden name. Publishing under a pseudonym has a lot of advantages, namely preventing any crossover between my academic identity and my author identity. You know, like in *Ghostbusters*: 'Don't cross the streams.'"

"But what about that collection of short stories?"

He shrugged. "A professor's gotta do what a professor's gotta do."

"You were young, you needed the money?" she teased.

"I needed *tenure*," he corrected. "My royalties from that short story collection couldn't buy us lunch at McDonald's."

She leaned back against the shelf and started to piece things together. "So all those FedEx packages are from your publisher?"

"Yep. I have a new series coming out this summer, back-to-back in June and July. Between teaching and writing, deadlines have gotten tight."

"Which is why you have to bribe your FedEx guy to come pick stuff up in the middle of the night?"

"Simon's a trooper. He always makes sure the manuscripts are back in Manhattan by noon the next day, and all it costs me is a hundred-dollar tip and my dignity."

"That does explain a lot." She raised her index finger. "Except for one thing: Who's Yvette?"

His grin broadened. "My literary agent."

"Is named Yvette? And sounds like Kathleen Turner?"

He nodded. "And negotiates a contract like a piranha in pearl earrings."

"And you're *sure* this is the story you want to stick to?"

"You can Google her right now." He gestured to the computer.

She ran her hands through her hair. "This is a lot to process."

"Take your time. I'm sure you'll have more questions."

"Just one for the moment." She knew it was inappropriate, but the aspiring author in her had to ask: "Is there any chance Yvette might be interested in signing a fresh and very steamy new romance novelist?"

He laughed. "First, finish writing your book. Then we'll talk agents."

"Finish the book?" She pouted. "You're no fun."

"Oh, I beg to differ. I'll be happy to give you a personal demonstration." He moved in for a kiss, but she held him at bay.

"Not so fast. You had to mention McDonald's and now I'm jonesing for fries. Let's go, Grayson." She tugged him back toward the hall. "My treat. We wouldn't want you overdrawing your royalty account."

"What?" He seemed confused for a moment. "Oh, you mean the short story collection. Yeah, that was art for art's sake." He indicated the rows of paperbacks. "These, on the other hand, paid for my cabin on Amelia Island."

"Where's that?"

"Off the coast of Florida."

"You have a house in Florida? Really?" Cait zipped up her coat with great purpose. "Screw lunch at McDonald's. Let's hop on a plane and go have a margarita on the beach. Do you have a private jet, too?"

"Whoa, there. I'm not J. K. Rowling."

"No, you're the dodgy and elusive G. C. Grayson, which is much more intriguing. Speaking of which, may I please read these?" She lifted the books in her hand. "I'm wild with curiosity."

"And I'm dying to read about your kick-ass heroine and her torrid adventures." He brushed his lips over hers in a whisper of a kiss. Then he stepped back and offered a handshake along with his most intimate proposition yet:

"I'll show you mine if you show me yours."

Chapter 25

"Authors and actors and artists and such
Never know nothing, and never know much."
—Dorothy Parker, "Bohemia"

"Hey, there, little lady. Which way to the weight room?"

Brooke glanced up from the paint cans stacked in a neat pyramid in the foyer of Paradise Found and threw Jamie a puzzled smile. "What are you talking about?"

"Your biceps." Jamie had draped herself across the brand-new living room sofa, which was still encased in thick swaths of plastic packaging. "You look like you could twist a crowbar into a pretzel."

Brooke began to unstack the cans, searching for the ceiling paint. "Well, who needs the gym when you have an endless source of backbreaking manual labor right under your own roof?"

"Not for long. You're almost done, right?" Jamie reverted to wedding planner mode. "You have to be almost done. We have wedding guests checking in next weekend."

"It's purgatory; I'll never be done. But don't fret; the wiring, bathroom, and porch issues are finally squared away." Brooke ticked off her to-do list on her fingers. "Now I just have to repaint the bathrooms and contend with all the linens, the furniture, and of course, the dozens of frilly freaking throw pillows I just *had* to have."

"Somebody's bitter," Anna trilled from the top of the stairs. "What hath Home Depot wrought?"

Jamie grinned up at Anna, who had descended to the landing, and then resumed tormenting Brooke: "So I take it you're no longer planning to take up quilting and hand-stitch a bedspread for every guest room?"

"Who has time for quilting?" Brooke glanced out the window at the heavy gray clouds amassing above the tree line. The first snowfall of the season was forecast for tonight. "I'm going to be spending all my time shoveling the sidewalk and clearing ice off the roof. And then, when spring rolls around, the grass is going to start growing again. Along with the weeds and the bushes and the tree branches. The deer are devouring the dormant flower beds already. Who's going to do all the landscaping? I can't afford to hire a gardener."

"You'll be making more money by the end of the winter," Anna said in a tone of hope rather than certainty.

"Ha." Brooke finally located the paint she needed at the very bottom of the pile. "I've already burned through most of my inheritance just buying this place and trying to get it open for business. Come April, I'm going to be forced to embark on a long and wretchedly dysfunctional partnership with John Deere."

"Wait," Jamie said. "Don't you get massive allergy attacks in the spring?"

"*Yes!*" Brooke cried, wondering if she could claim Claritin as a tax deduction.

"Will you stop baiting her?" Anna admonished Jamie.

"Oh, relax. I'm going to help her paint as soon as I finish my pedicure." Jamie shook up a bottle of dark red nail polish and propped her bare feet on the coffee table in preparation.

Brooke gasped in horror. "No!"

Anna and Jamie both froze and stared at her with huge, startled eyes.

"No nail polish allowed in the living room," Brooke decreed. "And no feet on the coffee table."

"Are you kidding me? The couch is still covered in plastic."

Brooke didn't argue. She simply extended her hand and waited for Jamie to hand over the bottle.

"I thought you wanted to make people feel at home," Jamie grumbled as she relinquished the nail polish.

"Not 'people,' darling—strangers. I want to make this a warm and cozy haven for strangers passing through. Close friends, on the other hand, must adhere to my draconian set of house rules."

"All those paint fumes have finally driven you over the edge. Next thing we know, you'll be forbidding us from making s'mores in the fireplace."

Brooke shuddered. "Perish the thought. I just had the carpets cleaned. Oh, and as long as we're talking housekeeping,

I should give you fair warning that you're going to have to vacate your rooms before next weekend. I need every available bed for paying guests."

"We'll pay," Anna offered. "You can charge us double our usual weekly rate."

"Too late. I'm already booked up."

"Then where are we supposed to sleep?" Jamie asked.

"One of you can bunk in my room with me," Brooke said. "The other two have a choice: basement or attic. We can set up cots."

"Cots in the basement." Jamie shook her head. "That is so Dickensian."

"Dibs on Brooke's room," Anna said. "You and Cait will have to huddle up near the furnace with your coal-smudged cheeks and your bowls of gruel."

"Where is Cait, anyway?" Brooke asked. "I haven't seen her since yesterday."

"Me, neither." Jamie made a grab to reclaim her bottle of nail polish, but missed.

"You haven't heard?" Anna said. "Cait's in Florida. With Gavin."

Jamie did a double take. "What the hell?"

"That's exactly what I said. She told me she'd be back Monday and hung up before I could ask any more questions." Anna patted Jamie's platinum hair. "I'm sure she'll tell you all about it during your sleepover in the basement."

"I'm the wedding planner," Jamie crossed her arms under her substantial bosom. "No way am I bunking in the basement."

"Throw yourself on the mercy of the bride," Anna suggested. "Maybe she can hook you up with a guest room at the president's house."

"It's the least President Tait can do," Brooke agreed. "After all, you are coordinating the happiest day of his life." She broke off when she saw Jamie's lips go white. "What is that face about?"

Before Jamie could reply, Anna's Counting Crows ringtone blared through the room. Anna dug the phone out of her pocket, muttered, "Here we go again," and then answered with artificial cheeriness. "Hi, honey, how are you?...I thought you said you'd be staying there for at least another month....Oh really? What happened?"

Brooke started backing out of the room to allow Anna some privacy, but Anna stopped her with a stern look.

"Well, I can't go anywhere right now, because I've committed myself to an important long-term project." Anna remained outwardly blasé, but Brooke knew from experience that this was a warning sign. "I'm baking for two now....It's a long story, but I'll be here at least through the holidays.... We'll see. Maybe I can make it back to Albany for a day or two, but I'll have to check my schedule." She ended the call abruptly and put away the phone.

Jamie and Brooke waited. Anna ignored them.

Finally, Brooke couldn't stand it any longer. "Mr. Move-In Condition resurfaces?"

"His business trip was cut short," Anna said. "He's coming back to the States next week." She shrugged. "Nothing juicy."

"You know, it's okay to express an emotion now and then," Jamie said. "We won't hold it against you. Unless, of course, you get nail polish on the couch."

"What's to get emotional about?" Anna sat down on the sofa and tucked her feet underneath her. "The man expects me to drop everything and pick him up at the airport and make everything at home all cozy for him. He thinks we're going to just pick up where we left off, like nothing happened. First he wanted me to, quote, 'distract' myself from all the infertility insanity with my, quote, 'hobby,' which I did, and now he wants me to come trotting dutifully back home. Well. I don't think so."

"So what are you going to do?" Brooke asked.

"I'm going to keep baking and helping Trish and waiting for the Bug to be born safe and sound."

"No, I mean about Jonas."

Anna tapped her fingers on the cherry wood console table flanking the sofa. "Let him eat cake." She started sorting through the day's mail, which was strewn across the table, and plucked out a magazine. "Who is this for?"

"Me!" Brooke snatched up the periodical. "Oh goody, now I've got something to read in the bathtub tonight."

"Is this for real?" Jamie peered over the couch. "I can't believe it. Up is down and black is white. Brooke Asplind subscribes to *Popular Mechanics?*"

"So?" Brooke scanned the list of feature stories on the magazine's cover. "It's cheaper than paying full price at the bookstore. Don't look so shocked. I *am* a product of one of the finest liberal arts schools in the country, you know. So well rounded." She grabbed the gallon of ceiling paint and started back toward the hallway. "Time to get back to work. Oh, and Jame—got your tickets?"

"For what?"

Brooke pushed up her shirtsleeve, lifted the paint can, and flexed for all she was worth. "For the gun show, baby."

When the doorbell rang just before dinner, Brooke assumed the furniture warehouse deliverymen had arrived with the new bedroom sets. She took a final swipe at the ceiling with her paint roller and yelled, "I'll get it."

She didn't even glance in the hallway mirror before she opened the door, but she knew her face was covered in perspiration and paint, and the earbuds dangling around her neck were blasting Duran Duran. She was completely unprepared to come face-to-face with the hot guy from the hardware store.

Everett stood under the porch light, holding a red metal toolbox in one hand and what appeared to be a folded strap of blue leather in the other. He was bundled up in a green wool coat, and he looked rangy and handsome and acutely self-conscious. His thick, unruly hair had gotten slightly shaggy since she'd last seen him, and his broad shoulders were dusted with the flurry of snow starting to come down.

For a moment Brooke stood motionless with her hand clamped around the antique cut-crystal doorknob. Faint refrains of "Rio" drifted into the still night air.

"Hi." He wiped his feet on the welcome mat and cleared his throat. "I came to help you run your wiring."

"Oh." Brooke's breath emerged in wispy white puffs. A blast of Arctic wind chilled the sweat on her face and back. As her mp3 player segued from "Rio" to "Hungry Like the Wolf," she turned off the music and addressed him with a detached cordiality that would do Anna proud. "I must say, this is very unexpected."

"I know." He flinched at her tone but held his ground. "I'm sorry about what happened last time you were in the store."

"Don't give it a second thought." She kept the smile fixed on her lips, but her voice was now chillier than the falling snow. "It's fine."

"No, it's not." He reached out and braced one hand against the doorjamb. "I wanted to call you. I should have."

"Hmm." Brooke glanced away, determined to harden her heart and ignore the hopeful, pleading look in his eyes. "Well, I appreciate your making the trip over here to clear that up." She brushed her palms against the hem of her paint-spattered Thurwell T-shirt. "Now, if you'll excuse me."

"Wait. I know I'm late getting into the game here, and you have every right to be angry."

"I'm not angry, exactly." She sighed and let the door swing open another few inches. "Everett, what are you doing here? Why now?"

"I'm ready to make up for lost time. I want to help you with your wiring project."

She nodded toward his shiny metal toolbox. "Is that new?"

"This?" He ducked his head. "No, I've had it for years."

She noticed a price tag still stuck to the bottom corner of the metal container but didn't comment.

"Oh, I almost forgot." He handed her the folded strip of leather. "This is for you."

She accepted his offering with some misgivings, then unfolded it to discover a streamlined baby blue tool belt scaled to fit a woman's waist. "I never thought I'd use this word in reference to hardware accessories, but this is fabulous! I had no idea they made these."

"I special-ordered it." Perhaps it was a trick of the light on the porch, but it almost looked like Everett was *blushing* beneath his five o'clock shadow. "Most of the ones we stock in the store looked way too big for you."

"And the color!" She couldn't help gushing a little. "It's so girly. I love it!"

"I picked blue because it matches your eyes." No doubt about it—he was definitely blushing.

Brooke felt the last of her reserve melt away. "That is so *nice.*"

"Close the door!" Jamie hollered from somewhere down the hall. "It's freezing out there!"

"Won't you come in?" Brooke smoothed her hair and stepped back from the threshold. "I apologize, I'm not dressed for company."

"You look great. You also look like you're right in the middle of something, so I won't hold you up. Just set me up with the wiring cable and I'll take it from there."

"Well, actually, I've already finished replacing all the wiring. But the insurance inspector is coming back on Friday, and there are a bunch of last-minute projects I'm trying to jam in. If you could replace the old outlet in the powder room with a GFCI outlet, I'd be eternally grateful."

He paused. "You're finished with all the knob-and-tube wiring replacement already? That was quick."

"Yep. You get off easy with a GFCI."

"Great." He threw back his shoulders. "No problem."

"Oh, but I should warn you: Be careful not to tear the gasket. Some of the upstairs outlets gave me a devil of a time."

"Roger that. Watch out for the gaskets."

"Oh, and Everett, I know this is appallingly rude, but may I ask you a question?"

"Shoot."

She bit her bottom lip. "How old are you?"

The corners of his eyes crinkled when he smiled. "Twenty-eight."

"Well?" She waited. "Aren't you going to ask me the same question?"

He laughed. "Just give me your word that you're over twenty-one and I won't check your ID."

"Handsome *and* tactful. A devastating combination." She looked at him. He looked at her. "Isn't there anything you want to know about me?"

"I want to know everything about you. But first"—he took off his coat and hoisted up his toolbox—"I've got to make the acquaintance of your electrical system."

*D*o you smell that?" Anna put down her book on Civil War cooking and wrinkled her nose at Brooke. "Is something burning?"

Brooke sniffed, but all she could smell was paint fumes. "I told Jamie thousands of times not to smoke in the house. If she gets ash on my clean carpets—"

A high-pitched electronic wail drowned her out. The fire alarm. Brooke raced out of the kitchen, down the hall, and into the entryway, where she found Everett balanced on a rickety wooden chair and jabbing at the ceiling-mounted smoke detector.

"Sorry," he said after he turned off the alarm. "That was me."

"Oh! I had no idea you were already in the wall." Brooke glanced at the overhead light fixture in confusion. "Didn't you turn off the circuit breaker?"

He stepped down from the chair. "Yeah, I probably shoulda done that."

"It's a miracle you weren't electrocuted."

"Everything was going fine—I made it past the gasket with no problem—but then the duct tape I was using to mark the lead wire caught fire."

She blinked up at him. "Why were you using duct tape to mark the wire? Duct tape is flammable."

"Yeah, so I've learned." He hung his head and rocked back on his heels. "Forget it. I knew this was never going to work."

"What's never going to work?"

"This. Me. My total incompetence." He kicked the gleaming red toolbox with the back of his heel. "As I'm sure you've already figured out, I know nothing about wiring or renovation or any of that stuff. I barely know a Phillips screwdriver from a flathead."

Brooke furrowed her brow. "But you work at a hardware store."

"Which makes everything worse. I know what everything is for, in theory, but knowing and doing are two different things." He shoved his hands into his pockets. "It's my dad's store, and he and my mom begged me to help out for a few months while they dealt with his medical issues. I said fine because it wasn't like I was making any money doing free-lance photography, but then you walked in asking for Romex wire and drill bits." His voice broke low. "And then you kept coming back. For the first time, I actually enjoyed working at my dad's shop."

She brushed her hand against his. "I'm so sorry to hear about your father. Is he feeling better, I hope?"

"He'll be okay, we think. He's had a rough autumn; in and out of the hospital." His eyes bore testament to the strain of the last few weeks; he looked older somehow. "But his doctors are optimistic."

"Wait." She was still trying to process his earlier confession. "So you don't know the first thing about replacing a GFCI outlet?"

"I don't even know what GFCI stands for. If it can't be fixed with duct tape, I'm out. That's why I haven't called you. I was trying to buy time so I could learn about wiring." He extracted a do-it-yourself circuitry manual from his toolbox. Yellow Post-its protruded from the pages he'd bookmarked. "And this damn thing is useless."

Brooke was flabbergasted. "Why didn't you just tell me?"

"I wanted to impress you." He flushed and kicked the toolbox again. "Stupid, I know. But you can do everything. I didn't want to be the guy who does nothing."

"Don't say that," she admonished. "Just because you're not mechanically inclined doesn't mean you do nothing."

"Yeah, that's the other thing I have to tell you." He rubbed the back of his neck. "I got a job offer. For photography."

"That's wonderful! That's your dream job, isn't it?"

"It's only a six-month contract for now, with a small weekly news magazine."

She studied his expression. "I have the feeling there's a 'but' here."

He nodded. "The thing is, I have to move down to Manhattan. And if it goes well, I'll be relocating for good."

"Oh."

"So it's not really practical for us to start dating."

She knew this was the time to say something along the lines of *Let's just be good friends*, but all that came out was, "I see."

Then he took her off guard with a big, warm grin. "But then I realized neither one of us is practical at all. Look at us:

me finally getting the guts to try to make it as a photographer, you building a bed-and-breakfast out of a falling-down firetrap of a dorm."

"Excuse me?" She laughed. "The only fire we've ever had here is the one you just started. Watch yourself, or I'll have you cited for violating code."

"We both go after what we want, even if it means hard work and delayed gratification. So I'm thinking, we go out this weekend. See how it goes." He paused. "And, if it comes down to it, I can always come up on the weekends to see you. As Kierkegaard said, 'Adversity draws us together and produces beauty and harmony.'"

"Nice. That philosophy degree comes in handy."

"Oh yeah. The ladies love old Søren K. And who knows?" He winked. "Maybe it won't be an issue. Maybe we'll find out we're totally incompatible."

"Maybe. But it's not every day I meet a guy who'll give me the contractor rate."

"It's not every day I meet a beautiful girl who can school me in how to install a GCFI outlet," he countered.

"GFCI," Brooke corrected without thinking. "For 'ground fault circuit interrupter.'"

"See? I'm learning already."

As soon as Brooke said good night to Everett and returned to the kitchen, Anna and Jamie pounced.

"What happened?" Anna demanded. "Tell us everything! Did you make him grovel?"

"Did you kiss him?" Jamie asked. "With tongue or without?"

"We replaced an outlet together," Brooke said. "Nothing more, nothing less."

Anna pretended to swoon. "It's a renovation romance."

"Not yet," Brooke said. "But we're having an official pizza-and-painting date tomorrow night."

"A date!" Jamie clapped her hands together. "Did you ask him or did he ask you?"

Brooke beamed. "He asked me."

"What's up with this guy? I thought he blew you off, callously and without remorse," Anna said. "Now he's turning up at your doorstep asking you out?"

"He had his reasons." Brooke picked up her paint roller. "Some better than others, admittedly. But he's not callous. Quite the opposite."

Then Jamie noticed Brooke's newest accessory. "Hey, check you out; I didn't know they made tool belts in pastels. I like it. Very contractor chic."

"Everett special-ordered it for me." Brooke couldn't resist adding, "He says it matches my eyes."

She waited for Jamie to come back with a snarky retort, but Jamie surprised her by softening. "Aw. What a nice guy."

"Here's hoping you'll have many happy years reading *Popular Mechanics* together," Anna said. "Oh, and Jame, that reminds me—something came in the mail for you, too." She pressed a slim, cream-colored envelope into Jamie's hand. "Looks like it's from Arden's attorney."

Chapter
26

*"There is nothing that makes a man suspect much,
more than to know little."*
—Francis Bacon, *Essays*

rden and I were supposed to get married." Jeff
Thuesen sat across the table from Jamie. He
watched her with unnerving intensity, seemingly
oblivious to the pub's lunchtime bustle. Since he'd spent his
morning conducting job interviews on campus, he was all
buttoned up in a well-cut dark suit and a subtly patterned silk
tie. He and Arden had made a great-looking couple with their
dark hair and classic features and Park Avenue dress sense.
Today, his conservative formality had the effect of making
Jamie feel as though she were being interrogated by a high-
ranking government official. "She knew it and I knew it."

"Oh boy." Jamie ran her thumbnail along the dull edge of

her butter knife. She was wearing a suit, too, but hers was a shapeless black poly-blend atrocity she'd bought without trying on at a thrift store in North Hollywood. The jacket fit her in the bust but nowhere else. All the better, she figured, for blending into the background and letting the bride shine. On her way out the door, though, she'd broken down and accessorized with high-heeled patent leather Mary Jane pumps. Brooke had advised her to wear comfortable shoes to prevent bunions, but a girl had to draw the line somewhere. "I'm sorry you didn't get married, Jeff, but what does that have to do with me?"

"That's what I'm here to find out."

Jamie accepted the laminated menu their server offered, then put it aside without even glancing at the text. "Listen, I'm going to level with you: My goal is to be out that door in thirty minutes or less. I just found out this morning that the tearoom we booked in Saratoga is shut down due to water damage, so we had to move the bridesmaids' tea to the college president's house, and I have about eight billion last-minute details to attend to."

He inclined his head slightly. "Then I'll get right to the point. Why did Arden break up with me?"

"How on earth would I know?" She stopped fidgeting and gave him her full attention. "Wait. Arden didn't break up with you."

"Yeah, she did. Believe me, I was there."

She sat back in her chair. "You broke up with her. I know you did. We all know it."

Now Jeff looked even more confused than Jamie felt. "Is that what she told you?"

"Yeah." She tried to remember exactly what had transpired all those years ago. "I *think* so. I mean, she must have said...Look, all I know is, people don't spend days at a time sobbing in bed and blowing off exams if they're the ones doing the dumping. She was devastated. I never saw her so upset about anything before or since that breakup."

He took off his suit jacket and loosened the knot of his necktie. "At least that clears up one thing."

"What's that?"

"Why you and your infamous lit clique all despise me so much."

"We don't despise you." Jamie paused. "Okay, fine, we hate your guts. But can you blame us? You broke our best friend's heart." She braced her forearms on the table and leaned forward. "You must have."

He maintained eye contact. "I did not."

"Are you *sure?*"

"Why do you think I came to her memorial service?"

"I don't know. To be hateful?"

"I loved her," he said with such conviction that Jamie finally believed him. "I was planning to propose at the end of senior year. Then she dumped me right before spring break, and to this day, I don't know why. What I do know is that something happened between the two of you right around the time she decided she was done with me."

Jamie schooled her expression into a stony poker face.

After a minute or two, Jeff gave up on waiting her out and asked, "What happened to her? How sick was she, and for how long?"

"She never told you?"

"She never spoke to me again after she told me she didn't want to see me anymore."

Jamie tried to remain as clinical as possible. "Arden was sick for a long time. I don't understand all the medical intricacies, but Cait tried to break it down for us a few weeks after the funeral. Lupus can cause your blood to coagulate, so you always have to worry about clots forming. For the past five years, she kept telling us she was going to die of a stroke." Jamie examined her hands and picked at her cuticle. "But then, randomly, a piece of a blood clot in her leg broke off and went to her lungs instead of her brain, so technically, she died of a pulmonary embolism."

"What is that, exactly?"

Jamie took a slow, steadying breath. "I don't know."

"Was it painful?"

"I hope not. I try very hard not to think about it." This clinical routine was not working. "I can tell you this, though: She was very calm and reflective about the whole thing. She had a much better perspective than the rest of us did." She shook her head. "I'm explaining this wrong. It wasn't like she was a martyr, she just...She was still *funny*, you know? She was still absolutely herself. It was like dealing with all that pain and stress pared her down to the most essential kernel of herself. The five of us, the 'lit clique'"—Jamie grinned in spite of the tears stinging her eyes—"spent a week every summer at her family's lake house, and every summer we picked up right where we left off. The dynamic was always the same."

"She was something," Jeff said with a small, private smile.

"Yes, she was." Jamie swiped at her nose with the paper napkin. "She knew everything there was to know about me—the good, the bad, and the very, very ugly—and she loved me anyway."

Another long pause, and then Jeff cleared his throat. "Which brings us back to the incident of senior year."

"Everything brings me back to that 'incident' these days."

Jamie stared over his shoulder and addressed the beer sign on the far wall. "The short version is, I did something I should not have done and Arden covered for me."

"Any chance I can hear the long version?"

"Fine. I did *someone* I should not have done." She resumed picking at her cuticles. "Terrence Tait, if you must know."

He couldn't have looked more shocked if she'd jumped up on the table and started stripping. "*President* Tait?"

She kept talking in a clipped monotone. "I was stupid and pathetic when we got together, but after he broke up with me, I took stupid and pathetic to a whole new level. I wanted his wife to find out about us, so I snuck into his house and left a smoking gun, so to speak, right on the desk in his study: a pair of black panties with a note reading 'Come hither to Henley House.'"

Jeff's eyes bugged out. "Holy crap."

"And his wife did find them, right in the middle of a trustee reception, and apparently, you could hear the shrieking all the way across campus. I wouldn't know because I wasn't on campus that night; I was busy getting drunk right here in this very bar."

"President Tait got busted sleeping with a student and he got to keep his job?" Jeff's mouth hung open. Jamie could see the glint of gold fillings in his back molars.

"He did not get busted," she corrected. "He claimed that he was being harassed by a delusional student with a crush. So campus security was dispatched to Henley House to ask around, and I guess they started with Arden's room. She knew I'd been seeing someone on the sly. Of course, when she saw a copy of the note, she recognized my handwriting and put two and two together. She figured I'd lose my scholarship if anyone found out the truth, so she swore to the security guy that she'd done it. She took the blame and let herself be known amongst all the administrators as the unhinged coed who went *Fatal Attraction* on the president. And since she corroborated his claim that nothing ever happened between them, the president got to keep his job, but I know for a fact people are still whispering about it."

"You let her take the blame for all that?" Jeff looked appalled. "What kind of friend are you?"

"A *bad* friend. I know!" Jamie dropped her head into her hands. "Believe me, I get it."

"Why didn't you come forward? How did you live with yourself?"

"I didn't come forward because, when I finally sobered up and found out about all this, she physically restrained me. Disconnected the phone, blocked the doorway. She was shockingly strong for such a skinny girl."

Jeff was having none of this. "But she couldn't hold you hostage forever. Ultimately, it was your decision to take the easy way out."

"Ultimately, yes, it was," Jamie acknowledged. "First, I was a home-wrecking hussy, and then I was a coward. I let her talk me into it because I was so afraid and she was so vehement. Arden said her family had given so much money to the school over the years that she could get away with anything because her last name was Henley, and you know what? She was right. At the time, I thought she was being noble."

"And now?"

Jamie sat back in her chair. "Now I think she was being even more self-destructive than I was."

"But Arden wasn't self-destructive at all," Jeff protested. "Not the Arden I knew. Why would she act like that?"

"I've spent a lot of time thinking about this," Jamie

replied. "And I'll never know for sure, but maybe it was because of the lupus diagnosis. She didn't tell us about it until she was halfway through law school, but she'd known for a while by then. Maybe she found out she was sick right around the time of the black-panty debacle. And then you broke up with her, and the downward spiral continued."

"For the last time, I didn't break up with her."

"So you say. But if you didn't, then this whole thing makes no sense. I thought you'd heard the gossip and dumped her because you thought she was, you know, trying to get with President Tait."

"I never heard any gossip, but even if I had, I wouldn't have believed it. Arden and President Tait?" He scoffed. "Give me a break."

Jamie's world shifted ever so slightly on its axis. "So it wasn't my fault that you two broke up?"

"Not as far as I know. And why does it really matter who's at fault at this point? It's been ten years."

"I'll tell you why." Jamie hesitated out of loyalty to Arden, but then decided that Jeff had earned her version of the truth by revealing his. "You got over her eventually, right? You've had other girlfriends since we graduated college?"

"Of course."

"Not Arden. She never went out with another guy after that."

He looked skeptical. "In ten years?"

"Not a single date. She never got over you, and it's my fault. I ruined her one shot at romantic happiness because I couldn't keep my underwear to myself."

"But you didn't ruin anything," Jeff said. "Don't you get it? It wasn't me that she never got over. It was the diagnosis."

Jamie shrugged. "We'll never know for sure."

"Knock it off. You just said she wasn't a martyr, so you don't get to be one, either."

"Um, ouch."

"When she broke up with me, she wouldn't say why. She just said, 'I can't.' I still remember that. And I asked what she meant, and she never gave me a straight answer. She said, 'I don't want you to waste your time.'" One corner of his mouth tugged up in a rueful smile. "The irony is, I can't even tell you how much time I wasted, wondering what I did and why things didn't work out. I got over it, but I always wondered. That's why I braved the wrath and showed up at the memorial service. I needed to see her through to the end. And now I know. It wasn't me, and it wasn't another guy. It certainly wasn't you."

"Closure." Jamie nodded. "It's supposed to help you heal. And yet, I still feel like crap."

"Go ahead and feel guilty for whatever else you want, but don't feel guilty about me and Arden." Jeff relaxed and perused the menu. "She and I had our own thing. Nothing you did could have changed that."

Jamie chugged the contents of her glass and pushed back from the table. "Well, thanks for the ice water. I'd love to stay and catch up, but I've got to run."

"I thought you had thirty minutes for lunch?"

She extracted the cream-colored envelope from her handbag. "I just remembered I have to make a quick stop on the way."

"I'd like to make a deposit, please." Jamie handed the reissued check from Arden's lawyer to the bank teller.

The teller glanced down at the deposit slip Jamie had

filled out. (She had listed Henley House as her permanent residence, because, well, what else was she going to put?) "Do you have an account with us, Ms. Burton?"

"I do. Well, I did, anyway. At one of your branches in Los Angeles."

Then the teller noticed the amount of the check and her whole demeanor changed. "Step right this way, please. One of our managers will be happy to complete all the necessary paperwork for you."

"Should I come back later? I'm kind of in a hurry."

"Don't worry, Ms. Burton. We pride ourselves on expediting these administrative matters for our preferred customers."

Ten minutes later, Jamie exited the bank with a deposit receipt in one hand and a pack of cigarettes in the other. She paused in the middle of the parking lot, shivering in her thin suit jacket and trying to avoid getting rock salt stains on her shoes. She flicked open her chrome lighter and rolled the notched metal spark wheel back and forth with her thumb, debating.

"Hey, any chance I can bum a smoke?" A college student sporting a battered backpack and a pierced eyebrow loped up to her.

Jamie shocked herself by handing over the whole pack. "Have 'em all."

The kid's eyes lit up like he'd just won the lottery. "Are you serious? Thanks, ma'am!" He seized the pack and strode away, obviously afraid she'd come to her senses and change her mind.

"Don't thank me," she called after him. "Those things'll kill you." She glanced down at her boxy black blazer and knee-length skirt. "And who the hell are you calling 'ma'am'?"

———

Ninety minutes into the bridesmaids' tea, Mrs. Richmond was clearly having the time of her life.

Maureen made the rounds of the president's parlor, fluffing her hair and glad-handing guests and doling out professionally gift-wrapped boxes to the bridesmaids.

"Thank you so much for coming all this way. Are you having a good time? Can I get you anything?" She would fawn over each new arrival for a few moments and then, without fail, turn the topic of conversation to her daughter. "Doesn't Sarah look beautiful? And just wait until you see her in her wedding gown. I broke down in tears at the final fitting last week. I'm so happy for her and Terry and I know her father would be, too."

Jamie lost track of Sarah soon after the guests started trickling in, but when she ran back to the kitchen to grab some extra spoons, she found the bride holed up in the pantry with a trembling lower lip and a mascara-smudged tissue.

"Uh-oh. What's the matter?" Jamie put her arm around Sarah. "Whatever the problem, I promise I'll fix it."

Sarah walked over to the doorway and nodded out toward the crowd in the parlor. "That necklace."

"What necklace?"

"On that woman."

Jamie followed Sarah's gaze toward the president's longtime administrative assistant, Linda. "What about it?"

"It's…"

Jamie waited for her to elaborate, but Sarah took one last swipe at her eyes with the tissue and made a beeline for the slim, stylish older woman. Jamie stumbled as her shoe heel caught between the wide, weathered planks of the hardwood floor. "Wait up. I'm right behind you."

"Hi." Sarah glided up to Linda with a radiant smile and offered her right hand. "I'm Sarah Richmond. I'm—"

"I know exactly who you are, dear. We've been introduced, don't you remember?" Linda clasped her hand over Sarah's and squeezed. "The alumni mixer in Manhattan last May. I'm Linda."

"Of course! Linda!" Sarah smote herself on the forehead. "I apologize. I've got a mind like a sieve these days, what with—"

"All the wedding activities. I completely understand. And you're just glowing, dear. You'll be such a beautiful bride."

Something about the way Linda kept repeating the word "dear" set off Jamie's infallible drama detector.

"Thank you." Sarah was still fixated on the pendant adorning the other woman's throat: a tiny gold apple with an underlayer of white gold peeking through where a "bite" had been taken out. It was simultaneously subtle and sassy. "You know, I was just telling my wedding planner here how much I love your necklace."

Linda raised her hand to her throat and preened. "How kind. I call it my Garden of Eden necklace."

"It's very unusual," Sarah said with just a hint of an edge in her voice.

"Isn't it?"

"Would you mind if I asked where you got it?"

"Oh, it was a Christmas gift." Linda held her smile for one more beat, then lowered the boom. "From Terry."

"Terry." Sarah swallowed so hard, Jamie could hear it over the clinking dishware and female chatter. "*My* Terry?"

"Yes, Terry—pardon me, President Tait—does have excellent taste, doesn't he?"

Sarah stared at her.

"He chose *you*, after all."

"Oookay. You'll have to excuse us, Linda." Jamie stepped in between the two women like a ref at a boxing match. "The lovely bride-to-be needs a drink."

"Forget a drink," Sarah said as Jamie hauled her bodily across the room toward the catering table. "What I need is a cigarette."

"Can't help you there."

"Don't hold out on me! I know you smoke."

"Smoked. Past tense. Sorry." Jamie snapped her fingers at Anna. "Crumpets and Chardonnay, stat."

Anna took her time walking over with a tray of doily-framed pastries. To Jamie, she said, "If you ever snap your fingers at me again, you'll have a hook where your hand used to be." To the bride, "May I offer you a petit four?"

The tiny cake was coated in baby blue fondant and topped with a spun sugar rendering of a diamond ring. "This is beautiful." Sarah took a bite and stopped freaking out long enough to tell Anna, "I never imagined I could love cake more than I already did, but you've proved me wrong."

Anna brushed this off. "Thank you, but I can't take the credit. Trish actually did most of the work."

"I thought she was on bed rest," Jamie said.

"She is," Anna said. "She lies on her couch and barks orders to me in the kitchen. We set up a card table next to the couch so she can do the icing designs. She says it's a great upper-body workout, but I know it's because she considers my piping abilities substandard." Anna got a load of Sarah's expression, shot a questioning look at Jamie, and then promptly excused herself to go check on something in the kitchen.

Jamie hustled Sarah upstairs into an empty bathroom and returned two minutes later with a suit jacket and a cigarette she'd cadged from one of the waiters.

"Menthol," she said with a shudder. "Sorry, but it's the best I could do on short notice." She cracked open the window for ventilation, then handed Sarah the jacket. "Bundle up. We don't want you sneezing and sniffling when you walk the aisle. Now tell me: What am I missing here?"

Sarah lit up the cigarette and took a long drag. "That necklace with the gold apple? Terry gave me the exact same thing two months after we started dating."

"Well, maybe he bought a few of them at once," Jamie suggested. "You know, like a go-to gift. A lot of guys hate picking out jewelry."

"Even if that's the case, don't you think jewelry is an inappropriate present for your secretary? I mean, a gift *certificate* to a jeweler, I could see, maybe, but—" Sarah took another drag. "And did you see her smug little smile? She hates me."

"Well, I'll admit she was a bit catty, but—"

"Do you think he slept with her?"

Jamie's face felt hot despite the frigid draft seeping in through the open window. "I have no idea."

Sarah turned to her with beseeching eyes. "If he did, do you think it was before or after I started seeing him?"

Jamie wrapped her shapeless black jacket tighter around her waist. "You should probably talk to him about all this."

"He was single for a long time after he got divorced," Sarah said. "He had almost ten years to sow his wild oats.

I'm sure he got it all out of his system. He must have, if he asked me to marry him."

"One would assume."

Sarah kept looking up at her, desperate for direction and approval. "Do you think I'm making a mistake?"

Jamie glanced out the window at the frost-encrusted garden where she'd help run the anniversary event just a few weeks ago. The flowers and lush green foliage had disappeared along with the warm weather, leaving only prickly shrubs and the bare wooden frame of the trellis. "It doesn't matter what I think."

"Do you think he's too old for me?"

"Sarah. I cannot have this conversation with you."

"You can and you will!" The bride was on the verge of tears again, so this came out as more of a plea than a command. "You're the one who opened this whole can of worms with your big morality lecture at the bar last weekend."

"And you told me in no uncertain terms to mind my own business," Jamie reminded her. "The only advice I can give you is this: If you're not completely, one hundred percent sure, don't do it. In my experience, you never regret *not* getting married to the wrong guy."

Sarah ashed her cigarette into an empty porcelain soap dish. "So you're telling me to call it off."

"No, I am not." Jamie reached out and squeezed Sarah's shoulder. "What I am telling you is that, if you do want to bail, this is the time. Just say the word and I'll take care of everything. I'm a full-service wedding planner, escape clause included."

"No, forget it. That's crazy. I can't call it off." Sarah wolfed down a petit four from the stash she had smuggled up from the reception. "I'm just delusional from all that dieting to fit into my Vera Wang." She reached for another pastry, then stopped herself. "Everybody gets cold feet, right?"

Jamie opened her mouth, but Sarah didn't give her a chance to comment.

"It's too late, anyway." The bride-to-be flushed the remains of her cigarette down the toilet, reapplied her lipstick, and headed back down the hallway, where they could hear Maureen's laughter drifting up from the foyer. "I made a commitment and I'm sticking to it. We'll work it out. We'll be fine. Everything's going to be perfect."

*"How it is I know not; but there is no place like a bed for
confidential disclosures between friends."*
—Herman Melville, *Moby-Dick*

J onas, I don't have time to talk. The wedding is tomorrow and I'm having a cake crisis. If you're that
desperate to see me, you'll have to come up here."
Anna clicked off her cell phone, carefully navigated the icy
path leading up to a weathered little cabin on the wooded
outskirts of town, and rang Trish's doorbell.

"Come in!" Trish called from inside.

Anna eased back the storm door, dredged her pockets for
the house key Trish had given her, and unlocked the dead
bolt.

What Trish's house lacked in square footage, it more than
made up for in rustic charm. The floor plan was open, with

a combination eating/cooking/living area and double doors that partitioned off the single bedroom. Firewood crackled and popped in the woodstove in the corner of the den. Trish was camped out on a saggy green sofa smack-dab in the middle of everything. Her russet hair hung limply over her face and her fingers were tapping away at the keyboard of a laptop. She barely looked up from the computer when Anna walked in.

"Well, it's about time you showed up. I was beginning to wonder if you'd fallen into the mixer at Pranza."

"You wish. I've got the cake in the car, along with a big tub of icing and enough gumpaste to choke a horse. Nice pajamas, by the way. You've been here alone all day?"

"No, my cousin came by with groceries this morning. And then my mom came by for lunch and a lecture on how I'm gaining too much weight, and I'm not doing enough to prevent stretch marks, and I'm going to regret getting that tattoo on my lower back when my child is old enough to realize that Mommy has a 'tramp stamp.'" Trish gritted her teeth. "Good times."

"What about your boyfriend? When do I finally get to meet this mystery man?"

Trish stopped typing. "I don't know. I don't even know when *I'm* going to see him again." Something in her tone warned Anna not to press, so Anna switched gears.

"How are you feeling?"

"Physically? Fine. Mentally? Eh. It turns out I'm further along than I thought, so they pushed up my due date. And bed rest is the opposite of restful. I hate not showering and wondering if every little flutter I feel is the rest of my placenta ripping away from my uterus." When Trish finally looked up, her expression was frazzled and fearful. "And I read all those pregnancy books you gave me."

"They upset you?"

"No, no, they were great. But then I had some follow-up questions so I went online, and now I'm afraid to wear nail polish, I'm afraid to eat anything that comes out of a can, I'm afraid to eat a damn doughnut."

Anna cocked her head. "Why?"

"Phthalates, heavy metals, trans fats." Trish's lower lip trembled. "Trans fats cross the placenta, you know. It's a scientific fact."

"All right, that's enough. You are officially banned from the Internet until further notice." Anna stepped forward and closed the laptop. "Pregnancy hormones and search engines do not mix."

"You can't ban me from the Internet; I need my bed rest support chat room! Plus, I need to shop online for all the crap I thought I'd be buying at the mall during the third trimester."

"Like what? Make a list."

"I have to figure out how to pick the safest car seat and baby bottles that won't poison my kid with Bisphenol A." Trish was practically hyperventilating now. "And you're not allowed to use crib bumpers anymore, because they're a suffocation hazard. And should I be blasting Mozart into my womb every morning? And should I be mainlining omega-3 or avoiding fish products altogether?"

"Scoot over." Anna made room for herself on the sofa and sat down.

"Before last week, I didn't worry about anything," Trish continued. "Now I spend all day, every day worrying about everything. And then I worry that I'm worrying too much, because stress isn't good for the baby."

"Whoa. Slow down." Anna took a deep, exaggerated breath and waited for Trish to do the same. "I promise I will help you hunt down the safest baby products on the planet. But you have to cut yourself some slack. The occasional doughnut isn't going to make the Bug grow horns and a tail."

"Says the chick who wouldn't even let me have an ibuprofen last month."

"You need to go take a shower and wash your hair. You'll feel much better, I promise."

Trish shook her head and sniffled. "My doctor says I'm not supposed to be on my feet for more than ten minutes at a time."

"So use combination shampoo and conditioner. I'll time you." Anna crossed the room to the kitchenette and rummaged through the cabinets. "And while you're in there, I'll make you some hot water and lemon. Surely you can't freak out about that."

"Actually, I've been reading some things about the local water supply," Trish said, her expression solemn. "I think I need to install a reverse-osmosis filter ASAP."

Anna rolled her eyes and pointed toward the bathroom. "Move."

"God, you're bossy." But Trish started to push herself off the sofa. "What's on our agenda today, anyway?"

"We have to finish the wedding cake this afternoon. Then we can go over the ingredient list for the next few weeks so I can special-order the more exotic stuff. And if you promise to stop obsessing, I'll send my housemate over on Monday to install a water filter."

"Which one?"

"The one who works in the alumni affairs office at the college. You've probably seen her around town. Brooke Asplind?"

Trish looked incredulous. "That tiny blonde who looks like a pageant contestant turned Sunday school teacher?"

Anna grinned. "The very same."

"You have the best housemates ever."

"Amen."

While Trish showered, Anna went back outside to retrieve the wedding-cake-in-progress from the back of her station wagon. She'd already baked and assembled the layers and covered the tiers in white fondant, but the finishing touches were trickier than she'd anticipated. It was relatively easy to pipe words and designs; it was exponentially more challenging to sculpt three-dimensional flowers and berries out of gumpaste.

She dragged the small, sturdy kitchen table over to the couch and set up the cake, along with an assortment of pastry bags and decorating tools. When Trish emerged from the bathroom in precisely ten minutes' time, Anna stepped back across the room to see if all the design elements came together. "Do the rosettes look a little wonky to you?"

"Wonky isn't the word." Trish heaved herself back down into the sofa cushions and finished toweling off her hair. "A drunken monkey could do better."

"Gee, thanks. Do you feel better now that you've showered?"

"Yeah," Trish admitted with a grudging smile. "Did you save any samples of the actual cake?"

"Right here." Anna pointed to a small bakery box at the edge of the table. "White cake with orange-cranberry filling. Very Thanksgiving-y."

Trish helped herself to a slice and took a tiny bite. She paused, took another little bite, then crammed the rest into her mouth.

"You don't have to tell me it's delicious," Anna said. "I already know."

"The inside's delicious," Trish mumbled through a mouthful of crumbs. "But these rosettes are a disaster." She finished chewing. "I'll fix them for you on one condition: You have to tell me how you made that Coca-Cola cake for Belinda Elquest's cocktail party."

"You heard about that?"

"Everyone heard about that. It's the talk of the freaking town."

"Done." They shook on it.

Trish grabbed a pastry bag and flexed her fingers like a pianist preparing to perform. "Sit back and take notes, Legacy. School is in session."

$\mathcal{A}$nna and Trish toiled over the cake for hours, pausing only for bathroom breaks and the high-protein snacks Anna insisted Trish eat. Dusk fell, then darkness, and the pair of bakers established a silent, cooperative rhythm. When the doorbell chimed, both of them startled and Trish mangled the tiny leaf she'd been adding to a rosebud on the cake's top tier.

Anna leapt up and headed for the entryway. "I'll get it." Her hands and back ached from the hours of detail work, and for once she was thankful she wasn't pregnant—she was free to pop ibuprofen at will.

"Whoever it is, tell them to get lost," Trish said.

Anna yanked open the door, not bothering to disguise her irritation.

"Oh good," said Jonas. "You're here." He'd lost a bit of weight since she'd last seen him, and if the dark smudges under his eyes were any indication, he was still jet-lagged from the flight home.

Part of Anna wanted to slam the door, throw the dead bolt, and go back to squabbling with Trish over mundane matters like rosette placement and the ideal sugar-to-liquid ratio in icing.

The rest of her wanted to throw her arms around her husband and never let go.

Finally, she composed herself sufficiently to ask, "What are you doing here?"

"You said if I wanted to see you, I'd have to make the trip, so here I am." He exuded a calming, casual confidence in hiking boots and jeans. "I went to Henley House, and Brooke and Cait told me you were still working on the wedding cake. So I drove down to that restaurant on Pine Street and asked around. The owner said you might be here."

"Oh." She started toward him, then stopped herself.

He shifted his weight. "Any chance I can come in?"

"Yes, of course." She stepped back and held the door for him. "Trish, this is my husband. Jonas, this is Trish."

He glanced back at Anna. "*The* Trish?"

"The one and only." Trish let out a diabolical little laugh. "Her archenemy."

Anna couldn't stop staring at Jonas. He looked so comforting and familiar, but something about him was different. Something had shifted over the last few weeks. "So what was so pressing that you braved the Friday afternoon Northway traffic?"

"This." He handed Anna a cordovan leather folder.

She ran her fingers over the smooth, flat surface. "What am I looking at?"

"It's our adoption portfolio."

Her head jerked up. "I told you, Jonas, I'm not—"

"Just open it."

She did, and inside she found several photo collages mounted on laminated binder pages. The first page featured her in her wedding gown, beaming up at Jonas as the minister pronounced them husband and wife. The next few pages were devoted to their home in Albany: the well-equipped kitchen, the cozy family room, and the grassy, sloping backyard that abutted a nature preserve. There was a snapshot of the local elementary school with the sign in front of the flagpole: "A National 'Excelling' School!" Finally, there were photos of the empty upstairs guest room that Anna and Jonas had designated as the future nursery, accompanied by a page torn out of a catalog featuring the crib, glider chair, and changing table Anna had selected during one of the interminable waits at a gynecologist's office.

"That's a cute crib." Trish leaned in for closer inspection. "And I like the upholstery on that chair. What catalog is this from?" She threw up her hand. "Wait. Don't tell me. Pottery Barn?"

"Pottery Barn Kids," Anna admitted.

"I *knew* it!" They both started laughing.

There were pictures of Jonas and Anna camping, gathered with friends at holiday dinners, wearing matching Yankee caps at the ballpark. Anna was struck by how much younger and how much happier they looked in these photos, most of which had been taken before they'd been on the receiving end of the infertility diagnosis.

She glanced up at Jonas. "This must have taken hours. When did you put it together?"

"Keep going," was all he said. "There's more."

She turned the page to find several shots of her vintage cookbooks and his Frisbee collection. And then came the cake photos. Anna had lost track of how many birthday cakes she'd created over the years for nieces and nephews and neighbors and godchildren, but Jonas had documented them all: a trio of goldfish in an aquarium, a canary singing in a cage, a colorful merry-go-round, a gold and silver floor harp, an orange striped tabby cat, the Eiffel Tower, steam engines, and spaceships.

"Holy crap," Trish marveled. "You made all of those?"

"Yep," Anna said with a mixture of pride and yearning. "Carved them myself, did all the decorating freehand."

"Those are unreal. Forget weddings; kids' cakes are your thing."

Anna kept flipping until she arrived at the last page, which featured a grainy photo of a shepherd-mix puppy with huge paws and floppy ears.

Jonas pulled up a chair, sat down next to her, and took both her hands in his. "I know you're not ready for all this yet. Believe me, I heard you loud and clear. But I called an adoption lawyer this week, just to get some information. I refuse to sit around doing nothing. Not when we're, you know, apart."

"A man of action." Trish nodded at Anna. "I approve."

"The attorney said we should put together a portfolio to

show to potential birth moms," Jonas continued. "Something that shows who we are as individuals, as a couple, and as a family."

"It's—" All of Anna's objections and questions lodged in her throat.

"Perfect," Trish finished for her. "I think my cold, Grinchy heart just grew a few sizes."

"Except for one thing," Anna said. "What's with the dog?"

"I was thinking we should get one," Jonas said. "I grew up with a dog, and I want my kids to have one, too."

"It's true," Trish agreed. "Every kid should have a dog."

Anna shot her a look. "I notice *you* don't have one."

"I'll put that on my to-do list, right after giving birth and getting back on my feet for more than ten minutes at a time."

Anna flipped through the pages again, dazed. "I can't believe you did this, Jonas."

"It's nothing compared to everything you've done." His voice deepened. "You've spent years tracking down specialists and making the appointments and taking the drugs and charting your ovulation and everything. And I shut down and let you do the heavy lifting because I didn't want to deal." He cupped her cheek. "I made a decision on the flight home from Brussels. I'm going to stop thinking about what I can't do and start focusing on what I can. This is the first step. We'll take the next one when you're ready."

She closed her eyes and pressed the leather folder to her chest. "It's time for me to concede defeat."

"It's not a battle," Jonas said.

But in a way, it was. Anna let go of the dream she'd been clinging to for so long and surrendered to the fact that she was not going to be that one-in-a-million who defied all the odds. She would not prevail through sheer force of will.

She and Jonas were never going to conceive a child.

This acknowledgment brought with it a bittersweet rush of relief. She could stop hoping for the impossible and finally start grieving the loss of a miracle that was never going to occur.

But through her grief, she might open herself up to new miracles. During the past few weeks in Henley House, she had witnessed with her own eyes the serendipity of second chances.

Anna opened her eyes to find Jonas and Trish shooting worried glances at each other and at her.

"Okay," Anna said to Jonas. "Let's go for it."

"You're serious? Just like that?"

"Yes. But I want more than a baby. I want a family, the kind of family we promised we'd be on our wedding night. Do you remember that?"

He nodded.

"You and me," she said. "First and foremost."

"You and me," he agreed. "We'll always be a team."

She ran her hand over the portfolio. "But what if nobody picks us?"

"Are you kidding me?" Trish broke in. "After browsing through that, I wish you guys would adopt *me*. Which reminds me, Legacy, I have to ask you something. Something big; brace yourself." She pushed her curly bangs back from her face. "Will you be the Bug's godmother?"

Anna sat back, stunned. "I'd be honored. But that's a huge deal. Are you sure you don't want to entrust that responsibility to someone you've known longer? And who's up to your culinary standards?"

Trish selected a book on infant care from her couchside library and opened to a random page. "Question: What's the ideal room temperature to set the baby's room at to help prevent SIDS?"

"Oh, that's easy," Anna said. "Between sixty-eight and seventy-two degrees."

"You're hired."

*A*t the end of the evening, Jonas helped Anna return the wedding cake to the safety of Pranza's freezer, then followed her back to Henley House and walked her to the front door. They stepped to one side of the porch to make way for a pair of arriving guests who were exclaiming, "Will you look at this place? It's so quaint!" and "Leave it to Maureen to find the perfect storybook inn to go with the perfect fairy-tale wedding."

"It's so weird seeing people who aren't, well, *us* waltz in here." Anna brushed her lips across her husband's cheek. "Are you sure you don't want to stay for the weekend? This place is booked to capacity, but we can find some other hotel nearby."

He drew her closer and rested his chin on her head. "What time do you have to get up tomorrow morning?"

"The cake has to be at the president's house by eight, but I promised Brooke I'd help her serve breakfast starting at six, and then Jamie asked me to help the caterers set up at nine, and—"

"Stay here, do your thing, and don't worry about me." He tightened his embrace. "Call me after the wedding and tell me how many compliments you got on your cake."

She tilted back her head and winked up at him. "Well, with Trish and me working our combined magic, how could any mere mortal resist?"

"It's not magic, Anna," he said. "It's you."

"How did everything change so completely and so quickly?" she murmured. "I let my guard down for one second—"

"Maybe that's the secret to happiness."

She laughed. "You went soft on me over in Europe."

"It's the dog."

"I haven't said yes to the dog."

"Yet." He waggled his brows suggestively. "I have ways of convincing you."

This time, their kiss was long and lingering.

"Are you sure you don't want to come up?" She nibbled his earlobe. "Just for a few minutes?"

His hands found their way under her coat. "I want to come up for a few hours. But didn't you just say there's no room at the inn?"

"Like that's ever stopped us before. Remember that outdoor shower next to the cabana on our honeymoon?"

"How could I forget?"

"Well." She went in for another steamy, openmouthed kiss. "Brooke's suite has a separate bathroom, and I happen to know that the shower pressure is superb in there. I'm sure she wouldn't begrudge us a quick little tryst while she's downstairs fluffing pillows and pouring cocoa."

He yanked off her jacket and started on her blouse buttons. "We're going to get in trouble."

She hooked her finger through his belt loop. "Maybe if we're really bad, they'll put us on probation."

When they finally stumbled through the front door, they were greeted by Brooke, who offered up a plate of warm oatmeal cookies and a hospitable smile. "Welcome to the Paradise Found Bed-and-Breakfast. We are officially open for business."

Chapter 28

"The last thing one discovers in composing a work is what to put first."
—Blaise Pascal, *Pensées*

*H*elena stretched her limbs and nestled into the luxurious ivory linens covering the feather bed. She'd never felt more feminine than here amid the masculine black walnut furniture in MacCormick's bedchamber.

She turned to him in the bed and sighed happily. He sat with his back against the headboard, his long legs out before him, a satisfied grin on his handsome face.

When he reached for the bottle of champagne resting on the bed stand and refilled their crystal flutes, she again marveled at their situation. "I truly had no idea that we were in such danger. And from such an unlikely source."

"You do no' know how badly I wanted to tell you. But I'd been sworn to secrecy."

She accepted the glass he offered and took a sip as she traced the scar that ran along his chest. "To think that all this time, you've been my protector."

"I knew from the moment I saw you that you needed a protector in more than one way," he said, the double meaning clear in his words.

She smiled against the rim of her glass. "Then it must have surprised you when I saved your life in the end."

"It's fortunate I'm so confident in my manhood. A lot of men would no' care for their women saving the day."

"Well, after these many hours, there can be no question of your manhood." She gave him a kiss before sipping once more. "You should thank me for continuing to ransack your chamber at every opportunity. Otherwise, I'd never have known where to find a sword in a pinch."

"For such a well-bred gentlewoman, you're quite handy with weaponry," he conceded. "Had you been taking fencing instruction on the sly?"

"No, but I've read all about the finer points of swordplay in those novels you dismiss so cavalierly." She frowned. "Yet reading about running a villain through is one thing; the reality is quite another. Truly, it was merely a stroke of abject terror and blind luck."

He reached forward to graze the back of his fingers along the line of her cheekbone. "I owe you my life. And now, you've stolen my heart as well."

"I shan't be returning it." She handed him her empty flute. "I believe all this celebratory champagne has gone straight to my head." With a nod toward the bottle on the bed stand, she said, "Won't you pour me another glass, my darling?"

He cast her that rakish grin she loved so well. "You are very improper, Mrs. MacCormick."

"You wouldn't have me any other way."

Cait didn't realize how long she'd been working, how terrible her posture was, or how much her neck muscles hurt until she felt the light pressure of Gavin's hands on her shoulders.

"You're up and dressed already?" His voice was thick with sleep. She could feel the warmth instilled by the down comforter radiating from his body. "It's the crack of dawn."

"I know, but I had an idea for the last scene of my book. I wanted to get it down on paper while 'the heat is in me,' as Thoreau would say."

"So you're finished with the first draft already?"

"If only. No, I still have to tease out a lot of plot points in the middle, but I'm getting there. And I have a ton of research to do." She double-clicked the icon on the computer screen to zoom in on a pen-and-ink sketch of London's Parliament building. "Are you upset that I'm using your office?"

"Not at all." He leaned over to examine the image on the screen. "What are we looking at?"

"Well, right now I'm reading about the Great Stink of 1858, when raw sewage overflowed the Thames. Every Londoner who had the means fled the city for the summer, and cholera decimated the remaining population. It was grosser than gross. Next up is a crash course in 1850s hairstyles and accessories." She nodded at the stacks of books she'd requested from the college library: *Inventing the Victorians, Love in the Time of Victoria,* and a compilation of lithographs from *Godey's Lady's Book.* "Makes me want to slip into some puce kidskin gloves and a gown with a gilt leather sash."

"Sounds like you're making progress."

She sighed. "I've pretty much figured out the love story, but I need to go back to the beginning and work on the action scenes and layer in all the details. What style shoes my heroine has, what she eats, what she reads."

He brushed aside her hair and kissed her temple. "Whether she wore plaid boxer shorts under her petticoats."

"Exactly. And then I'll have to go back through again and focus on character development, now that I have a better idea of who these people really are. It's like the more I write, the more I have left to write." She sat up straighter. "I just keep telling myself that if Brooke can single-handedly remodel Henley House, surely I can renovate a manuscript of my own making." She waited for him to weigh in with advice. He just kept rubbing her back and looking at the picture of Parliament, so she prompted, "Don't you have any words of wisdom to impart?"

"Nope. You know what you're doing. In fact, I'd say you've accomplished quite a lot for seven A.M. on a Saturday. Don't you want to come back to bed?" He took a step back. "Or would you prefer I make you some coffee and leave you alone to work?"

She couldn't detect any trace of resentment in his tone, and was startled to realize she'd expected it. Over the last few years, she'd allowed her boyfriends to prioritize their own goals—both personal and professional—before her own. But Gavin considered her his equal. More importantly, so did Cait.

"No, stay." She swiveled in the chair to face him. "This isn't at all what I expected."

"What isn't?"

She spread out her hands. "Everything. My book isn't what I expected it to be. You're not who I expected you to be. Even *I'm* not who I expected me to be. 'Real life' is not as advertised." She smiled. "It's much better."

He smiled back. "I love you."

The words hung between them for a few seconds while

she stared up at him. He laughed and said, "From the look on your face, I can tell you weren't expecting that, either."

Cait didn't bother trying to be eloquent or original. She simply replied, "I love you, too."

He tugged her to her feet, then toward the hallway. "Come with me. I have this research project I'm working on."

"You don't say."

"Yeah. I'm investigating what insomniac historical romance novelists wear underneath their pants."

"You and those plaid boxer shorts. You're obsessed."

"That's not fair; I'm always willing to try new things. Let's get you some gilt leather sashes and see what happens." He urged her toward the bedroom.

She gave him a hard, quick kiss on his cheek. "I promised Anna I'd help her transport the wedding cake to the president's house and she'll be here to pick me up in five minutes."

His hands slid down to her hips. "We can cover a lot of ground in five minutes."

Ten minutes later, there were clothes strewn all over the hallway and a car horn was blaring outside. Cait yanked her bra straps back into place, pulled on the black pants and white shirt Jamie had instructed her to wear "to blend in with my staff," and combed her fingers through her hair.

She peered out the window, waved to Anna, and turned back to Gavin. "Do I look presentable?"

"You look—how would the Victorians put it? Beauteous. Like an angel in human form. Although I should probably tell you that your shirt's inside out."

"Jamie would rather I be on time than well dressed. I'll be back by—" Cait glanced at the clock, then considered the unpredictable demands of her friends' jobs. "I'll be back

eventually. Hopefully tonight, but definitely by tomorrow."
She blew him one more kiss on her way down the stairs. "I
promise I'll make it worth your wait."

"Have fun. Stay out of trouble."

"Having fun is a given," Cait assured him. "But staying
out of trouble has never been our forte."

*A*m I hallucinating, or does this bride have a *mustache?*"
Cait squinted at the delicate porcelain statue atop the
wedding cake. She, Brooke, and Anna were attempting to set
up the cake table in the back parlor of the president's house,
and as the morning sunshine intensified, she had started to
discern an unmistakable shadow on the upper lip of Mrs.
Richmond's expensive, European, hand-painted masterpiece.

"Damn it." Anna stopped arranging ivory rose petals on
the dark red tablecloth and frowned at the cake. "You can
still see that? I spent hours trying to scrub it off."

"I didn't notice it at first, but yeah, it looks like her 'something borrowed' is facial hair from the groom. Should I even
ask what happened?"

"It would probably be better if you didn't." Anna turned
the base of the cake so that the bride's face was no longer in
direct sunlight. "And for the love of all that is good and holy,
don't let Jamie see this."

Brooke approached with a fresh cup of coffee poured
from the silver carafe in the corner. "Here you go, Anna. You
look exhausted."

"A little bit." Anna yawned.

"Another all-nighter in the kitchen?" Cait asked.

"No." Anna's eyes sparkled. "Jonas came up to visit me
last night and we—"

"*Defiled* my bathroom," Brooke interjected. "And what's worse, you got water stains on the rug in the downstairs hallway."

Anna choked on her coffee. "Are you kidding me?"

"I haven't had time to install glass doors in the upstairs showers, so in the meantime, we have to make do with those flimsy vinyl curtains," Brooke explained to Cait. "Well, some of us got a little carried away last night."

"Pulsating shower head." Anna grinned. "I only have so much self-control."

Brooke was not amused. "The water sloshed onto the bathroom floor, leaked down through the ceiling, and ended up on the hallway rug. It was like an indoor rain forest."

Anna busied herself with rose petal placement. "Relax, I'll buy you a new rug."

"I don't want a new rug." Brooke closed her eyes. "What I want is to remain blissfully ignorant of all the sexual escapades going on under my roof."

Cait laughed. "What do you expect? When people go away for the weekend, they want a little vacay nookie."

"Last night was like a Regency house party! Nothing but compromised virtue and midnight assignations!" Brooke shook her head. "I was up till all hours listening to headboards banging and glasses clinking and drunk people stomping up the stairs. And these are well-heeled, middle-aged couples!"

"Those are the people most in need of sexual escapades," Cait pointed out. "They're ditching their jobs and their kids and their stress for a few days. They need to cut loose."

Anna glanced at Cait. "Hey, speaking of vacay nookie, how was Florida?"

"We defiled a few bathtubs ourselves." Just the memory

triggered a little quiver. "Also beach dunes, a sailboat, and a hammock—that one was a little tricky."

"Sounds heavenly. Where did you stay?"

Cait hesitated, then decided that her best course of action was to stick to the truth. "A cute little beach bungalow, right on the water."

"In the middle of the season, on such short notice?" Brooke looked impressed. "Professor Clayburn must have some connections."

Cait sidestepped the issue by saying, "I think you can call him Gavin at this point."

"Especially now that we know about his sexual proclivity for hammocks," Anna added.

Brooke put her hands over her ears. "I'm not listening! La, la, la!"

The next few hours passed in a flurry of activity as the three of them carried trays of food in from the caterer's van, helped the florist drape the mantel in fresh greenery, and lined up rows of elegantly carved ballroom chairs in the living room for ceremony seating. Their efforts were rewarded by a brief appearance from the groom himself.

"Everything looks wonderful." Terrence bowed down to kiss Anna's hand with old-world gallantry. He looked tall and dashing and Spencer Tracy–esque in his charcoal gray morning coat. Cait finally understood what a vibrant younger woman like Sarah saw in him. He exuded power and stability. "The cake is a work of art, truly."

"Thank you." Anna beamed. "I just hope it tastes all right. I know orange-cranberry filling is a little unconventional, but Sarah was brave enough to let me take the risk."

"This is no time for false modesty." The president chuckled and kept Anna's fingertips clasped in his own. "Your reputation precedes you, my dear: You cook as good as you look."

Anna pulled her hand free with a flustered laugh. "President Tait! Who knew you were such a flirt?"

His reply was drowned out by Jamie's rallying cry:

"English majors! Please report to the master suite immediately!"

Cait, Brooke, and Anna raced upstairs to find Jamie clutching a clipboard and offering a box of tissues to a tearful Maureen Richmond.

"What happened?" Cait asked.

Jamie pointed wordlessly into the master suite, where a lacy wedding gown hung on the door of the armoire and the makeup artist awaited with her tools of the trade arrayed on the bureau. A quartet of bridesmaids milled around the doorway, whispering and glancing at Maureen.

"Where's Sarah?" Cait asked. "Shouldn't she be here by now?"

Jamie nodded. "She should be."

Maureen blew her nose with a mournful honk and retreated into the bathroom.

"Oh no," Brooke breathed.

"Oh yes." Jamie addressed the other three with flinty-eyed determination. "Let's mobilize, ladies. We've got a bride on the lam."

Chapter
29

"... She saw that they were in for what is known as 'quite a scene...'"
—E. M. Forster, *A Room with a View*

Jamie dialed Sarah's cell phone number again and gnawed her thumbnail. "I definitely should've waited til next week to quit smoking."

"You quit?" Cait asked.

Anna patted her on the back. "Jame, that's great!"

"Don't congratulate me just yet; I'm going to relapse with a vengeance if we don't find this chick in the next fifteen minutes." When Sarah's voice mail picked up (again), Jamie hung up her phone and turned to Brooke. "Time check."

"Forty-five minutes until the ceremony is scheduled to begin."

She moved on to Cait. "Groom check."

"He's still downstairs mingling." Cait leaned over the railing and peered down at the guests starting to file into the front room. "As far as I know, he has no idea Sarah's gone."

Jamie pushed up the sleeves of her black blazer. "All right, Brooke, you keep Maureen and the bridesmaids corralled. Everyone stays upstairs with their lips sealed until further notice. There are extra boxes of tissue under the sink in the guest bathroom. Cait, you're running defense on the groom, and Anna, you're going to help me go door-to-door looking for our fugitive."

Anna's eyebrows shot up. "Door-to-door?"

"Well, bar to bar."

Brooke blinked. "Why do you think she's in a bar?"

"Hello, where else is a bride on the verge of a nervous breakdown going to go?"

"Maybe she went to a spa," Brooke suggested. "Or, I know! In the movies, the jilted bride always goes off on her honeymoon alone."

"Who's broken off three engagements here, you or me?" Jamie said. "Trust me, girlfriend's holed up nearby with a bottle of booze." She jingled her car keys. "Come on, Anna. We'll start down on Pine Street and work our way out."

Five minutes later, Jamie pulled up the car in front of Pranza to drop off Anna—"Call me immediately if you see, hear, or suspect anything!"—and then continued on to the Pine Street Pub. The stools were stacked next to the long, brass-trimmed bar and the dining area was practically deserted at this hour on a Saturday morning, but Jamie strode over to the cash register and introduced herself to the short, spiky-haired waitress who appeared to be the only employee on the floor.

"Have you by any chance seen a doe-eyed brunette in here? Pretty, petite, probably weeping?"

The waitress tilted her head toward the far wall, indicating the booths beyond the flickering neon beer signs and the deserted pool table.

Jamie found Sarah huddled in the back corner booth, surrounded by a veritable buffet of carbs: French toast, hash browns, blueberry pancakes.

She slid into the bench seat across from Sarah and helped herself to a hot buttered biscuit. "Hey, hon. How you feeling?"

Sarah didn't look up from her plate. "You found me." She heaved a weary sigh and shoved another forkful of pancake into her mouth.

Jamie rested her chin in her hand and waited.

Finally, Sarah stopped gorging herself long enough to say, "I'm starving. I can't stand it anymore. It's been six weeks since I had a bagel with cream cheese. All I do lately is fantasize about cheesecake and French fries and penne alla vodka. Vodka. I could do with a bottle of that right about now."

"There's a whole cake waiting for us back at Terry's house," Jamie said quietly. "I could have Anna put together a preceremony pastry sampler, if you want."

Sarah put down her fork. "Are the guests already there?"

"They're starting to arrive, yes."

"Is the harpist set up for the ceremony?"

"She was plinking out a stirring rendition of Bach's 'Ode to Joy' when I left."

Sarah began shredding the paper napkin draped across her lap. "What about my mom? Is she—"

Jamie leaned in. "Forget your mom for a second. What about *you*?"

"I can't go back there. I thought I could go through with this, but..." The bride's lower lip quivered, and then she clamped her mouth into a tight little moue. "She's going to be devastated. She's been looking forward to this since the day I was born, basically."

"Maureen will be fine." Jamie pushed aside the plates and silverware and patted Sarah's forearm. "I promise. Don't get me wrong, I'm not saying you should hit her up for a loan tomorrow, but she loves you. She wants you to be happy." She echoed Sarah's own words from the week before: "You know how mothers are."

Sarah slumped down even farther. "It's not a good sign when you're more upset about the prospect of upsetting your mom than you are about the prospect of losing the groom." She glanced up, her expression strained. "I don't know what happened. We were the perfect couple; you saw us. And then I spotted his assistant wearing that necklace. Do you know what he said when I confronted him about that? He said I was making something out of nothing. He said he loves me, but that he can't be responsible for my insecurities." Her eyes watered. "I don't know if it's him or if it's me or what, but I physically couldn't force myself into that wedding dress."

"It's not you," Jamie said emphatically. "Trust me."

"What am I going to do?" Sarah pressed her face into her palms. "Isn't it kind of late in the game for me to pull a U-turn on my entire future?"

"Not at all," Jamie said. "Ever heard that old saying, 'Marry in haste, repent at leisure'?"

"No. But I think I just found my new life motto. I almost called it off a few months ago, when I first heard all the rumors about, well, you know what they were about. That's why we didn't have a June wedding. But Terry finally convinced me that I was crazy to doubt him."

"He's good at that."

Sarah cast a long, speculative look at Jamie but didn't ask any questions. She went back to attacking her pancakes and said, "You'll have to tell everyone. I know I'm a wuss, but I can't face them right now."

"No problem," Jamie said. "You take care of yourself; I'll take care of everything else."

Sarah glanced over Jamie's shoulder, then shrank back against the wall.

"What?" Jamie whipped around.

"Don't look now!" Sarah hissed, but it was too late. Jeff Thuesen had just entered the restaurant. He noticed Jamie and waved.

"Did he see us?" Sarah asked, her eyes huge.

Jamie nodded. "He's heading this way."

Before Sarah could duck underneath the table, Jeff arrived with a smile and a Styrofoam cup of coffee.

"Hi." Jamie reciprocated with a wave and a refresher introduction. "Jeff, you remember Sarah Richmond."

Jeff's smile faded as he took in the bride's expression. "Sorry. Am I interrupting a big wedding planning summit?"

"Actually," Sarah said, "the wedding's about to start without me."

Jeff froze, the cup halfway to his lips. "Right now?"

"Yes. I had an epiphany. Unfortunately, I didn't have it until the catering staff arrived and started passing out pre-ceremony canapés, and now I've been reduced to a cute little cliché: the runaway bride. Except, let me assure you, when you're the bride doing the running away, there's nothing cute about it."

"I see." Jeff glanced over at Jamie, then back to Sarah. "Where are you running to?"

"I have no idea. I already gave up my apartment in Manhattan." Sarah's tone changed from defensive to defeated. "I can stay with friends, I guess, although most of them are at Terry's house right now, waiting for me to walk down the aisle."

"Do you want me to call someone?" Jamie asked.

"No. I've dragged too many people into this mess already." Sarah thought for a moment. "Book me a suite at the Gansevoort for the weekend, please. I'll come out of hiding on Monday, but first I need forty-eight hours to pull myself together."

"Will do." Jamie scribbled the hotel name down on a napkin.

"I can give you a ride back to the city," Jeff offered. "I just came in to grab a coffee to go. I'm heading back to Brooklyn right now. You can make a clean getaway before the next bus leaves town." He paused. "But you probably want to be alone."

"No, let's go." Sarah dug out her wallet and tossed some cash down on the table. "I'm ready. The sooner, the better."

"What about your luggage?"

"Oh." Sarah faltered. "Everything I own is in storage of at Terry's house."

"Sounds like some retail therapy is in order," Jamie said. "Don't worry. I'll collect all your stuff and ship it back to you when you're ready. Just send me an address."

"I love her," Sarah told Jeff. "Isn't she amazing?"

"One of a kind," Jeff said drily.

Jamie walked them both out to the curb. She gave Sarah a hug while Jeff jogged around his car to open the passenger door.

His eyes met Jamie's as he walked back to the driver's side, and they shared a poignant smile.

"Take care," Jamie said.

"You, too."

Before he closed the door, Jamie asked, "Hey, did you find any good candidates for that internship?"

"Yeah." He laughed. "An English major, actually."

"We're the best; we do it all. Safe trip, you guys." She banged her palm on the car roof and waved good-bye.

Then she returned to the pub, bought a pack of gum from the vending machine, and shoved two minty squares into her mouth. After a few minutes of deep breathing and furious chomping, she dialed up Anna.

"Where are you? I'll swing by and pick you up in two minutes. I've gotta go break some bad news to a houseful of guests and one soon-to-be-former fiancé."

When Jamie pulled up in front of the president's house, Terry was waiting for her on the front lawn. He'd removed his morning coat and vest, despite the whipping wind and the frost on the grass. Anna took one look at his face and prepared to bail out.

"One of the bridesmaids must have blabbed." Anna reached for the door handle. "You don't have to stop, just slow down and I'll tuck and roll."

A preternatural sense of serenity seeped through Jamie as

she parked the car and prepared to confront the man she'd once allowed to determine her worth.

"Well?" Terry scowled down at her. He seemed to almost vibrate with anger.

Jamie stood her ground and kept her voice low. "She's gone."

"Is she coming back?"

Jamie shook her head.

"What did you say to her?"

"Nothing, really. I simply asked—"

"You told her about us, didn't you? This is your fault!" He jabbed an accusatory finger at her. "*You!* You did this!"

She stepped back and let his rage run its course. When he at last sputtered into silence, she turned on her heel, took one last look back over her shoulder, and told him, "Wrong. You did this all by yourself."

Chapter
30

"You never know what is enough unless you know what is more than enough."
—William Blake, *The Marriage of Heaven and Hell*

always wanted to open a bed-and-breakfast like this."
The paunchy, gray-haired man settling into the sofa
cushions wore dark green twill trousers and a plaid
flannel shirt still creased from its original packaging. "But I
was too cowed. I listened to my parents and my teachers,
took the 'practical' route and went to law school. Ugh.
Thirty years of corporate meetings later and look at me."

"You look very successful." Brooke set down a tray of
Anna's boudoir biscuits next to the assortment of cheese and
fruit on the coffee table in front of the fireplace. She had
arranged the sterling silver tea service set she'd inherited from

her grandmother alongside a row of flowered china cups. Mr. Croucher had shown up at three-thirty for Paradise Found's four o'clock tea, but Brooke saw no reason to keep a hungry guest waiting.

"Success is subjective, young lady, and don't you forget it." The attorney helped himself to a biscuit and glanced around the living room. "This is quite a life you've made for yourself. No meetings, no commute, no deadlines."

Brooke smiled and poured a cup of tea for the older man. "No end-of-the-year bonuses, no cushy retirement plan."

"Money isn't everything. I'm getting ready to retire and if I had a chance to do it all over again, I would've done things differently. Taken more risks, spent less time at the office."

"It's never too late to follow your heart." Brooke used the ornate antique tongs to extract a pair of sugar cubes from the silver bowl.

"True enough." Mr. Croucher propped his ankle on his knee and stared contemplatively out the window. "I've been thinking about moving out of Westchester County and buying a home upstate, here in the mountains. Why, if I had half a chance, I'd buy this place right out from under you."

Brooke prepared to take a seat and share a few tales from the dark side of B-and-B ownership, but before the back of her knees even touched the chair, she noticed a drop of water plop down from the foyer ceiling onto the hallway rug. She slammed her teacup into its saucer and raced toward the staircase. "Won't you please excuse me for a moment? I'll be right back."

The bathroom in Brooke's suite was empty, of course, but the bathroom on the other side of the wall adjoined a guest room. Even out in the hallway, over the rush of running water, Brooke could hear the laughter and guttural moans emanating from within.

After a full minute of agonized deliberation, she worked up the nerve to rap lightly on the door. "Excuse me?"

The moaning continued, accompanied by more splashing. Brooke envisioned a chunk of ceiling collapsing onto Mr. Croucher's head. Mr. Croucher and his thirty years of litigation experience.

She pounded on the door. "Hello? Excuse me? I'm sorry to disturb you, but there's, uh, would you please make sure the shower curtain is tucked in?"

For a moment, there was silence on the other side of the door, then sloshing as the faucet turned off. "It's tucked in," a raspy female voice called.

"Thanks," Brooke said. "I apologize for the interruption. Carry on!"

The guest room door opened and a middle-aged woman with dripping black hair stuck her head into the hallway. "Wait. You're the owner?"

Brooke stared down at the baseboard. "Yes, and again, I hate to disturb you, but we have a slight plumbing situation."

"Did you hire a decorator?" the guest asked.

"Oh no, I did it myself."

"I love it." The woman nodded, splattering droplets of water across Brooke's shoes. "Very authentic to the region without being over the top."

"Well, thank you. I put in the tile myself, too," Brooke boasted.

The towel-clad guest didn't bother to conceal her skepticism. "You did?"

"Yes, ma'am."

"By yourself?"

"Mm-hmm. The cast-iron toilet flanges gave me some trouble, let me tell you, but I had better luck with the tile and the sinks and installing those showerheads everyone seems to be enjoying so much."

The woman opened the door wider and leaned back into the bedroom. "Did you hear that, Mitch? She renovated this place herself."

"I also did the wiring, the painting, and the ceiling retexturing."

"Mitch!" the woman hollered. "Get out here, pronto!"

Two seconds later, the nearly nude female was joined by her nearly nude male counterpart. The woman pointed at Brooke and crowed, "Look at her. Listen to her."

"I'm looking," the man said. "I'm listening."

The woman clutched his shoulder. Her expression could only be described as giddy. "Are you thinking what I'm thinking?"

Unnerved, Brooke edged back toward the stairs. "What?"

"We're in television production." The woman accepted the dry towel her partner offered and wrapped it around her hair. "I'm Barbara Berkman; this is my husband, Mitch. Right now, we're partnered with a cable home improvement network. We're in talks to shoot a pilot for a concept called *Four-Wall Face-Lift*, and we're still looking for a host. The show targets Gen-X females and we need someone adorable. Articulate. Accessible."

"Really? That sounds..." Brooke tried to appear blasé. "Interesting."

"You're exactly what we're looking for. You should come down and audition. Mitch! Where are our business cards?"

The ever-helpful Mitch ducked back into the bedroom

and returned with two business cards and a pair of terry-cloth robes.

"I'm going to take down all your contact information before we check out tomorrow," Barbara Berkman said. "Do you have a head shot, by any chance?"

"Oh, goodness, no. Although I do have an official staff photo from the college alumni affairs brochure."

Barbara waved her hand dismissively. "No matter, a Polaroid will do for now. The only catch is, if the network picks up the show, we'll be filming in Manhattan. You'd have to relocate to New York City."

Brooke paused for a moment, considering. She thought about how comfortable and safe her life in Thurwell had become. She considered how easy it would be to stick to the routine she'd established. Then she thought about Everett and Professor Rutkin, and how she'd started to love the feel of hardware in her hands. And how many more times she could realistically bring herself to reprimand mature, professional adults for having sex in her showers. "That wouldn't be a problem for me."

When she returned to the living room, the burned-out attorney was waiting for her with crumbs on his shirtfront and a wistful expression on his face.

She offered him a fresh pastry along with her most dazzling smile. "Mr. Croucher, were you being sincere when you said you would buy this place if you had half a chance?"

"Absolutely." He rubbed his chin. "I've been trapped at a desk under fluorescent lights for too long. I'd love to finally get a crack at my dream job."

"Well, your dream may be about to come true." Brooke batted her eyes and offered him a pen. "Make me an offer."

Chapter 31

"My friends are my estate."
—Emily Dickinson

ine coolers again?" Jamie shook her head when Anna brought the six-pack into the living room. The sofa and love seats had been draped in old bedsheets and the contents of the bookshelves had been packed into boxes, but the fire blazing away behind the old masonry hearth kept the dark, drafty room warm and cozy. "You're killing me. It's New Year's Eve! We should be cracking open the champagne."

Anna glanced at the label on the package. "Would you prefer peach or strawberry-kiwi?"

"This is seasonally inappropriate," Jamie protested.

"There's two feet of snow on the ground. What about Irish coffee? Hot toddies?"

"Peach or strawberry?" Anna repeated.

"I hate you." Jamie paused. "Peach, please."

Anna handed over a bottle. "Wine coolers may not be strictly traditional, but they're *our* tradition. It's our last night in Henley House, and we need to mark the occasion."

Jamie muttered under her breath and propped her ratty plaid-slippered feet up on the coffee table. "Do we at least get some fresh-baked goodies to soak up all the cheap alcohol and artificial flavors?"

Anna conducted a quick mental inventory of the kitchen. "I made an eggnog trifle and some chocolate marshmallow cupcakes. Oh, and I have an English plum pudding left over from the holiday party I catered last night."

"I love you." Jamie grinned. "Cupcake, please."

The front porch creaked as Cait and Brooke hurried up the steps and into the foyer.

"Holy Kelvin." Cait shucked off her mittens and blew into her cupped hands. "It's, like, absolute zero out there."

The glass pane embedded in the doorframe rattled as Brooke dropped her ski boots onto the bristled black floor mat. Her eyes widened when she saw the six-pack on the end table. "Wine coolers? Don't start without us!"

"So?" Jamie asked. "How was the double date?"

Cait wriggled out of her hat, jacket, and scarf. "It was fun, except Brooke and her knight in shining hardware were so busy making out that we barely got onto the slopes."

"We only see each other every other weekend right now," Brooke said. "Besides, don't think I didn't see you and Gavin accosting each other on the chairlift. Maybe you wouldn't be so cold if you'd keep your coat on."

"My extremities may be chilly," Cait said, "but my heart is on fire."

"Your *heart*?" Jamie laughed.

Cait grabbed one of the cupcakes Anna offered. "Bless you. I don't know how you found time to bake for us with the whirlwind of Christmas parties you had to cater, but I'm eternally grateful." She sat down on the floor next to a pile of boxes and warmed her hands by the fire. "So now that the holidays are over, are you heading back to Albany?"

"Not yet," Anna said. "I promised Trish I'd stay here and help her until she has the baby. It's tough being apart from Jonas, but he understands, and luckily, he doesn't mind driving up here to see me on the weekends."

"He's my favorite houseguest ever," Brooke said. "Always up first thing to shovel the walk and start a fresh pot of coffee. And those waffles he made last week! Is he always this helpful?"

"Not always." Anna smiled mischievously. "Let's just say I give him lots of incentive to keep coming back. Which reminds me—you're going to have to give me the make and model of that showerhead so we can do a little remodeling of our own when I finally do go home."

"Hey, speaking of Trish, did her boyfriend ever resurface?" Cait asked.

Anna shook her head. "Just long enough to tell her he couldn't handle the responsibility of impending fatherhood. Then he vanished back into the ether."

"How's she handling it?" Brooke asked.

"All bluster and bravado. Typical Trish." Anna sighed. "I know she's scared witless, though."

"Who wouldn't be?" Cait said. "So what's she going to do when the baby's born?"

"Well, I'm trying to convince her to move to Albany and open a bakery with me. Thanks to Arden, I have plenty of start-up money."

"You two would be quite the dynamic duo. What'd she say?"

"She said she'd only relocate if I proved I was serious by enrolling in culinary school and training with a professional pastry chef."

"And?" Cait prompted.

"And." Anna spread open her hands. "Classes start this spring."

"More over, Julia Child!" Jamie crowed.

"What about the adoption stuff?" Brooke asked.

"We finally got all the paperwork filed and approved." Anna picked at a fluted paper cupcake liner. "Now the waiting begins."

Brooke nodded sympathetically. "That's the worst part, huh?"

"You know, I thought it would be, but now I'm realizing that it's going to be less excruciating than waiting for the outcome of all those fertility treatments. Because this time I know I'm not in control. At least I can stop blaming my body, you know? I've done everything I can, but ultimately, it's not up to me. It'll happen when it happens."

"Soon," Brooke assured her. "You and Jonas are going to be great parents."

"And just think," added Jamie, "someday you'll be able to tell your little tyke that you knew Brooke Asplind when."

Brooke squinched up her pert little nose. "When what?"

"When you were a humble B-and-B owner," Anna said. "Back before you skyrocketed to fame and fortune as the host of *Four-Wall Face-Lift*."

"Oh please." Brooke gulped her wine cooler and flushed. "Let's not get ahead of ourselves. We've only taped a few episodes so far."

"I know." Anna glanced toward the TV in the corner. "We just watched the rough cut of the one where you show us how to refinish hardwood floors."

"I told you not to touch that DVD!"

"But you left it where we could find it," Jamie replied. "Knowing damn well we have no self-control."

Cait nodded up at Mr. Wonderful. "This *is* the house of boundary issues, remember?"

"That reminds me." Brooke snapped her fingers. "I've got to dismantle Mr. Wonderful and pack him up before the movers arrive."

"You're taking him to Manhattan?"

"I couldn't possibly leave him here after all we've been through together." Brooke looked aghast at the very suggestion. "The sales contract specifically states that 'the decorative bronze finial atop the newel post does not convey to the buyer.'"

"We'll find the perfect spot for him in our new apartment," Jamie assured her.

Cait spun around to face Jamie. "You're moving to New York City, too?"

"That's right. I'm using my inheritance to start my own event-planning business. I figure I can use my Maureen Richmond contacts as a jumping-off point. Lots of the guests from Manhattan told me it was the most elegant and entertaining nonwedding they'd ever attended. So I'm going all in. You know I can't do anything halfway." Jamie shrugged and took another sip of wine cooler. "Besides, Scarlett here needs a roommate."

"You're not moving in with Everett?" Anna asked Brooke.

"Are you kidding me?" Brooke's hand fluttered up to her throat. "I've only been dating him for two months. My mother is already wringing her hands about my relocating to the big city. She could never face her bridge club again if I started living in sin." Brooke glanced at Cait and murmured, "No offense."

Cait laughed. "None taken. I'm not moving in with Gavin, either, FYI, although sinning is very much on the agenda. I need my own time and space to write. When Gavin and I get together, we tend to get somewhat undisciplined."

"Hearts on fire and all?" Anna teased.

"Precisely. Separate living quarters is the best option for both of us right now. I'm hoping to sign a lease by the end of next week and live off my Arden Henley Literary Fellowship funds until I sell a book or five. The starving-artist routine is highly overrated. I need food and health insurance and TiVo."

Brooke dug a chunky knit blanket out of one of the half-packed moving boxes and wrapped it around her shoulders. "It's chilly in here. Let's build up the fire and make s'mores, just like the old days."

"I thought we weren't allowed to violate the sanctity of the clean carpet," Jamie said.

"I'm closing escrow next week. In less than seven days, this carpet—along with the rest of the house—is no longer my problem."

"Can I do my toenails?" Anna asked.

"Knock yourself out."

Jamie and Anna high-fived. "I still can't believe that old lawyer guy actually followed through on that offer."

"With a lot more cash than I expected." Brooke raised her wine cooler. "Here's to unloading my dream job."

Jamie chimed in with, "To new beginnings and old friends."

"To Arden," Cait said.

Anna grinned. "To the English majors. We may not always be practical, but we have infinite potential."

Four voices rang out in unison: "Cheers!"

Photo: Kevin McIntyre

BETH KENDRICK got her B.A. in English at a small liberal arts college before earning her Ph.D. in psychology and then pulling a professional U-turn to pursue her dream job of becoming a novelist. Her previous women's fiction titles include *Fashionably Late, Nearlyweds,* and *The Pre-Nup.* She lives in Arizona with her family and a pair of unruly rescue dogs. You can visit her website at www.BethKendrick.com.